LULU SINAGTALA

AND THE CITY OF NOBLE WARRIORS

BOOK 1

GAIL D. VILLANUEVA

HARPER
An Imprint of HarperCollins*Publishers*

Lulu Sinagtala and the City of Noble Warriors

For information address HarperCollins Children's Books, a division of HarperCollins Publishers, 195 Broadway, New York, NY 10007.
www.harpercollinschildrens.com
Library of Congress Control Number: 2023936891
ISBN 978-0-06-325536-4
Typography by Joel Tippie
23 24 25 26 27 LBC 5 4 3 2 1
First Edition

To my grandmas, the strongest and snazziest ladies in the whole wide Worlds,
Mama Nena, Lola Goco, and Lola Polly,
I love you.

To Tita Nanette,
I'll never, ever forget your kindness.
And I'll miss you.

AUTHOR'S NOTE

This book was inspired by the myths and legends I grew up with.

I know, I know. You've heard it many times before. But there's a reason why authors mention it often.

Myths and legends have existed long before we were born—like, way, *way* before. Philippine mythology specifically has been around even before colonizers arrived on our shores. These stories were told by our ancestors who worshipped the deities that were in them, and have been passed on from one generation to the next.

It goes without saying that the interpretation of Tagalog mythology in this book is by no means the only one out there. Some of my depictions of the deities, heroes, and magical creatures in the story even deviate from the original myths. Not to disrespect them, but to pay homage to the source while staying within the context of modern times.

That's the great thing about our mythologies—the beautiful tales we pass on evolve with their storytellers. We add a little bit of ourselves every time we tell these stories, these stories that become time capsules of who we were, who we are, and who we will be.

I hope you enjoy reading *Lulu Sinagtala and the City of Noble Warriors*. You might be surprised to find Lulu's story similar to yours, but just a bit more magical. After all, anybody can be a hero. Even you. . . . Especially you.

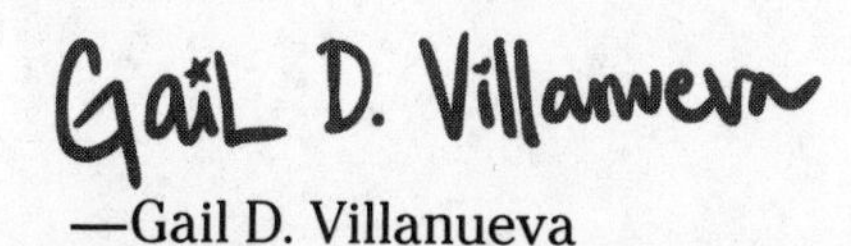

—Gail D. Villanueva

CHAPTER ONE

Beware the Creepy Lady with the Isaw Sword

SOME LEGENDS SAY HE WAS A GIANT, WHILE OTHERS CLAIM HE WAS AN ordinary-sized man. There are people who believe he was a supernatural being who caused earthquakes, while others say he was just a human king. But if there's one thing all these stories agree on, it's that Bernardo Carpio was a man with great power—and a symbol of freedom.

My favorite tale of Bernardo Carpio says that he was a revolutionary fighting against our Spanish colonizers. It describes him as supernaturally mighty and strong, kind of like the Filipino version of the Greek hero Hercules. It says Bernardo could carry a ship full of armed men without breaking a sweat. He could even crush a stone house to dust with a single punch. Sounds unbelievable, but for some reason, there are people who consider this version of Bernardo's story historically accurate.

Weird, right? I thought so too. But our teacher said that the scholar who wrote this Bernardo Carpio tale was just being poetic, equating "mighty" with someone who had a lot of money or friends in politics.

I mean, Bernardo Carpio won so many battles, he could have single-handedly freed the Philippines from Spain. And I only say "could have" because our colonizers found a way to defeat him. They hired a local shaman (a corrupt nobody, I'm sure) to capture Bernardo Carpio using magical means. He tricked our hero into a cave. Then the shaman trapped him between two mountain-sized rocks, trying to crush him in a boulder sandwich . . .

"'Traitor! How dare you betray your own people to those colonizers?' Bernardo Carpio bellowed," I narrate the hero's last words as dramatically as I can. Well, I suppose those were his last words, because that's what it says in our textbook. I squeeze my eyes shut and hold out my arms, reenacting the event. "Every muscle in Bernardo Carpio's body screamed as the giant rocks tried to crush him—"

"AHH-TEH LOO!" My younger sister, Kitty, is on the sidewalk, her hands on her hips. She's far enough away not to get sprinkled with tire dirt from my Bernardo Carpio impersonation. But she's close enough to scold me. "Get down from there before those stacks of tires collapse on you. They don't seem very stable."

"I heard you. Don't shout." I roll my eyes. My sister and I are both eleven and only three months apart, but sometimes she acts like a stuffy old lady. The old tires I'm stepping on are stacked perfectly like Lego blocks around Silverio Auto Repair Shop, further supported by the concrete wall. And the tire towers aren't very high either. The one under my feet is about half a meter tall, and the ones on either side of me are barely higher than my head. "Geez. Just chill, Meow."

"Meow" is my nickname for Kitty. "Kitty" as in "kitty cat."

I know, I know. It's not very imaginative, but I think it fits her well. She gets scared easily, especially when it has something to do with me.

Kitty bites her lower lip. "I just don't want you to be injured."

"I won't."

Now, you're probably wondering how it's possible for us to only have a three-month age difference. Mom adopted me as a baby when she was pregnant with Kitty. So, it's understandable that Mom and I look nothing alike, but Kitty is her total miniature.

They both have miraculously straight brownish-black hair. Mine is very black, and it's always a mess. They're tall and willowy, while I'm short and as thin as a toothpick.

Their eyes are so small, they disappear when they smile—the total opposite of my big, deep-set eyes. They're Chinese Filipino. I am not.

But the most obvious differences of all are Mom's and Kitty's fair complexion and high-bridged nose. My very dark-brown skin and nose as flat as the rice plains of Central Luzon make it super clear that we're not related by blood. It's a fact that mean kids and tactless adults never fail to point out. Because to them, my being dark and flat-nosed means I'm not "pretty" like my sister and mother.

"Let Lu stay on the tires and break as many bones as she wants. We won't be the ones who'll spend Christmas break stuck at home." My best bud, Bart, comes up behind Kitty on the sidewalk, joining the "Let's Scold Lulu" campaign. He has big eyes, and they're made even bigger by his thick glasses. His skin is as light as a brown Filipino's can possibly be, even fairer than Kitty's.

"Fine." I snort, causing a cloud of dust to scatter from the tires on my left. Kitty and Bart step back to avoid my sneeze. "Move over, unless you want to catch me."

Bart and Kitty take a couple more steps to the side, giving me space to land between them.

"Be careful, Ate."

Even though I'm not that high up, I can still see a bit of a view from the stack of tires, because Silverio Auto Repair Shop is located on the elevated side of the road.

Silanganan Village, our little subdivision in Caloocan

City, has a hilly terrain. But I like it here. It has this eclectic, old-but-modern vibe. The buildings are mostly small, a bit dilapidated, and built close together. On every street, though, there's at least a house or two with glass balconies, white concrete walls, and bamboo gardens. Modern, but the traces of Old Manila are still very visible.

For a boring subdivision where nothing fun happens, Silanganan Village has quite an interesting history. Mom said that people have lived here since the nineteenth century, during the time when Spain still colonized our country. It's near Balintawak, where one of our national heroes, Andrés Bonifacio, and his comrades made the historic Cry of Pugad Lawin. This monumental event marked the beginning of the 1896 Philippine Revolution against the Spanish Empire.

It's nice to live near a place where Filipino heroes were made. Who knows? Maybe their hero-ness might rub off on me, and this place will finally see a bit of excitement.

I leap off the pile of old tires, landing on both feet. Then I drop to one knee with a hand on the ground and the other outstretched behind me, Black Widow style.

"Ate!" Kitty protests, groaning. Bart simply shakes his head in disapproval.

"Where have you been?" I ask Bart before Kitty can start nagging again. "You were behind us when we left school. Then you were gone after we went past the beauty parlor. Did you get a mani-pedi?"

"No." Bart clears his throat, fussing over his T-shirt collar. "I had to take care of something."

I peer at him. "Does that 'something' have anything to do with my Christmas gift?"

"Maybe."

"Ate, Christmas isn't only about receiving gifts," Kitty says, shaking her finger like I've just gotten myself on Santa's Naughty List. "That's a very materialistic point of view. Christmas is about spreading love and holiday cheer to everyone."

"Okay, then." I raise an eyebrow. "Bart can just give me your materialistic Christmas gift instead. You can have all the love and holiday cheer you want."

"No way!"

Bart, Kitty, and I burst into laughter. We all know that Kitty loves receiving presents as much as she enjoys giving them. But I get what she means. When you live in a country where the holiday season starts in the first "ber" month—as in Septem*ber*—it's hard not to feel the Christmas spirit. Even the Grinch would have a hard time ruining the holidays here. I mean, can you just imagine trying to steal Christmas stuff daily even before Halloween decorations are up? That would be a very exhausting, Grinchy nightmare.

"Anyway, I gotta go," Bart says. "I just wanted to check on how much trouble you've gotten yourself into already." He smooths his hair, even though he doesn't really need to. Bart's black hair is always neat and clean—closely shaven, kind of like those really short haircuts people in the army are required to have. It suits him, making him kind of cute. . . . Well, not BTS's Jungkook cute, but cute-in-a-friend-way cute. "My lolo is having some friends over today. He needs help serving drinks and stuff."

"Oh!" Kitty claps her hands in glee. "We'll come with you and help too."

"No, we won't," I say. Running errands for Bart's ancient grandpa and his equally ancient friends is not how I want to spend my first day of Christmas vacation. I love Bart and all, but our best friendship has its limits. "*You* come with us. I want to have isaw first before heading home."

"No thanks." Bart shifts his backpack on his shoulder. He's been using that same backpack for as long as I can remember. And that's a very, very long time. Kitty and I have been friends with Bart since we were babies. It sounds weird, but it's as if his backpack has grown up with him. It's always had the same plain gray design, and it only gets bigger every year.

"Say hi to your lolo and his friends for us." Kitty smiles at Bart. "See you tomorrow!"

"Yeah," he says, walking up the street and running into a tall, college-age guy. But Bart's still too busy texting. Typical. He could run into a boulder and probably never notice it unless the boulder ruined his phone. For his safety, Kitty and I watch him until he turns right at the corner and disappears.

"You really shouldn't do dangerous things like that, Ate. You're lucky you didn't get a seizure while you were on the tires. You could have seriously hurt yourself." As Kitty tosses me a small bottle of hand sanitizer, we hear a soft chime from her pocket. She takes out her phone, turning off the alarm. "It's time for your epilepsy medicine."

"I haven't had any seizures in a while, thanks to you," I say, beaming. Kitty brings out a plastic medicine box and a water bottle from her messenger bag. I take them from her without hesitation, swallowing my medicine like an obedient trouper.

Kitty can be an annoying worrywart, but I understand where she's coming from. Four months ago, I didn't notice that I'd been missing taking my pills a bit too often. And because of that, I had a major seizure in school and nearly fell off the stairs. My social status took a nosedive along with my unconscious, shaking body. From "respected athlete" I became "Tremor Girl, the Girl Who Shakes." Never mind that *I could have died*. . . . There are just some kids who choose to be mean to people with conditions they don't understand.

Since that day, my sister has taken it upon herself to make sure I don't skip any scheduled medication. I didn't want to become an added task for her to do, but she insisted.

My biological parents are gone, but fate has made up for it by leading me to Kitty. I'm super happy to have her.

I put an arm around my sister. "Let's get isaw."

Kitty returns my grin with her usual bright smile. That's another thing she shares with Mom—a smile that can brighten up a gloomy day.

And it's definitely not a gloomy day today.

The late afternoon sky is blue with featherlike clouds that say it won't rain anytime soon. The residents and shop owners showcase their holiday spirit by hanging garlands, parols (star-shaped bamboo and paper lanterns), and fairy lights. They're awesome reminders that we won't need to go back to school until after New Year.

Woof! Woof!

A tiny black shih tzu approaches us as we arrive at the barbecue stand. It's Tannie, our neighborhood handylady's beloved pet. Tannie is always well-groomed, with his breed's typically long fur cut super short. His owner loves to dress him in dog clothes, and his attire always depends on the season. For example, he wears a sleeveless Kobe Bryant jersey in the summer. Then he'll don a waterproof coat in the rainy season. Today he's wearing a red-and-white-striped Christmas sweater with gold ruffled cuffs as garish as our neighborhood's holiday decor. Tannie is a shaved canine fashionista with a closet full of clothes.

Tannie's human got him four years ago. Though we often see her taking him on walks in the neighborhood, Tannie usually follows Kitty and me around, bumming treats whenever he chances upon us eating.

"Hey, there!" I greet the dog. Kitty does the same, bending down to pat the shih tzu on the head. As usual, Tannie avoids her hand. He's like Bart—they're both allergic to affection. "Grouch."

"He'll be friendlier once we have food," Kitty says with a laugh. The barbecue stand is usually crowded around this time. Luckily, there's only a couple of customers ahead of us, a middle-aged lady and a teenage boy ordering inihaw.

We *love* street-side inihaw. The food from the street-side grill is cheap and delicious, plus it's all cooked right in front of you. It's kind of like a lemonade stand, except they're selling grilled pork and innards marinated in this sweet and slightly spicy barbecue mixture. You dip it in either sweet sauce or spicy vinegar (I prefer a mix of both), straight from the grill. Yum!

"Apat na isaw baboy, anim na isaw manok, dalawang pork barbecue, isang balunbalunan, at isang dugo." I order four sticks of pork intestines, six chicken intestines, two pork barbecue, one gizzard, and one dried chicken blood. Kitty will have the dugo and I'll have the gizzard. I don't like dried blood, while Kitty has trouble eating the tough and chewy balunbalunan.

Kitty tells the vendor we want our orders toasted. "Tustado po."

"One hundred pesos," the inihaw vendor says. He spreads our selection on the hot grill. "You can pay after you eat."

"I'll get us melon juice," Kitty says, pointing her thumb at a nearby cart. Then she shakes her index finger at me. "Behave. Don't pick a fight. I won't be long."

"What do you mean— Oh. *Her.*"

As Kitty makes her way to the juice stand, I look to my right, where a girl our age is crossing the street. We're not in the same class, but I know Carmen and always avoid her. She's the one who seeks me out and calls me a freak. Carmen is the reason why Bart and Kitty are my only friends in school. Nobody wants to annoy her, but they don't mind being on the bad side of the infamous Tremor Girl.

I brace myself for a round of Carmen insults, but thankfully, she doesn't see me and keeps walking. She joins her family at the secondhand store. I'm sure they're her parents and older brother, considering they all look like her.

It must be nice, being part of a family like that. You know, the kind of family that other people don't doubt you belong to.

Sighing, I touch the pearl-like, oval-shaped pendant inside my shirt. On the back, flat side of the pendant, there's a silhouette of a man in a squat, his arms folded on his chest, but it's barely noticeable. This jewelry was a gift from Mom's best friend, and I love to wear it. It's so simple and light and doesn't stick out at all.

Don't get me wrong. I'm happy to have Mom and Kitty. But I'm always the odd one out—in school, in my family, everywhere. Sometimes I wish I could just blend in.

"What the—" I jump as something wet touches my toes. Tannie is sniffing my foot. "Oh. It's just you."

Tannie doesn't answer, of course. Thank goodness. I'd freak out if he did.

The inihaw vendor switches on his mini electric fan, pointing it in the direction of the grill. The coals turn redder, blasting my face with smoke.

"Hey!" I cough, stepping backward. My heel lands on someone's foot. I look up and see a teenage boy in a basketball jersey who's also waiting for his order. "Sorry po."

"Okay lang—" As the boy tells me it's fine, his head slides back and his brown irises turn red. Like, literally bright red. He stares at me with his odd crimson eyes and spits on the ground beside Tannie. "Fraternizing with spineless followers. How typical."

"Huh?" I try to put distance between us, but instead, I bump into another customer, the middle-aged lady. "Sor—"

"Run and hide under the Balabal, little brat," the lady customer says in the same monotonous tone. Her eyes are red like the teenage boy's. "Once he reclaims what is rightfully his, even the gods can't stop him."

Balabal? As in, "veil"? Why would I hide under one? I don't even *own* a balabal.

"What's your problem?" I demand. But the lady and the boy just stare back at me with their red eyes and blank, expressionless faces.

My pendant starts to feel warm on my chest, as if it's come alive in the presence of these weirdos. Tannie, who's usually so friendly and chill, snarls at the lady and the boy. He crouches down, ready to pounce.

Goose bumps prickle my skin. What in the world is going on?

The inihaw vendor turns around to face me, pointing with the brush he uses to baste the meats. His eyes have also turned to that creepy red color. "And he shall."

Kitty. My heart is pounding so fast and so loud I can almost hear it. *I need to get to Kitty!*

But the teenage boy blocks my way. He slowly tilts his head to one side. "Soon, our brethren shall all break free."

Behind him, I see my sister patiently waiting for our drinks at the juice cart. Across the street, Carmen and her family are still busy sifting through preloved clothes. It's as if the bubble of weirdness is just around the inihaw stand.

The middle-aged lady holds her half-eaten isaw baboy in the air as if it were Excalibur. "No more suffering!"

The inihaw vendor nods in agreement. "It is our time to shine."

“From the darkness”—the teenage boy’s face forms a grotesque grin—“we will come and take what they stole from us.”

I clutch my pendant, only to realize it’s not only warm, it’s also starting to glow blue. Tannie keeps barking angrily at the super weird people.

The three of them take a step toward me and Tannie, boxing us in. They look at my pendant and then at each other, their faces contorted with identical sinister sneers.

“Go away!” I exclaim, my voice cracking. The three just keep moving closer and closer. My heart pounds louder. Tannie is shaking in fear, but he doesn’t leave my side.

“It has begun,” the vendor says.

The middle-aged lady lets out a shrill, hyenalike laugh. “He shall rise to power once again!”

The boy lifts his cup of spicy vinegar, as though making a toast. “The sun will fall.”

“And the worlds are ours,” the inihaw vendor says. His head rolls back, and dark smoke leaves his body. He cracks his neck, then takes a plastic cup and looks at me. To my surprise, his eyes have returned to a normal dark brown. “Matamis o maanghang? Sweet or spicy.”

“Halo, please,” I blurt out, taking the bundle of grilled skewered meats from him without thinking. I shake my head. “Wait. What? Are you talking about the sauce or the sun or the worlds or whatever?”

“The sauce, of course.” The inihaw vendor raises an

eyebrow as he hands me a cup of my preferred dip—a mix of sweet sauce and spicy vinegar. "Are you all right?"

"I'm fine," I murmur, exhaling deeply as my pulse slows down. My gaze falls on Tannie. He's scratching his chin with his hind leg. It's as if he's been calmly waiting for a piece of meat beside me all along, and not on the verge of going into battle in his ugly Christmas sweater.

The teenage boy is making his way to the junk shop across the street with his cup of vinegar and bag full of inihaw takeout. The middle-aged lady eats her skewered isaw, the same one she brandished at me like a sword, then pays for her meal. She tells the inihaw vendor to keep the change, smiles at him, and leaves. The inihaw vendor himself is humming under his breath as he fulfills orders for delivery.

Everyone who was super weird just a minute ago now looks normal. Their irises are ordinary brown in color, no red in sight. It's as if that creepy moment never happened at all.

"Let's just wait for Kitty over there," I tell the dog, sighing. "No one is going to believe me even if I have you for a witness. It's not like you can talk. Or can you?"

Tannie tilts his head to one side, raising an ear. For a second, it's almost as if he's throwing the question back at me.

"That's ridiculous. Dogs can't do pseudo-intellectual

question-and-answers," I say to no one, chuckling at myself. With Tannie in tow, I take a seat on a wooden bench reserved for inihaw customers. The dog lies in a comfortable sprawl beside my right foot, the perfect spot to bum leftovers from both Kitty and me.

Still, I keep an eye on the inihaw vendor. This time I'll be ready with my cell phone. I'll take a video of him being weird for proof. Proof for others, but mostly for me.

"Ahh-tehh Looooo!" Kitty calls, arriving with two cups of melon juice in her hands. "Drinks are here! What did I miss?"

I don't really feel like eating anymore, but Kitty will notice if I don't. There's no use worrying her about something that I'm not even sure happened. I force myself to smile as I take a bite of isaw with one hand and give my sister her share with the other. "Here's your food."

I've always had a very active and vivid imagination. Like, I had a clear picture in my mind when I did that Bernardo Carpio dying reenactment on the junk tires. I imagined the falling debris and crushing boulders so well, they seemed real.

But seeing random strangers act like they're possessed by creepy spirits reciting bad poetry? I shake my head. Schoolwork and mean girls like Carmen must have finally gotten to me.

I toss my remaining half stick of pork barbecue to Tannie. I've totally lost my appetite now.

“Are you okay, Ate?” Kitty studies me, her small brown eyes brimming with concern. “You’re awfully quiet.”

“I’m okay, just stuffed.” Well, I’m not totally lying. Really. I *am* full, and I’m okay *now* because Kitty is here. I give her a smile—a genuine one, this time.

We watch the dog carry the barbecue meat in his mouth as he makes his way up the street. He’s probably heading home to his human, to that person he calls his family.

Like Tannie, I also have my people—my family, my Kitty. Everything is going to be fine. I’m sure of it. . . . And it’s all because I have my sister with me.

CHAPTER TWO

Hello from Inarawan Street

It takes around ten minutes for Kitty and me to reach the crossroads leading to Inarawan Street from the inihaw stand. Thankfully, we don't meet any more spooky rambling people along the way. Still, I can't help but breathe a huge sigh of relief as Inarawan Street's Sangang-Daan Tree comes into view. For once, I'm glad to see this ancient, sinister-looking tree.

The Sangang-Daan Tree is exactly as its name indicates in Tagalog; it means "crossroads tree." Because, well, it's an old tree that's right in the middle of a crossroads. It's not in a traffic island and doesn't have fancy landscaping; it's literally *just there*. The city builders obviously didn't want to cut down the tree, so they just constructed the road around it.

A tree in the middle of a street like the Sangang-Daan Tree isn't unheard of, though. There's another tree in the middle of the road in Antipolo City, and that one is right smack in front of a mall. Interestingly, trees left untouched by city builders are almost always balete trees.

A balete tree is basically a strangler fig that starts out as an innocent seedling beside another healthy tree. As it grows, the balete engulfs the host tree with its vines until it totally entraps and kills the host tree.

Maybe that's why most people think there's something sinister about the balete. They say bad things will happen to anyone who tries to harm a balete, because magical creatures live on it. Or that the balete is under some powerful being's protection. I don't really believe in myths or superstitions, but I totally get it. I mean, if you're a tree that lives and thrives on the death of another, you shouldn't have to wonder why you have such a bad rep.

"The tree looks brighter today," I say, taking my sister's hand as we cross the street. "It doesn't have its usual gloomy feel to it. Like it finally woke up after a hundred years of sleep or something."

"It looks the same to me." Kitty takes a step forward. "Well, they seem to have cut some leaves—"

Beeeeeeeeeeeep!

"Watch out!" I pull my sister back to my side just in the

nick of time. A bucket truck drives by on the very same spot where Kitty's foot had been. "Geez. If you don't watch where you're going, you'll end up like roadkill, Meow."

"Sorry." Kitty gives me an apologetic smile, and I find myself smiling back. It's hard to stay mad at my sister. I hold her hand tight as we cross the street, making sure that there aren't any passing vehicles this time.

"Thank goodness we're almost home," I say. A huge wave of relief washes over me as soon as we step onto the corner of Inarawan Street. It's like covering your head with a thick blanket while a storm rages on outside your bedroom. The noise and the chaos seem muffled, and you finally feel safe.

But my relief turns to annoyance when I see the bucket truck that almost ran Kitty over parking beside a utility pole. The service crew brings out their equipment. Judging by their uniforms and the logo on their truck, they're from the electric company.

"Oh, great. Wala na namang kuryente," I say with a sigh, watching the boom lift a worker in the basket. "No electricity again."

I don't envy the lineman. I'd pee in my shorts going up on a bucket truck that's parked at a forty-five-degree angle. I'm sure he's got a great view, though. Well, probably not as awesome as the view he'd get from our apartment building (which is at the end of the street and its highest peak). But it's pretty enough that he'll want to bring out his phone and snap a picture if it's his first time seeing it.

Inarawan Street is one of those places blessed by the sun god, Apolaki. Okay, fine, I'm exaggerating. But really, whoever designed our street knew a great deal about the positions of the sun. Our neighborhood is the best place to watch the sunset, and the view at sunrise is even more amazing. It's like being inside an oil painting—it's surreal.

"The transformer must have overloaded again." Kitty purses her lips, shaking her head. "Don't forget to put citronella oil on your skin before bed, Ate. The mosquitoes will feast on you again if you don't."

"Yeah, I know," I say with a groan. Mosquitoes love to bite me, but they leave Mom and Kitty alone. For every twenty bites I get, they only get one, or even none. Bart said maybe the tiny vampiric insects just find my blood yummier, the same way I prefer seafood over beef. "I'm like an all-you-can-eat buffet for them—a Lulu buffet!"

"Oh, we can't let that happen. The mosquitoes might get indigestion," quips a beautiful trans woman in her early twenties, flashing us a dazzling smile from behind the overgrown bush she's trimming. She has this thick, very curly black hair that goes past her shoulders, and big brown eyes. Her skin is dark like mine. Unlike me, though, she's tall and has a high-bridged nose, so she still fits people's definition of a "morena beauty."

"Ate Mariel!" Kitty and I grin.

Ate Mariel is the "handy-lady" of Inarawan Street, and she's Tannie's human. Technically, Kitty and I should refer to Ate Mariel as "tita," or auntie, out of respect. But she says it makes her feel old, so we just call her "ate," or older sister, instead. Ate Mariel is also our next-door neighbor, so she's like an older sister to us already.

"Nice shirt," I tell Ate Mariel, admiring her purple shirt that has a huge black-and-white print of her favorite BTS member, V. Ate Mariel loves BTS, the world's awesomest Korean boy band, just like I do (though my favorite member is Jungkook). I'd buy BTS stuff too if I could, but it doesn't come cheap. Ate Mariel takes a lot of odd jobs here and there, so I guess that lets her afford nice things.

To be honest, I'm 100 percent certain that Mom would buy me expensive things if I asked. But Mom's job as a medical assistant in the neighborhood clinic doesn't pay much. It's hard enough for her to make ends meet as it is, with my epilepsy meds and regular brain checkups. I don't want to add another burden.

"You never know, Santa might give you a Jungkook shirt this year," Ate Mariel says with a wink. She chops the top of the shrub with her pruning shears, making the air around us smell leafy. The plant now looks like the top of Bart's semi-shaved head. "Hang out with me and Tannie outside the store later if you want. I'm manning it tonight. It'll take a while before the electricity comes back."

"We will!" I say while Kitty thanks Ate Mariel, who waves her away with a pretty grin.

Everyone in Inarawan trusts Ate Mariel. If she were able to split herself into many Ate Mariels, the whole neighborhood would probably hire her and her clones to do everything for them. Well, except for me. It's not that I don't trust her . . . it's just that I prefer to do things on my own, you know? Because if something goes wrong, the only one I'll have to blame will be myself.

Kitty and I continue our walk up the hill. Every neighbor we meet is ready with a smile and a cheery greeting. It's like this every day, but today something feels different. Not in a creepy way like at the inihaw stand, but there's just something off about the too-friendly greetings from the too-beautiful people of Inarawan Street.

"Don't you find it weird that our neighborhood handyperson is a gorgeous lady like Ate Mariel?" I ask my sister as another person offers us a good afternoon. "Everyone seems so perfect, even Tannie, with that adorably perfect fur-cut of his. Inarawan Street is like a movie set for a Hollywood flick."

"I never really thought about it, but now that you mention it . . ." Kitty frowns, looking around as we keep walking. "Yes, I have to agree. It's almost like being in a different realm."

"You mean like the Mirror Dimension in *Doctor Strange*?"

“Sort of,” says my sister. K-pop is my thing, and Asian dramas are Kitty’s, but we both love watching superhero movies. “I’m thinking more like the Realms of Tagalog mythology, the ones we learned about in school. None of the funky stuff and psychedelic lights of Marvel’s Mirror Dimension.”

“Ah. Yeah. I get it.”

Ancient Tagalogs believed that the universe is made up of three Realms—the Upperworld, the Middleworld, and the Underworld. The Upperworld is where the gods and other immortals live, like a heaven of some sort. The Middleworld is here, where we mortals live. And the Underworld is where spirits go when they die. Good souls go to Maca, while corrupt souls are made to suffer eternal punishment in Kasanaan.

“If Inarawan Street is too extra to be the Middleworld and too sunny to be the Underworld . . .” Kitty tilts her head to one side, something she always does whenever she’s thinking. “Maybe the Upperworld—”

“Oh, definitely *not* the Upperworld.” I point to the neighborhood sundry store that comes into view. “Something with a name and a sign that ugly can’t be in heaven!”

Kitty and I laugh at the sari-sari store’s funny sign.

Like most sari-sari store signs, it’s made of wood and perched above the wide, metal-barred window in front of the shop. But the fairy lights around it make it look as if the Grinch had tried to take them, then changed his mind midway, leaving half a strand of lights hanging awkwardly on one side. The sign itself has this unique but badly drawn cartoon painting of Bugs Bunny wearing sunglasses and smoking a cigarette.

Bads Bunny Sari-Sari Store is the only convenience store on the entire stretch of Inarawan Street. You know, "Bads" as in "bad" and "Bugs" combined. It's a ridiculous pun, but absolutely something that its owner would think of.

Bads Bunny belongs to Manong Sol, as does the Sikaran gym beside it and the whole multipurpose building where they're located. There are apartments on the second floor, one of which we're renting, while the other three are rented by Mom's best friend, Bart's family, and Ate Mariel. So that makes Manong Sol our landlord and, unofficially, my Sikaran teacher.

I say "unofficially" because I don't pay for formal lessons and only join the classes whenever I want to. I'm not allowed to spar with anyone at the gym except Manong Sol himself, though. Maybe it's because I'm so tiny. But to his credit, Manong Sol has never kicked me out of his gym when he holds classes.

I'm so glad he hasn't, because Sikaran is such an awesome traditional Tagalog martial art. It involves hand fighting but mostly kicking. Imagine being able to take down somebody as tall as a doorway using only your foot when you're as tiny as I am. Sikaran makes me feel like I can protect Mom and my sister, even though I'm so small and scrawny. It makes me feel powerful.

"Hoy! Bumalik ka dito. Kulang bayad mo!" Manong Sol's loud voice carries all the way down the street to where we're at. One of the Sikaran gym regulars, a man who's, like, twice as wide and twice as tall as Manong Sol, stops dead in his tracks. From the looks of it, this guy didn't pay enough for whatever it is he bought at the store and is now being called back by the grumpy old man. Even from here I can see the big guy hunch his shoulders, cowering in fear as he does what Manong Sol orders him to do.

I don't blame him. Manong Sol scares a lot of people, even those who are bigger and younger than he is. He's around seventy years old (he's wrinkly and everything), but he's really buff and strong. Just imagine a grandpa who's built like Captain America—that's Manong Sol.

"Look, Meow. Tita Cecile is back!" I exclaim. Crossing the street to Bads Bunny are Mom and Tita Cecile. Kitty and I refer to Tita Cecile as tita, or auntie, even though Tita Cecile is Mom's best friend and not her sister. Like me and Kitty, they look nothing alike. Tita Cecile is a plus-sized lady with short, bleached hair, and she's a head shorter than Mom. She has dark-brown skin like me. But Mom and Tita Cecile are such besties, they might as well be siblings. "I hope she got us stuff from Baguio. The strawberries and ube from there are super yummy."

"And peanut brittle!" Kitty quickens her steps to match my stride. "Glad to see Mom's off early from work today too."

Mom's boss must have known it's the first day of Christmas break and, being the world's greatest and nicest boss, let Mom off early to spend the rest of this awesome day with us.

Maybe the start of our school holiday isn't so bad anymore. I almost forgot about that weird thing at the inihaw stand—well, *almost.*

"Mom! Tita Cecile!" Kitty and I call, waving our arms out of their sockets.

They wave back. Tita Cecile gestures for us to hurry, taking a seat on the wooden bench in front of Bads Bunny Sari-Sari Store. Mom walks up to the counter, probably ordering karioka for each of us. Every afternoon around this time, Manong Sol sells these yummy fried and skewered rice balls covered in caramel sauce.

They're my absolute favorite. I may be full from the inihaw, but I always save space in my tummy for karioka.

"Even Tannie is already here." Kitty points to the dog lounging on the wooden bench across from Tita Cecile. "He runs so fast— Oh! I feel dizzy."

The ground beneath our feet shakes.

"Lindol!" People scream "earthquake" around us.

"Get down, Meow!" I yell.

Kitty and I drop to the ground at the same time, bracing

ourselves. I cover Kitty's head with my hand. It won't do much if an electrical post or some structural thing collapses on us. But it's better than doing nothing. I'll always do everything to protect my sister, no matter how hopeless it is.

"We're okay. We're okay," Kitty murmurs, almost like a prayer. I can feel the fear in her voice. I hold her tighter. I can't stop the earthquake, but I'll protect her with every last inch of my body.

"It'll be over soon," I assure her, wincing as we hear a loud crash behind us. My heart is racing, but I'm trying my best not to show Kitty how terrified I truly am. I'm her ate, after all. I need to keep her safe and calm. "Earthquakes don't last long—"

A tremor ripples through the ground. It lifts the asphalt layer of the road, curling into an arched form as it moves toward us. It's like when the sea rushes in and breaks on the shore. But unlike those harmless shoreline waves, this ripple upends the people who are running to safety as well as the vehicles parked on the sides of the road.

One of those vehicles is the bucket truck. The linemen who were working on the electrical lines somehow managed to get to safety. But the driver is still stuck behind the wheel, screaming for us to move. "TABI!"

The loud screech of metal plowing through the asphalt drowns out his voice and the truck's honks. The driver seems to be desperately trying to stop the vehicle from crashing into us, but he can't. Gravity and the road's steep slope are making sure the truck annihilates everything in its path. Everything, including me and my sister.

Kitty and I have nowhere to go.

We're going to die.

Everything around me slows down, even my pounding heart. On the other side of the street, I see Tita Cecile holding on to a hysterical Mom while Tannie pulls on Mom's shirt. They're obviously trying to stop her from coming toward us.

Listen to them, Mom. There's no use. You won't reach us in time. Just save yourself! I want to shout, but nothing comes out of my mouth.

I need to think.

There must be a way.

There has to be.

I can't let Kitty die.

I look down at my sister, who's frozen in terror and trembling in my arms.

"Please help me!" I pray to God and Papa Jesus and Mama Mary. If Tagalog deities exist and there's a god who watches over desperate kids like me, I beg them too. "Help me save my sister!"

Luningning, listen to me. I hear Manong Sol's voice in my head. *Stand up and spread your arms in front of you.*

"But I can't let go!" I say, holding Kitty tighter. I'll do anything to save her.

Do as I say! You do not have any other choice.

I must be so close to death that I'm hearing the old man's voice in my head. Manong Sol runs toward us from across the street. He even begins to resemble a streaking ray of light. Kind of like the sun when it's shining bright.

I hold my arms out in front of me. My hands glow blue, and so does my pendant.

Be ready to catch the truck.

That's ridiculous. I'm just a tiny toothpick of a girl.

I believe in you.

The bucket truck will probably toss us into the next street when it hits. But what choice do I have? We're going to die anyway, so I might as well listen to this imitation of Manong Sol's voice in my head.

I am not an imitation. I am real. You can do it, Luningning. You will save your sister.

The bright light around my hands grows brighter as the truck gets closer. I don't know how or why it's doing that, but I keep my hands in front of me.

The truck will plow right over my tiny body, but maybe I can get it to slow down a little bit. And maybe—just maybe—my desperate act will give Kitty a fraction of a chance to live.

I brace myself for the impact.

The truck's front grille touches my fingers, and I'm surrounded by intense bright-blue light.

CHAPTER THREE

My Weird Neighbors Get Even Weirder

My dream is really weird. And I don't just mean "weird." This one is next-level weird. Like, weirdest of the weird kind of weird.

In this dream, I am Bernardo Carpio, complete with the long hair and bahag, a loincloth worn by men in ancient Tagalog times. I'm pushing against two giant rocks that are trying to crush me. These rocks are as big as mountains, exactly like in the scene I tried to reenact outside the auto repair shop.

"Get me out of here!" I scream. But no one can hear me.

I look down and notice that I'm also wearing my pendant, but it's strung on an abaca fiber rope instead of the metal chain I always wear.

The dream scene changes.

This time, though, I'm stopping a bucket truck with my bare hands—bare hands that are glowing with blue light.

It doesn't end there. The blue light explodes, and the sun falls from the sky while a snakelike shadow slithers in the clouds. Then a beautiful woman in a traditional Tagalog baro't saya suddenly appears in front of me. She seems to be about the same age as Mom, but her eyes make her seem older—much, much older.

The lady looks at me, as if she realizes that I'm staring at her. She says my name. "I'm so sorry, Luningning, but it's almost time. The Salamangka in you has awakened. Soon you will have to choose."

"What do you mean? Who are you? What's awaken—" I try to hold on to the lady, but something pulls me backward. It's like getting into a fight with someone and you have long hair for them to grab on to. But this is unlike any fight I've had with Carmen and her crew. The force pulls me so hard, I feel as though my soul is getting yanked out of my body. Everything around me is moving fast, but in reverse.

Then I wake up.

I'm suddenly blasted with sunlight. I rub my eyes. As my vision clears, I realize I'm not in our bedroom. I'm not even at home.

"Where am I?" I yawn. The strong scent of nail polish and hair spray wafts under my nose, making me gag. "Gross!"

The person leaning on my shoulder stirs. It's Kitty.

"*Yoo-kay-ah-teh*," she mumbles. Kitty's asking me if I'm okay. Having been roomies since forever, I've long learned to decipher her sleep talk.

"I'm fine, go back to sleep," I whisper, tucking a stray hair off my sister's face and behind her ear. I gently lay her head on a throw pillow on the sofa's armrest so she'll be more comfortable.

I stand and stretch, looking around. Somehow, my sister and I are camping out in the reception area of Marites and Tolits's Beauty Salon. On the receptionist's counter there's a dancing Santa beside a miniature Christmas tree. The ugly Santa is moving its hips to the beat of the Christmas music coming from the speakers mounted on the ceiling. The partition walls separating the styling area from the lobby are decorated with plate-sized paper snowflakes. Beside the sofa, the edges of the floor-to-ceiling glass windows and glass door are sprayed with fake snow.

I just can't remember how we got here. Or why we're even here.

"Wake up, Meow." I poke my sister on the cheek. She just grunts. I squeeze her nose gently with a "Boop! Boop!" Still, she doesn't stir. Kitty must be really tired to be so deep in sleep.

Marites and Tolits's Beauty Salon is usually where Mom brings me and Kitty for a haircut (or trim, in my sister's case). It's on the first floor of the house Tita Marites shares with her brother, Tito Tolits. This sibling-run business is the only place for pampering near Inarawan Street, so it's always packed with customers.

Well, it's *usually* packed with customers. There's no queue here in the waiting area, which is odd. Did Tita Marites and Tito Tolits get a bad review on social media that scared everyone off or something?

As the speakers play the third stanza of Mariah Carey's "All I Want for Christmas Is You," the ugly Santa tries to keep up with the increasingly brisk tempo. It's wiggling its plastic butt so fast, it causes its base to sway like a utility post in an earthquake.

An earthquake. I gasp. Yes, that's what happened! There was an earthquake on our way home.

Thank goodness Kitty is all right. I hurry to the glass door to look outside. I hope Mom's okay. I hope Bart, Tita Cecile, Ate Mariel, and Manong Sol all made it to safety. I hope— "What in the world?"

We learned in school that quakes happen when the earth's crust moves. An earthquake as powerful as the one we experienced would have been felt many kilometers away. Inarawan Street is just a fifteen-minute walk from this beauty parlor. There's no way this street remained untouched while the rest of Metro Manila shook as if the world were ending.

But it did. It's as if the earthquake didn't happen at all here.

Everyone is just going about their usual one-week-before-Christmas thing. No one's bothering to check if there are cracks on their walls. The roofs seem like they didn't collapse. And the utility posts look as sturdy as before. There is absolutely no sign of earthquake damage.

"I need to think." I close my eyes and take a deep breath. This doesn't make any sense. I try to remember how Kitty and I survived the runaway truck. Did we run? We couldn't have—the ground was shaking too much to even stand. So how did we escape?

The blue light.

There was this superbright, will-burn-right-through-your-brains-if-you-look-at-it blue light.

Maybe the blue light saved us.

"Don't be silly," I tell myself. The blue light couldn't have saved us. It's like saying *Captain Marvel* is real and not just a movie. That I'm like Captain Marvel herself, who's superstrong and basically indestructible. That I used blue light to stop the runaway truck from crushing Kitty and me.

"I'm not Captain Marvel," I say out loud with a laugh, opening my eyes. "I'm just dreaming—"

"Ahem." A man clears his throat, followed by muffled voices coming from the styling area. I follow the sound as carefully and quietly as I can, hiding behind the partition wall.

Kitty will scold me when she finds out I've been eaves-dropping, but adults usually tell each other things that they don't like kids to hear. And after today? I want answers. Real ones, not the "you're too young for this" kind of answer.

From where I'm hidden, I see Mom and Tita Cecile sitting side by side on styling chairs while Tita Marites works on Mom's hair. A male customer is in the mani-pedi chair. Manong Sol is walking back and forth behind everyone like a nosy supervisor. Tito Tolits soon enters with a tray, carrying two glasses of what looks like iced lemonade.

"Thanks, Tolits," says Tita Cecile, taking a glass from the tray for herself and handing the other one to Manong Sol. "It came from the Underworld. I felt it."

The Underworld? Like, that place where dead people go?

I pick my ears. No, that can't be it. I just heard wrong.

"Ah. Much better," Manong Sol says. "Mapulon's tonics never fail to energize me." He takes a sip of his drink. "Has your father reached out to you yet?"

Tita Cecile shakes her head. "Tatay and his minions haven't even sent me a text or anything."

Tatay. Tatay means "father."

I'm surprised that Tita Cecile's dad is still alive. I always assumed he was dead, as she never talks about him. Mom said it was a "sensitive issue." Usually, when someone says that about their parent, the parent is either already in heaven or on bad terms with them.

"He would have at least rubbed it in our faces about the work we had to do." Manong Sol gulps down the last of his drink, letting out a loud burp. Gross. "We're all exhausted trying to fix this world while he sits pretty on that throne."

Tita Cecile heaves another defeated sigh. I guess they have father-daughter issues, after all.

"I know. It's unlike him," she says. "Tatay is dealing with trouble. He just doesn't want to admit it."

"Are you really sure it came from there?" Mom asks. Her voice is muffled by the towel Tita Marites is using to dry her hair. But I recognize that tone—it's the same one Mom uses whenever she's worried about something.

"Yes, I'm sure. There's no doubt about it." Tita Cecile finishes her drink, wincing. "It takes a great deal of power to affect another Realm like that. The only explanation for the recent events is that something huge happened down there."

Recent events? I frown. So even the adults noticed the weird things going on. It isn't just me or my imagination.

Now the question is . . . which of those weird things are for real? So far, everything I've supposedly witnessed makes me wonder if I have a different kind of epilepsy. You know, the kind that makes people hallucinate before a seizure. My neurologist told me my epilepsy isn't like that, but now I wonder if I should get tested again.

"I've heard rumors"—Tito Tolits soaks the male customer's fingers in solution—"that the Maligno has indeed escaped and he's coming for the child—"

"Do not speak of such a thing, brother!" Tita Marites stops applying the dye solution to Mom's hair to scowl at Tito Tolits. As she faces him, I notice her face changing. Like, literally changing. It becomes sharper, almost birdlike. But as Tita Marites squeezes Mom's plastic-cape-covered shoulders, the stylist's face returns to normal. "Don't mind him," she says. "He's just very gullible. Our parlor is everyone's favorite place to gossip. Unfortunately, he'll believe anything he hears around here."

Tito Tolits throws his sister an equally sharp birdlike look. But he doesn't take the bait and just goes back to giving his customer a mani-pedi.

"Sir, medyo matagal-tagal na kayong di nagawi dito sa parlor para magpa-pedicure ha," Tito Tolits says, telling the man that it's been a while since he came to the parlor for a pedicure. He pulls up a stool in front of him and removes the man's shoe. But instead of toes popping out, the shoe reveals a hoof—a horse's hoof. "Your hooves will take a while to file."

Hooves?!

"I've got time." The man lifts a hand, revealing bony fingers. He snorts, and his head morphs into that of a horse.

My jaw drops.

Horse head. Horse hooves. Bony and disproportionately long limbs. The man looks exactly like the half horse, half man of Tagalog lore described in my Filipino textbook.

"You're a tikbalang!" The words fly out of my mouth before I can stop them.

The adults turn to look at me. Mom gasps, covering her mouth. Tita Marites drops her dye brush. The customer's feet jerk up in surprise. Tito Tolits falls off the stool, narrowly avoiding a kick to his face.

But Manong Sol and Tita Cecile are unperturbed.

"Don't be rude, Luningning," Manong Sol says, waving his hand. "I agree this fella over here is very unattractive, but it is not polite to tell him he looks like a horse."

I blink. I look back at the customer and see that he's a normal man. He's not handsome, just as Manong Sol says, but 100 percent, definitely not a tikbalang man. "Okay—"

"It's rude either way." Tita Cecile frowns at Manong Sol. "Didn't you say you were leaving today? Now is a great time for you to go."

I bite my tongue and stop myself from saying that she's also being rude to Manong Sol, who's, like, many, many years older than Tita Cecile. Surprisingly, Manong Sol doesn't seem to mind. Something's still bothering me, though. "But . . ."

Tita Cecile flicks her hand like Manong Sol. "Yes, kiddo?"

"Um . . ." I scratch my head. "I can't remember."

The question is on the tip of my tongue, but right now I'm drawing a blank. It's the same feeling when you try to recall a word for something but just can't find it in your head. Like, deep down you know what it is, and you're pretty certain you've used it before. But for some reason, you can't say what exact word it is at that moment.

"It'll come back to you," Manong Sol assures me, his usually gruff tone softening. He meets Mom's gaze through the mirror. "I'll return after solstice. It will be all right, Jenalyn."

"Thank you po."

"Behave yourself, Luningning." Manong Sol bids the beauty parlor siblings and their customer goodbye, then leaves.

Tita Marites and Tito Tolits busy themselves with their respective customers. Tita Marites with Mom and Tita Cecile, and Tito Tolits with the mani-pedi dude. Mom and Tita Cecile exchange a glance through the mirror.

"Mom, what's going on?" I really feel like I'm missing something here.

"You'll find out soon, my sweet. We'll tell you when we get home," my mother says, biting her lower lip. She looks like she's about to cry. "Stay by my side for a bit. Bart's on his way. He said you promised to play some online game with him."

I did? I don't recall promising something like that to Bart. The games he plays bore me. I try my best not to look surprised for Mom, though. It's too trivial a thing to argue about when she looks so sad already. "Okay, Mom."

* * *

"I'm hungry." I rub my growling tummy as Bart, Kitty, and I leave the internet café. "You should treat us at the ini-haw stand. Your team wouldn't have won if not for Meow and me."

"No, Kitty's the only one who helped. Your avatar and its pet bird kept getting in everyone's way," Bart says, snorting. Tannie the shih tzu does the same thing if I give him pork fat instead of barbecue meat. "Anyway, you're always hungry. Just wait a little. Your mom wants you home after the game, so we do as she says."

I roll my eyes. Bart is what I call selectively stingy. He'll save money on everything except whatever he's obsessed about—like his favorite online game, *Dambana Wars*. Every week he spends half his allowance for power-up items and virtual coins. He needed me and Kitty to join his team for this special online game event, but we have only one computer at home, and it's very old and slow. So he paid three hundred pesos' worth of computer rental for us at the internet café.

"No worries. It was fun helping you." Kitty yawns. "I just want to go home and sleep. I don't know why, but I feel like I've been hit by a ten-ton truck."

"Same." I massage the back of my neck. I'm tired too, but I can't remember why. This usually happens after I've had an epileptic seizure. The seizing and shaking are like blank spots in my memory, but I get super exhausted after each episode. Kitty doesn't have epilepsy, but we're experiencing the same thing, so we must have done something else together.

The internet café is about a ten-minute walk from Marites and Tolits's Beauty Salon, which is fifteen minutes away from Inarawan Street. On a usual day, I don't mind walking. But Kitty is tired, and the sun has set. My phone clock says it's half past six already. I point to a covered waiting area on the intersection up ahead where a couple of motorcycles with passenger cabs are parked. "Let's just take a tricycle. I don't want to walk in the dark."

"Great idea," says my sister. She hugs herself and rubs her arms as cold wind blows at us. I put an arm around her even though I'm shivering too. "Thanks, Ate."

We're almost at the intersection when Bart suddenly stops.

"Wait," he says, holding his arm out in front of me like a boom gate on a roadway. Bart's skin is warm against mine. He's so close that I can see how curly his dark lashes are.

"What are you doing?" I yank my arm self-consciously, turning away. My gaze lands back on the waiting area, and I'm surprised by what I see. "Where did all the tricycles go? I know I saw at least two of them!"

A frown forms on Bart's red lips. He sniffs the air. "Oh no."

"Is something wrong?" Kitty tilts her head. "Are you okay?"

Eek! Eek! A bat shrieks above us.

Across the street, somewhere within the branches of a mango tree, another bat shrieks. Then another. And another. It's like having front-row seats in a creepy orchestra of agitated, screaming winged rats. Even from where we are, we can hear their wings flapping furiously.

Kitty holds on to my arm tight. "What's going on?"

"I don't know. Bart—"

But Bart isn't paying attention. He's staring at the bats, and the bats are staring back at him.

"Hoy. Tama na yan." I tell my friend that's enough in a low voice. A bat nearby lets out a loud screech, showing us its sharp teeth. I put an arm around Kitty and pull her close to me. "Let's just walk away slowly."

Only Kitty follows my lead. Bart's frown deepens.

"A warning," he mutters. His voice is so low that I feel goose bumps appear on my arms. Bart's nose flares as he sniffs around like a dog. "I need to tell her."

"Ate . . ." Kitty's voice shakes. "Ate Lulu . . ."

The fear in her tone is enough to shake me into action.

"Seriously, dude, stop it." I snap my fingers in front of Bart's face. "Yo!"

Bart blinks, finally turning to look at us. "I need to go back to the parlor. She has to know what's going on."

"Tell who? What are you— Ack!"

A cloud of bats dives toward us. Kitty and I cover our heads, but Bart doesn't move. He's unfazed by the creepy bats, watching them as they land on the tree in front of us.

"Just trust me, okay?" Bart says. He takes both my hands in his. I try to yank them back, but he holds on tight. His hands are very warm. "I promised to protect you with my life. That's all I can tell you right now. So please. For once, listen to me. Run straight home. Don't stop until you reach Inarawan Street. You'll be safe there."

"Bart, you're scaring us," Kitty says.

Bart doesn't reply to her. He looks straight at me. Maybe it's a trick of the light from the streetlamps above, but I'm pretty sure I notice a red glint in his usually dark-brown eyes. He gives my hands a squeeze before finally releasing them. I wish he'd hold on much longer. His touch made me feel . . . I don't know . . . safe.

"Run home." Bart repeats his instructions and dashes back to the street we've passed.

"Ate, what are we going to do?"

Before I can answer, we hear a flapping of wings. Loud flapping wings of something big.

The hairs on the back of my neck stand up. I know Bart said we should run straight home. But home is still too far away.

"We need to take cover. Meow, stay close." I pull her with me to the nearest alley. The mysterious flapping sound is softer from here. I should feel we're safer now, but I don't. Still, I give my sister's hand a squeeze. "Don't worry, it's far—"

SCREECH! A flying humanoid creature lets out a piercing cry above us. It has batlike wings on its back and feathers peeking through the collar of its shirt. It has huge talons for feet. The creature is like a cross between a bat, an eagle, and a cranky school principal in a very bad mood.

A wakwak. That creature is a wakwak. A very real wakwak in bright-pink leggings and an oversized orange shirt.

I blink in disbelief and turn to my sister. I must be dreaming again. "Are you seeing this?"

Instead of answering, Kitty just stares at the wakwak with bulging eyes.

Yep. She can see it.

The wakwak cackles. "I've been looking forward to meeting you, Luningning Sinagtala."

CHAPTER FOUR

I Vaporize My Self-Appointed Number One Fan with a Snake Lightsaber

Kitty and I have read about wakwaks in school. But I never imagined I would come across a wakwak in real life, especially one that actually knows my name.

"How do you know who I am?" I ask nervously.

"Of course I know your name. I'm your number one fan." The wakwak sneers, showing its sharp, sharklike teeth. "And I also know you, Katrina Sinagtala."

"I don't know who *you* are," I snap, trying my best to keep the shakiness out of my voice. We're stuck between two apartment buildings and a dead end. We're trapped. The only way out is to pass beneath the creature.

I made a mistake thinking we'd have shelter in this

alley. But how was I to know the thing that was chasing us was a living, breathing, horribly dressed wakwak?

This is all Bart's fault. He should have said that a wakwak was after us. I would have run faster when the sound of the flapping got softer—wakwaks are known to mislead their prey by making it seem like they're still far away when they're actually very near. If he'd been honest, I wouldn't be in this situation in the first place. Bart and I are going to have a serious friendship talk if I get out of this alive.

"I've been watching you for so long, but that dog is always sniffing about when you're not on Inarawan," the wakwak says in a voice that sounds like she's whining. Kind of like me when Mom orders me to wash the dishes and Kitty is too busy with homework to help. The wakwak brings out something from under her ugly orange shirt. I can't see clearly, though, as she's at least six feet in the air. But it looks like a glass vial with something black in it. "Those selfish gods think they're the only ones who can manipulate the Balabal. Ha! They are so wrong. Well, I have this now. They can't hide you from us anymore. . . . I can do anything I want with you, torture you till the worlds end. And no one will hear your screams."

So ironic that her T-shirt says "Good Vibes Only!" Threatening to torture someone is definitely not promoting good vibes.

Kitty squeezes my hand so hard it hurts.

"Gee, thanks," I say. A wave of irritation starts to overcome my fear. This creature is scaring Kitty. No one, and I mean *no one*, is allowed to bully my sister. "Listen, bird-lady. We're only eleven. We don't know you. Nor do we care about your issues. So why would we hide? Kitty and I have nothing to do with old people problems!"

"Ate, please don't," Kitty says in a small voice. "Don't make her mad."

My anger dissipates. I clear my head, thinking of a way to escape. My gaze lands on an electricity post nearby. Its dark wires are almost invisible in the night sky.

Aha!

"Run when I say so," I whisper back, looking pointedly to our right, where the utility pole is. Let's hope the wak-wak isn't great at disentangling herself from wiring. "On three."

Kitty squeezes my hand. I'm glad she understood.

"One . . ." I start the countdown.

"The gods are weak, thanks to my master," the wakwak says. "And you have no idea what power you hold." Her creepy grin fades a bit. "But you're still so well-guarded. They even made an entire street just for you!"

I always find it annoying when movies feature villains who yak about their plans and marvel at how brilliant they are. Instead of, I don't know, just doing what they say they will.

Well, this villainous wakwak can keep yakking all she wants so Kitty and I can make our escape.

"Two . . ."

"Those meddling deities!" the wakwak hisses. "It's so hard to terrorize you when they and their annoying little minions are always hanging around. But that doesn't matter now. Master has made sure the tremor drained their powers. They are no match for his genius!"

"Thr—" I stop mid-whisper and frown at the wakwak. "Deities? You don't mean gods and goddesses?"

"What else would deities be?" The wakwak rolls her eyes. "I thought your kind was smart, Salamangkero. Of course I meant gods and goddesses. They're everywhere, like pests. Like cockroaches. Like mosquitoes—"

"Salamangkero? What's that?" My frown deepens. Sounds like a reptile or something. Whatever it is, this creature can't be referring to me. "I'm not a Salamangkero. You're mistaking me for someone else."

"Oh, wow. You *really* don't know." The wakwak lets out a cruel laugh. "He's right again, as usual."

"Who's right?"

I feel a tug on my hand.

"Ate," Kitty says. She keeps her voice low, but I can hear the urgency in it.

Oh yeah. Our escape.

I squeeze Kitty's hand to let her know I understand.

"Your guards don't stand a chance against my kind

without those gods." The wakwak preens. "Prepare to suffer, Luningning Sinagtala."

Nope. We're getting out of here.

As if by coincidence, the stars twinkle bright in the sky. I don't know how that's possible since it's too early in the evening for stars to be that bright. But I never thought I'd be needing to escape a wakwak either. Thanks to the stars, Kitty and I can see our escape route better.

"He is going to be so pleased. You're falling right into his trap—"

"NOW!"

My sister and I run toward the utility post, veering right before we hit the pole. As expected, the wakwak follows us and flies smack into the tangle of wiring. We don't stop, and her furious screeches tell us that my plan worked.

"It's not going to hold her for long!" I say, throwing a glance at my sister, who's running behind me. Her face is red and dripping with sweat and fear. I'm not sure if we're safe at home or anywhere. But at least we won't be out in the open. "We have to hurry, Kitty. We're almost there. You can do it."

"Ahhhhh!"

I glance over my shoulder to find Kitty sprawled on the ground. She's holding her knee and it's bleeding.

"KITTY!"

“I tripped.” My sister sobs. “I’m sorry, Ate.”

“We’ll patch you up later.” I crouch low on the ground. “Put your arms around my neck and your legs around my waist. You’re going on a piggyback ride.”

“I’ll just slow you down, Ate. Leave me—”

“DO AS I SAY OR WE BOTH DIE!” I feel bad shouting at her, but there’s no time for drama. Thankfully, Kitty finally does what she’s told.

As I stand with my sister on my back, a warm feeling washes over me. I get a sudden surge of strength, and I’m able to lift her easily. She’s surprisingly light. Very, *very* light. It’s as if she weighs nothing at all.

“Hold tight, Meow!” I run up the street as fast as I can. I really don’t know how I’m doing this, but who cares. Up ahead, the Sangang-Daan Tree gets nearer and nearer. Starlight shines on the balete like a giant trophy at a finish line. We’re almost there.

Watch out, Lulu. The wakwak is near, says a voice in my head. It sounds like someone our age, though I can’t be sure, as I’ve never heard it before now. *I’m sorry I can’t do anything except light your path in this Realm. But help is on the way.*

I don’t know where this voice is coming from or who’s talking. But it gives me the encouragement I need. We will be okay.

But as we’re about to reach the balete tree, the wakwak suddenly lands in front of us, blocking our path. Her face is contorted with a sneer, making her birdlike features resemble a hungry pterodactyl's.

"You can't escape, Luningning Sinagtala," the wakwak squeals in wicked glee. "His brilliant magic made sure of it. He'll be even more powerful, thanks to you."

I put Kitty down. I'm not ready to give up yet.

Suddenly, I feel the weight of something in my pocket. I reach inside, finding a balisong—a small butterfly knife. I have no idea how it got there, but I'm glad it did. "We're not dying. Not today."

The balisong feels natural in my hand. As if this isn't the first time I've used it. A memory flashes in my mind—a memory of me sparring with someone using this very same knife.

I don't think an adult would ever let a kid spar using weapons. But the memory feels so real, even if it's probably just a dream. It feels as real as me pushing the runaway bucket truck away from me and Kitty.

"I can do this." Dream or not, something tells me I know how to use this knife.

"Ate, the ground is inclined. You need to throw it at an arc—"

I ignore Kitty and throw the balisong straight at the wakwak. It soars with more speed than I intended . . . and grazes her left wing.

Oops.

The wakwak screeches in pain.

"Ate Lu!" Kitty groans. "You should have aimed for its heart."

"I *was* aiming for its heart," I grumble. "It's dark. I can't see well."

EEEEEEEEEKKKK!

The wakwak screeches once again. This time it's so loud I feel like my ears will burst.

I take a step back and pull Kitty close to me.

The wakwak lunges for us.

I hug my sister and turn her away from the wakwak, shielding her. I close my eyes and wait for the creature to bite my neck.

The wakwak lets out another ear-piercing shrill, but the bite doesn't come.

"STOP!"

Mom and Tita Cecile suddenly appear. Mom runs to us as Tita Cecile holds the wakwak by her ankles with a whip. A thick, long whip that's glowing blue like a *Star Wars* lightsaber.

"It's all right, girls," says Mom, hugging us close. "It's going to be okay."

"Jen, take the girls and run home!" Tita Cecile says, wiping sweat from her shoulder. "You'll be safer inside."

"Let me go before I fly away with you, *my lady*," the wakwak snarls. "He's weakened all of you, and it's all part of his plan. But you . . . I see your strength isn't what it used to be. Is it because of this child?"

“I will let you go only if you swear to leave this family be.” Tita Cecile tugs on the whip, and the wakwak screams in pain. “Or you’ll suffer my wrath.”

“Die with her, goddess!” The wakwak dives at Tita Cecile, loosening the whip’s hold on her feet.

Goddess? I snort. What a weirdo. This wakwak seriously needs some villain-ing lessons. Villain-ing lesson 101: you don’t compliment your enemy when you’re attacking them.

Tita Cecile steps back, but the creature digs its claws into her shoulders. She lets go of the whip and screams in agony.

“CECILE!” Mom cries.

Tita Cecile and the wakwak slug it out. I had no idea Tita Cecile has such a nasty uppercut punch!

Mom picks up Tita Cecile’s fallen whip and hands it to me. “Use this, Lu. You’re the only one who can. Your tita is powerful, but right now, she needs your help.”

My jaw drops in shock. “Me?”

Kitty steps between Mom and me. “No. Are you serious, Mom? Ate Lulu might get hurt. You’re *our mother.* You’re supposed to protect us. You should know better.”

“I know, my sweet. I will protect you both with my dying breath. But I can’t wield the whip’s power even if I wanted to—but your ate can.” Mom bites her lower lip. It’s like she wants to say more but changes her mind. “Trust me. I’ll tell you more later. You’ve been trained to defeat creatures far worse than a wakwak.”

"What do you mean?" I say. "I don't understand— Ow!" My temples throb in pain as the wave of memories rushes into my head. The scenes flash in my mind like a movie on fast-forward, then suddenly slow down.

That's when I remember using a variety of weapons. Like, for example, failing miserably with the bow and arrow. Accuracy just isn't my thing. But I also remember using a practice balisong to defeat a one-eyed giant by stabbing it at close range, wielding a single-edged sword with a tapered training blade against a ghoul, and cracking a rubber whip at a flying creature. I remember actually kicking a thousand banana trees in a forest where plants regrow perpetually. I remember a voice whispering instructions in my ear.

My memories are still fuzzy, but there's one thing I'm sure of. I was trained for this.

"You can do it, Lulu." Mom gives me a sad smile.

"But . . . Ate . . ." Kitty says.

"I'll be fine. Mom's right. I can do this." I give my sister a quick hug, then take the whip by the handle. The weapon glows blue at my touch like it did when Tita Cecile was using it.

"I need a little help here!" Tita Cecile says, narrowly avoiding getting punched by the wakwak. "Vanquish this brat, Lulu!"

That's easier said than done. "How?"

"My gods! Didn't they teach you self-defense?"

"I know Sikaran, but it doesn't include using a snake lightsaber!"

The wakwak screeches and disentangles herself from Tita Cecile's hold. She flies up in a flash.

I let out a huge sigh of relief. "Oh, good. It's gone."

"It's not gone, just building momentum. Look." Tita Cecile points at the sky. She then slumps to the ground, wiping sweat off her forehead with the back of her hand. "Also, that weapon is a buntot pagi, a stingray's tail, not a snake lightsaber."

I spot the wakwak barreling her way back down toward us, her arms and wings tucked to her sides like a skydiver in a high-speed descent, an orange-and-pink bullet from the sky. In a few seconds we'll know what it feels like to be hit by a ten-ton truck.

"I don't care what this is. Tita Cecile, HELP ME!"

Tita Cecile coughs. She looks exhausted. "Just crack the whip, kiddo. Let your instincts kick in. Your body will remember what your mind doesn't."

The wakwak lets out an ear-piercing scream as she dives. "Die, human. DIE!"

"You talk too much." I do the first thing that comes to mind—I spin the buntot pagi above my head until it resembles a mini tornado.

The wakwak lands straight into my trap. "NOOOOOOOOO!"

"That's it. Keep spinning, Lulu!" Tita Cecile says, crawling out of the way. Mom and Kitty help her up.

The creature screams as she's sucked into the vortex.

I feel almost sorry for her. But the wakwak tried to harm Kitty, Mom, and Tita Cecile. No one's allowed to touch my family.

The wakwak glows as blue as my whip, then dissolves into mist. There's a swooshing of air, and the creature is no more.

CHAPTER FIVE

My Peanut People Dwindle to One

I DROP THE WHIP IN SHOCK.

"Ate!" Kitty runs to me and throws her arms around my neck. Mom joins our group hug under the balete tree.

For once, I don't hug them back. I want to push them all away, but I can't bring myself to do anything. I just stand there, staring at my hands.

"What did I do?" I feel awful. To think I couldn't even bring myself to squish a cockroach just last week. Granted, the cockroach was only passing by, whereas the wakwak bragged about how it planned to torture me. . . . But *still.* The wakwak was a living being. It was talking, flying, breathing—that is, until I made it disappear with that whip.

Tita Cecile walks up behind Mom and Kitty as they release me. She's sweaty and winded but still manages to give me a proud smile. She carries the buntot pagi with one hand and pats my back with the other. "You did well."

Did well? I step back, recoiling at her touch. "You made me kill her."

"No, you didn't kill her." Tita Cecile shakes her head. I want to believe her. Really. "You just sent her back to her home in the Underworld."

"The Underworld?" Kitty's eyes nearly pop out of their sockets. "You don't mean the *Underworld Realm* from Tagalog mythology?"

"Yep. The one and only." Tita Cecile cracks the buntot pagi. It extends out, glows blue, then rolls up into the handle.

I'm super glad I'm not a wakwak murderer, but I'm not going to admit that to anyone. Because I'm still upset that they kept so many things from me. And that is just as bad as outright lying.

"Kiddo—" Tita Cecile turns away before she can finish what she's saying, coughing loudly. Mom strokes her back as Tita Cecile takes a deep breath and squares her shoulders.

"So, all the things they taught us in school as Tagalog myths are real?" I ask. I feel a bit guilty making her talk when she's obviously exhausted, but I can't wait anymore.

"How come we've never seen all these magical things before?"

"One question at a time." Mom tries to put an arm around my shoulders, but I pull away before she can. I don't want a hug right now—I want answers. "It's okay, my sweet Lulu. You're angry. Let's just go home, and we'll explain everything."

"No, Mom." I cross my arms over my chest. I try to keep my tone respectful. But it's getting so, so hard. "You've just made me send a horribly dressed wakwak to the Underworld via Dissipation Express. I deserve to know what's going on."

"She's right, Jen. I'll answer what I can," Tita Cecile says, offering her hand to me. I pretend I don't see it and keep mine in my pockets. Thankfully, she doesn't push it, and begins walking. "Very well. Some stories have changed as they're told and passed down through generations, but they are based on the same truth: that magic is real. You just couldn't see magic before because of the Balabal that the gods cast upon this world—the Middleworld Realm."

"Well, that's just great," I snap. Like I said before, "balabal" is "veil" in Tagalog. Which means one thing. "So this giant magical veil hid everything from everyone. Were any of you even planning to tell me about this magic if that wakwak didn't show up wanting to torture me?"

"Yes, we would have told you," Tita Cecile says, looking around warily. "We really need to hurry home. It's only

Lulu who's untouchable on Inarawan Street. But we'll be fine once we're in the apartment building."

"How come I'm the only one safe here?" Great. Even in the magical world I'm singled out again. No wonder I'm like a walking magnet for bullies like Carmen. The whole world—or maybe even the entire three Realms—ensures that I'll never, *ever* fit in.

Tita Cecile sighs. It's weird. Walking up a sloped road should have made her feel worse, but she seems less tired with every step she takes. "Unfortunately, that question requires a long answer—"

"Yeah, yeah. I get it!" I stomp past her. To be clear, I'm only agreeing for everyone's protection. But once we're at the apartment, "I'll tell you later" just won't cut it anymore. "Isn't there anything you *can* tell me now?"

"Kiddo, wait." Tita Cecile grabs my arm. I shrug her off, and she holds up her hands in surrender. "I know you're mad at me, but this is important. What's the last thing you remember before you went to the internet café with Bart?"

"We were at the salon, Ate," Kitty says helpfully. "They let us out from school early since it's the first day of Christmas break." She frowns. "We met Bart on the way home. And Ate Mariel. I think we even saw Mom, Tita Cecile, and Manong Sol at Bads Bunny. But I don't remember going inside the apartment."

I massage my temples. It's hard to think clearly while

we're hurrying home, especially when the timeline isn't adding up. We left school at one o'clock and reached Inarawan by around half past two. I woke up in Marites and Tolits's Beauty Salon at four p.m. But I can't remember what went on between those two events. It's like it's been deleted from my memory. "Where did that hour and a half go?"

"You really won't remember entering your home when you saw us at Bads Bunny, nor will you remember going to the salon," Tita Cecile tells my sister in a gentle voice, waving her hand. She notices me watching her, but I turn away before she can meet my gaze. "Because they didn't happen. You never went into the house or the salon on your own. The gym rat carried the two of you after Lulu collapsed."

My stomach churns as I finally look at Tita Cecile. "So, the earthquake . . ."

"It happened, kiddo. You saved yourself and your sister by stopping the truck from running over you," she says. I can hear pride in her voice. "Kitty's memories of today will return little by little. But yours—"

Suddenly, everything comes back to me with dizzying speed.

The earthquake. The bucket truck. The blue light. The tikbalang getting a mani-pedi.

All these things actually happened.

I massage my temples. The sudden gush of memories

is making my head hurt. Still, I continue walking. "The linemen and truck driver. What happened to them?"

"They're fine. The linemen are wakwak and their driver is an aswang," Tita Cecile says, steadying me. "How are you feeling? I know it's a lot to take in, kiddo, but you must get used to it. There is a lot more you must know about this magical world—"

"A lot to take in?" That's the understatement of the year. "A wakwak just attacked me. The three Realms are real, and oh . . . the 'myths' mentioned in last week's quiz are actual living and breathing creatures walking around me under this giant magical veil. A lot to take in? YOU THINK?"

"Luningning. Watch your tone," Mom warns in a stern voice. "Calm down, and let's talk about this like a family."

"Families don't lie to each other! We don't keep secrets as huge as this." I wipe a tear off my face. I'm so angry, my insides hurt. "You knew about all this too, Mom. You knew, but you didn't tell me!"

"I'm really sorry, my Lulu," my mother says, her voice cracking a bit. "But I wanted you to have an ordinary life with me and Kitty for as long as possible. I still do, but we can't stop the magic. It would have come for you sooner or later."

Don't do that, Mom. Don't make me feel worse.

"Oh, my sweet. Come here." Mom holds out her arms, but I sidestep her.

I hear her sigh behind me, but I ignore it. We walk the remaining stretch of Inarawan Street in silence.

Truth is, I totally get it. I wanted an ordinary life with Kitty and Mom too. Learning that magic is real is already turning my world upside down. And if what Tita Cecile said is true, things are going to get even wilder from this day forward.

But keeping all this from me, literally altering my memories . . . it's betrayal.

Trusting people comes in different layers. Kind of like a peanut M&M. It melts in your mouth and not in your hand because of this thin, crispy candy layer. It protects the chocolate layer. When you melt the candy and chocolate layers in your mouth, you finally reach the peanut inside.

I don't trust people easily. Many will stay in the candy layer while a few will break into the thicker chocolate layer. But very, very few can make it into the peanut layer.

Mom and Tita Cecile have always been in that peanut layer. Now I'm not so sure if they should be.

And that thought makes me feel even more alone.

"Are you okay?" my sister asks as she falls into step beside me. I notice the adults walking ahead, probably giving us space.

"What do you think?"

"I'm sorry." Kitty bites her lower lip. "That was a silly question."

I instantly regret snapping at her. I know I shouldn't

push her away too. But I just can't help myself. "Are you also hiding something from me?" I ask.

Kitty's eyes narrow, seemingly offended by my question. "Why would you think that?"

"Are you?" I'm honestly very afraid of her answer. What if she's been lying to me too? I don't know what I'll do.

"Of course not! If I knew anything about this, I'd have told you in, like, five seconds." Kitty stops walking and stares at me. "We're sisters. No secrets, remember?"

"No secrets," I say, smiling. Kitty for sure still has my peanut-level trust. This time when my sister offers me her hand, I take it without hesitation. We walk home together, side by side. Before long, the slope of the road becomes steeper, and the ugly Bads Bunny sign comes into view.

But as we get nearer to the apartment building's sari-sari store, the slightly nice feeling dissipates like a wakwak being sent to the Underworld.

"MARIEL!" Tita Cecile runs the rest of the way to the sari-sari store on the ground floor of our apartment building. We hurry behind her.

My jaw drops at the scene in front of us. If Kitty hadn't been gaping like me, I'd have thought I have that kind of epilepsy where, just before a seizure, the epileptic sees things that aren't real. Because my brain is trying its absolute best to process what my eyes are seeing at this very moment.

In front of Bads Bunny is Ate Mariel. Well, more like Ate

Mariels. As in, plural. And I don't mean her having a clone or any of that sci-fi stuff. I really do mean the *two pieces* of Ate Mariel.

One half of her, from the waist down, remains standing by the store entrance. Her torso, on the other hand, is on the ground a few meters from her lower body. And she has wings. Batlike wings. But her face remains the same—beautiful and brown like a Tagalog princess.

"She's a . . ." Kitty looks like she's really struggling to find the words. I don't blame her. "Ate Mariel is a . . ."

"A manananggal, yes." Mom cradles Ate Mariel's head on her lap. "We need to wash off the salt that her attacker put on her lower half. She'll be okay once we get her body parts to rejoin."

I stare at my mother. "How and where did you learn that?"

"At the clinic. My boss heals magical creatures." Mom says it like it's the most obvious thing in the world. "My sweet, I know you have a lot of questions, but Mariel needs our help. C, Mariel's torso—"

"I'll get water." Tita Cecile hurries into the store.

"Mariel's in a cold sweat. Her fever's really high." Mom wipes Ate Mariel's forehead with her hankie. "We need to bring her in. Girls, be careful with her wings. They're very delicate."

Kitty and I carry Ate Mariel's upper body inside Bads Bunny. Mom pushes plastic containers off the cashier's counter and helps us lay half of Ate Mariel on it. After a couple of minutes, Tita Cecile brings in Ate Mariel's lower body and puts it on the table.

The space between Ate Mariel's upper and lower halves glows with blue light. Then the light disappears, and Ate Mariel is whole again.

Mom uncaps a small, clear bottle with pearl-like stuff inside. She puts a few drops of the tonic into Ate Mariel's mouth. "Swallow it, Mariel. It'll make you feel better."

Color returns to Ate Mariel's face. She begins to mumble incoherently "Tolome . . . Dog . . ."

"Shh . . ." Mom strokes Ate Mariel's hair. "It's okay. We're here now. You're going to be fine."

"She's saying something." I cock my head to one side. "I don't understand—"

"Bartolome?" Kitty suggests.

"Yes!" Ate Mariel gasps. "Alley . . . Help him."

Bartolome. Bart. She must mean Bart. My best friend, Bart.

My stomach drops. I run out of the sari-sari store, ignoring calls from Mom and Tita Cecile. Kitty is close behind me.

If something happens to Bart, it'll be my fault. We went by the alley, but I was too busy feeling sorry for myself. I should have been paying more attention!

We hurry down the street and turn right into the alley beside Tita Cecile's office building. But instead of finding

Bart, we see Tannie the shih tzu. The poor pup is lying on his side.

Kitty and I immediately check Tannie for injuries. But we don't stop looking for Bart.

"Bart!" I call out. Kitty does the same. "Where are you, Bart?"

Mom arrives. "Stop shouting, girls," she says. "We don't know what might still be lurking around."

"But Bart—"

Tannie yelps in pain. He raises his head slowly.

"Thank goodness," I say, relieved. "You're still alive—"

The shih tzu's irises suddenly turn red. His short black fur starts to retreat. He grows bigger and bigger, and his dog body molds itself into humanlike form. Soon he's no longer a dog, but a fully clothed eleven-year-old boy lying on his side.

Bart.

Bart is Tannie. Tannie is Bart.

They're one and the same.

Is this for real? My best friend is a dog?!

"I'm an aswang," Bart explains in a very weak voice. He can't look me in the eye. He knows he's betrayed my trust.

The aswangs are shape-shifting creatures of Philippine mythology. There are different types of aswang, but from the looks of it, Bart is the were-dog kind. A were–shih tzu, to be specific.

"You're a dog." My guilty feelings turn to anger. Like smoldering, building anger.

Everyone lied to me. My neighbors. My best friend. My mother.

Everyone.

Kitty is the only Peanut Person I have left.

"I'm so sorry, Lu." His pained expression really does look like he *is* sorry. "I promise I'll explain later."

Everyone keeps promising me explanations for later.

Thing is, you can bite the peanut M&M and eat it in one go. You might get lucky and see the peanut whole. But chances are, you'll crush the peanut and it'll break into pieces.

Like the peanut, it'll be hard to put trust back together again.

Being an aswang and not telling your best friend is guaranteed to crush the Trust Peanut. No explanations later can fix that.

"Let me see. . . ." Mom studies Bart's arm. It's covered with cuts and bruises. "You're hurt."

"I'll be fine, Tita," Bart croaks. "They ambushed us. She knocked me out. I couldn't see her—it's as if she came out of nowhere."

"You did well, Bart." Tita Cecile joins us. She hands Mom a bottle of mineral water. "The wakwak was using Balabal magic. You couldn't have seen her."

"Help him up, my sweets," Mom says. She brings out a

vial of the same pearl-like stuff she gave Ate Mariel from her pocket and hands it to Bart with the bottle of water. "He needs to take this. It tastes awful, but it will help him heal faster."

Kitty and I help Bart take the tonic. I feel Bart's eyes on me, but I ignore him. He needs to get well so I can be openly mad at him.

"Thanks. Ate Mariel—" Bart stops at the sound of flapping wings. Batlike wings.

I reach around for a weapon but come up empty. Ugh. Still, I ball my fists and ready myself for battle.

Wait. Didn't I banish the wakwak already? How can it return to Silanganan Village from the depths of hell so fast?

"Hey! It's just me," Ate Mariel says, landing on the ground and studying her arms. "So this is how tenderized meat feels."

Kitty is staring at Ate Mariel's wings in awe.

"Mariel! You scared us!" Mom exclaims, putting a hand on her chest. "You shouldn't be walking . . . er . . . *flying* about just yet."

"I'm better. Thank you, Tita. Thanks to all of you." Ate Mariel gives us a smile. She massages her torso as her wings retract and disappear into her back. "You really should go back inside. That snazzily dressed wakwak did quite a number on me."

I shake my head. The attack must have messed up Ate

Mariel's sense of fashion too. "She wasn't well-dressed," I say. "That orange shirt didn't really go well with her pink pants."

"No . . ." A frown creases Ate Mariel's smooth forehead. "*He* was smartly dressed. Black pants, white polo shirt. He even had specialty sneakers made for his talons."

Mom, Tita Cecile, Kitty, and I all look at each other in alarm.

My pulse jumps from normal to lightning fast. The hair on my arms stands up.

"Everyone, get inside now!" Tita Cecile brings out her buntot pagi and cracks it. The whip glows blue, whizzing with power. "Show yourself, wakwak!"

That's when we hear the distant flapping of wings.

A wakwak swoops in, grabs Mom by the shoulders with its sneakered talons, and flies away into the night sky.

CHAPTER SIX

A Choice Between What's Harder and Harder-er

"That's not fair! I'm not done being angry at you!" I scream at the sky. My throat hurts, but I don't care. "Come back, Mom!"

"Mom. Mommy . . ." Kitty shakes her head, her voice breaking. "She can't be gone."

"Come here, Kitty." Ate Mariel takes my sister into her arms. Kitty burrows her face into the woman's chest, muffling her sobs. "Let's go inside," Ate Mariel says. "Your mom wouldn't want you in danger out here."

"MOM!" I drop to my knees. It hurts, and it'll probably hurt even more later, but I don't care. I ball my fists, feeling a surge of power rushing into them. This can't be real. Mom has never failed to be there for Kitty and me. Even when she needed to work overtime, she still found a way to help us with our homework and cook us a nice dinner.

Mom *can't* be gone.

A cry of anguish escapes my lips, an animalistic sound I can't recognize.

"It's going to be okay, kiddo." Tita Cecile holds out her hand, but she lets her fingers hover an inch from me.

"It won't! It *can't* be okay." I feel like every bit of my heart is getting torn apart. Even my pendant is throbbing now. "That thing took our mother!"

Tita Cecile takes a step back and withdraws her hand, as though I just bit her. She gestures at Bart and Ate Mariel to move away. "Lulu, you have to control your emotions or you'll put everyone here in danger."

"Ate Lu—" Kitty disentangles herself from Ate Mariel and reaches for me. The sight of her tearstained face is like a stab in my gut.

I was wrong. Mom is still one of my Peanut People. *Just come back, Mom. We'll talk through everything the way you wanted us to.*

Tita Cecile stops my sister. "Kitty, stay where you are."

"This is all my fault." I feel my pulse beat faster as I walk back and forth in the middle of the street. "I should have listened to her! I should have gone inside when she told me to."

"There was nothing you could do. Come on, kiddo. Let's go in." This time Tita Cecile touches my shoulder.

"NO! We need to find Mom NOW!" I shrug off Tita Cecile's hand, but she tries to pull me into a hug.

"Lulu, kiddo, we *will* find Jenalyn. But first we need to—"

My fists emit a haze of blue light, and I push Tita Cecile away. Like, away *away*. She goes flying off the street and is swallowed by the darkness.

Kitty, Bart, and Ate Mariel all stare at me at the same time, their mouths hanging open.

"I'm sorry." I stare at my hands. They no longer have the blue light around them. "I don't know how that happened."

Ate Mariel hurries to my side, taking me by the shoulders. "Look at me, Lulu. Her identity is not mine to share, but you can rest easy that she is going to be fine."

"Tita Cecile," I say, my voice shaking. I can't believe it. "Is she . . ."

"Well, I'm not dead."

We jump at the sound of Tita Cecile's voice. She's standing behind us, thankfully whole. "I was planning on telling you later, but I guess this will do." She massages her nape and stares straight at me, unblinking. "I'm a goddess, kiddo. I'm an immortal being tasked to protect you."

No way.

"But you're a family lawyer! You just assist people with getting their inheritance and help unhappy married couples break up." I shake my head. This can't be true. "You *can't* be a goddess."

"I can be both." Tita Cecile gives me a kind smile. "The same way you can be a tiny, epileptic eleven-year-old and have the strength to single-handedly throw a goddess three streets away."

"I'm really sorry." I hang my head. "I didn't mean to throw you, Tita Cecile. I don't know what's wrong with me."

"Nothing's wrong with you, kiddo. You're just . . . well . . . You're just very strong."

"Yeah. Like, very, very, *very* strong," Kitty says, taking my hands and squeezing them. "But you're still my Ate Lulu. My superstrong Ate Lulu."

"You're not afraid of me?"

"No." Kitty puts an arm over my shoulders. Since she's taller than me, it's like she's the ate this time. "I don't know how to explain it," she says, "but it's a sister thing. I can be asleep and still worry about you. You can have the biggest of tantrums, but I know your powers will remember not to hurt me."

That's true. It's a huge relief knowing I still have Kitty. And Tita Cecile can't be scared of me (she's a goddess, after all). "But Ate Mariel and Bart—"

"Lulu, dear, I'm a manananggal," Ate Mariel says, rolling her eyes. She grunts, and her batlike wings pop out behind her. "Your people have written a whole bunch of spooky stories about my kind."

Bart morphs into Tannie, the little fashionista shih tzu. "And I'm an aswang," he says. It's so weird seeing and hearing a dog talk, especially when the voice that comes out of his canine mouth is very much Bart's. "*You* should be scared of *me*."

"Yeah, right." I snort. Bart and I still need to have a long talk about him keeping his aswang nature a secret. But I'm glad he and Ate Mariel aren't afraid of me. "You're like a dog version of Chucky."

"Chucky?"

Tita Cecile bursts out laughing. "It's the ugly possessed doll in that old horror movie *Child's Play*." She shakes her head. "The things you kids stream. . . . Hay naku! I'm going to tell Jen."

We walk back to Bads Bunny in silence.

"We *are* going to find Mom, aren't we?" I ask Tita Cecile as she locks the door behind us.

"Yes, we will." Tita Cecile brings out two bottles of mineral water from the store's fridge and hands them to Kitty and me. "Drink up and sit down. We have a lot to talk about. Mariel, prepare our gear, please. Bart, go to Aman Sinaya's assistant and tell him we'll be needing a bag that Lulu can carry around."

"Yes, Lady Cecile." Ate Mariel and Bart bow at the same time, then leave. It's odd to see them treat Tita Cecile like she's royalty, but I don't blame them. If the mythology stories we learned in school are true, I wouldn't want to get on the bad side of a deity either. I mean, I'm pretty sure Tita Cecile won't turn me into a frog if I get too cheeky, but you never know.

"Okay . . . where was I?" Tita Cecile takes a seat behind the counter while Kitty and I sit on the chairs in front of it. "As I was saying, we're going to find your mom. I don't know exactly where she is right now, but I know a goddess who can point us in the right direction. Anagolay—"

"The goddess of lost things!" Kitty finishes for her. "In the myths, she's been known to willingly help ancient Tagalogs whenever they lost something or someone."

"That makes sense," I say, feeling a surge of hope. We're going to get Mom back after all!

"Yep. We'll ask for Anagolay's help. That wakwak can't hide from her magic. No one ever has. . . ." Tita Cecile stares at me so intently, I see a flicker of blue light in her eyes. "Do you remember anything suspicious that the female wakwak said?"

"More suspicious than wanting to torture me?" I start to shake my head but stop midway. "I think I remember something. The wakwak didn't say who sent her, but she did mention her master knowing how to manipulate the Balabal when immortals—I mean, you and your godly folks—thought they were the only ones who did."

"The Maligno," Tita Cecile murmurs. "He really did escape."

"Maligno? As in evil spirit?" I try to lessen the impatience in my voice, but I can't help it. "You and Mom promised me answers, Tita Cecile. Mom's not here now to keep that promise, but you still are."

"I know. I'm sorry." Tita Cecile heaves a long sigh. "I'll do my best to honor that promise. But for you to understand who the Maligno is . . . Do you remember what you've learned in school about the Anito?"

I glance at Kitty, raising my eyebrows questioningly.

"It was in our last homework, Ate." My sister shakes her head in disapproval, but she tells us what she knows anyway. "Before the Spanish came, our ancient Tagalog ancestors believed that everything—rocks, trees, humans, animals, everything—has a spirit. The collective term for the spirits is Anito."

"Very good." Tita Cecile smiles at Kitty. "Now, here's what your textbooks don't mention. Magic comes from the life energy of the Anito, and this magical life energy is called Salamangka. Salamangka is what keeps order and chaos in balance within the universe, making sure that the realities of the three Realms intersect in harmony. It's also the source of the gods' powers. Some beings, human or magical, might have the talent to use this energy in a very, very limited capacity."

"The blue light!" I exclaim. So that's what it's called. "But what does that have to do with me?"

"I'm getting there. You see, there are times when that balance is threatened," Tita Cecile continues. "The

Anito then gifts someone with the power to use Salamangka in totality—the Salamangkero, who will wield the power of the Anito and save the universe from falling into chaos."

The hairs at the back of my head stand up. *Salamangkero* . . . I'm pretty sure I've heard that word somewhere. "You don't think . . ."

Tita Cecile reaches over the table to cover my hands with hers. When she lets go, my hands are glowing with bright-blue light. "Your powers—this is a gift from the Anito. You're the Salamangkero, Lulu. You're the one the Anito has chosen to protect the Realms."

No. Tita Cecile must be mistaken. "I'm only eleven! It can't be me!"

"We've asked ourselves so many times, couldn't it be someone else? Or at least, couldn't the Anito have given you this power when you're all grown up?" Tears well up in Tita Cecile's eyes, but she simply blinks them away. "Still, the Anito chose you. We don't know why or how this happened, but the Anito must have a reason for it. All we can do is prepare you for this monumental task and keep you safe as long as we possibly can."

I try to pull my hands away from her, but she holds them tight.

"Listen to me, Lulu. Many want this power," she says in an urgent tone. "One of them is the being we call the Maligno. He was a sorcerer in his lifetime, a powerful one at that. But he wasn't satisfied—he wanted to overthrow the gods and hold dominion over the Realms. The Salamangkero of his lifetime defeated him, and he died in obscurity. But his corrupt soul festered with such great hatred that he became a powerful evil spirit. He tried to take the Anito's gift from you once, and from the looks of it, he's trying again."

"You don't mean . . ." My stomach turns. "He took Mom because of this?"

"Yes. I think he's trying to bait you into going after her."

I have a thought that's so horrifying, I almost don't say it out loud. But I need to know. "When you said 'trying again' . . . you don't mean my biological parents—"

"Yes, kiddo. I'm afraid you guessed right." Tita Cecile looks as though everything she's saying pains her. "He is the reason why your biological family cannot be with you in this Realm."

The goddess's words cut through my heart like a magical balisong slicing a wakwak's wing.

Mom and Tita Cecile always said that my biological parents were "involved in an unfortunate incident ending in tragedy." I assumed it was a car accident, since there wasn't any major disaster here in the Philippines the year I was born. But it never occurred to me that *I'm* the reason why they're gone. Now the Maligno has taken Mom, and it's because of me again.

I ball my right fist, watching blue light engulf my hand.

They gave me this power when I didn't even ask for it. "I don't want this. I never wanted anybody to get hurt because of me."

"It's not your fault, Ate. Maybe—" Kitty's voice breaks. "Maybe we can get Mom back and then have someone else do this Salamangkero thing."

"Yeah. The Maligno can have it!" I meet Tita Cecile's eyes, begging her. I don't want Mom to suffer the same fate as my biological family. "You're a goddess. Just remove this from me so we can get Mom back!"

"It doesn't work that way, kiddo," Tita Cecile says, her voice gentle. "Think about it. While we still don't know what the Maligno plans to do, we're certain it won't be good. Do you really want to give your power to someone who intends to wreak havoc on the universe? Kitty, Jen, Bart, Mariel, that gym rat . . . Your family and friends are all part of these Realms. If the Realms fall into chaos, everyone you know and love will be gone."

I bite my lower lip. "That makes sense."

"No, it does not!" Kitty wipes a tear off her face. "We've already lost Mom. I can't lose you too, Ate!"

I lower my head. I can't lie to my sister or make a promise to her that I can't keep.

"You won't lose Lulu," Tita Cecile says. I throw her a grateful look. "Like you said, I'm a goddess. I'll protect both of you. And we'll get Jenalyn back."

I wish I could be as confident as Tita Cecile. I mean, I'm

only eleven. What can a kid like me do against a maligno with a grudge so great it can literally bring the universe to its knees?

To be fair, I do have Hulk-like super strength, thanks to the Anito. And Hulk totally knocked out Thor, the god of thunder, in that arena battle scene in *Thor: Ragnarok*. Granted, Hulk cheated with the Grandmaster's help. . . . Well, I also have a goddess and the blessing of the Anito to help me, not to mention an aswang best friend, a manananggal neighbor, and the best sister support system in all the Realms.

I take a deep breath. We just need to do this one step at a time. We find Mom first, get her back, then worry about the universe later.

"Weapons delivery!" Ate Mariel exclaims as she arrives with Bart. She gives Tita Cecile a black tote and Kitty a yellow messenger bag. "We found the balisong, Lady Cecile."

To my surprise, it's the knife I threw at the wakwak. "Hey, that's mine!"

"It sure is. Let me make sure you don't lose it again." Tita Cecile takes the balisong from Ate Mariel. She brings it close to her lips, whispering an incantation. The knife glows blue for a few seconds.

Bart carries his usual backpack, but this time he has a purple belt bag around his waist. He takes it off and places it on the table in front of me. "This is yours, Lu. We couldn't find a bag with a Marvel or BTS design. But I know you love purple and don't like carrying stuff around, so we got this for you instead. It's made of special material—you won't even notice it's there once you put it on."

"It's pretty." I'm still upset at him for not telling me he's an aswang. In spite of that, it's nice he remembers what I like.

"I've put an enchantment on your balisong," Tita Cecile says, handing it to me. "It's now bound to your belt bag. The knife will materialize in there within minutes no matter where you throw it. As long as you have your bag with you, you'll never lose the balisong again." As I take the knife, I feel like I'm meeting an old friend. I remember it now. The knife is mine. It's always been mine. Manong Sol gave it to me when I turned four. I thought it was odd that a responsible adult like him would think it was a good idea to give a knife to a little kid. Even odder, my mother allowed it. But now I know. I needed a weapon to survive this impossible task to save the worlds.

A wave of memories reminds me that I've been through a lot with this balisong. Manong Sol trained me to use it, just like he trained me to use a buntot pagi, to punch through walls, and to deliver a Sikaran death kick.

I clench my fists and feel the power surge through them. Manong Sol has been training me all along. He's been helping me get strong all these years. Rescuing Mom and saving the universe is becoming more and more doable.

“Where’s Manong Sol?” I ask. Being such a huge part of my life, he should be here giving me advice or something. I remember a moment during the earthquake when he spoke in my head and streaked toward me like a fiery ray of light. “Is he a god too? Or maybe some kind of a fire creature?”

Bart, Ate Mariel, and Tita Cecile exchange glances. But only the goddess answers me.

“He’s urgently needed elsewhere,” she explains, frowning. “I’m sorry, kiddo, but it’s up to the gym rat to reveal his identity. Remember what your mom told you?”

“Yeah.” How can I forget? It was an evening like this, quiet, and the sky outside was clear. Kitty, Mom, Tita Cecile, and I were hanging out on the apartment building’s roof deck. I asked Mom if it was wrong to find Jungkook cute and, at the same time, think Blackpink’s Rosé just as pretty. Mom said there wasn’t anything wrong with that. My identity wasn’t anyone’s business, and it should be up to me if and when I wanted to tell other people I liked boys and girls.

I guess the same thing goes for magical creatures and immortal beings.

“This belongs to you too, kiddo.” Tita Cecile takes a small leather pouch from her handbag and hands it to me. “The balisong is good for close combat, but you need something else if your enemy is in the air or a couple of meters away. I’d give you my kampilan, but the gym rat said you prefer these weapons over a sword.”

Inside the pouch is a dark-brown tube thing that looks like a flashlight. On one end of it is a carving of a man in a squat. It's exactly like the one on my pendant. As soon as my skin touches the carving, the top of the tube expands, becoming a whip. "Oh! Cool."

"Just like your balisong, the handle is made from the horn of a sacred carabao," Tita Cecile explains. "It'll protect you from malicious creatures that are out of your reach. You must always keep the pouch with you—the pouch and buntot pagi always go together. Without it, the buntot pagi won't be able to return to you. Just put it on the belt bag and you should be good."

"Okay." I secure the pouch as Tita Cecile suggests. "What about Kitty and Bart? And Ate Mariel?"

"Mariel and Bart already have their own weapons."

Bart nods while Ate Mariel gives me a thumbs-up sign.

"I have something here for Kitty." Tita Cecile gives Kitty a Pringles canister and a small baton. "This was designed by the deity of crafts themself. Try it out."

"What's she going to do, have snacks with her enemies while doing a dance routine?" I know I'm being sarcastic. But we're going on a quest that's obviously a trap by the universe's most disgruntled evil spirit. This stuff just won't do—Kitty must be able to protect herself.

Thankfully, my worries vanish. As soon as Kitty grasps the baton, it expands into a bow. She opens the Pringles canister, and arrows suddenly materialize inside it. My sister stretches the bow excitedly. "It's perfectly balanced!"

"And you won't run out of arrows either," says Tita Cecile, beaming at my sister. "You can put it inside your bag when you're not using it. Like Lulu's weapons, they'll always materialize in the bag, so you can't ever lose them."

I watch Kitty fiddle with her bow and arrow. She's really good with them. I remember Manong Sol used to bring Kitty, Mom, and me to an indoor archery range in Pasig City. Mom stayed at the archery range's café reading a book while Kitty and I shot arrows at zombie targets with Manong Sol.

Well, they weren't really zombies. More like printouts of zombie illustrations with a target on them. Kitty hit those targets every single time, while my arrows usually ended up below or above the target's frame.

But who knows what we'll encounter on this quest? I'm pretty sure they won't be zombie illustrations. I don't like the idea of leaving my sister behind. But seeing her with an actual weapon, the danger feels even more real. "Maybe Kitty should just stay here."

"No way!" Kitty puts down her bow and crosses her arms over her chest. "I'm coming with you, Ate. We're in this together."

"Why are you so stubborn?" I groan in frustration at my sister's defiance. I'd be lying if I said I didn't expect her to insist on coming, but I had to try. It's not worth fighting over it, though. Because honestly? I'm just too tired to argue. "Fine."

"It's settled, then." The goddess gestures at Ate Mariel. "Say your goodbyes."

"Goodbyes?" I frown at the beautiful manananggal. "What does she mean?"

"I'm sorry, Lulu, but I can't come with you. It ends for me here," Ate Mariel explains sadly. "My family is bound to the gods. I need to look after Manong Sol's building and sari-sari store."

"That's not fair!"

"It's complicated." Ate Mariel tucks a strand of hair behind my ear. "When you bring your mom back, we'll all have lumpiang toge at Bads Bunny."

As much as I want her to come with us, I totally agree that she shouldn't get in trouble with Manong Sol. I mean, he's a god. My memories have been coming back to me in chunks. And from what I've seen so far, he's quite a powerful god. Getting fired will be the least of Ate Mariel's worries if he gets mad.

"Keep safe, Ate Mariel!" Kitty and I give her a hug each.

"Take care of one another, okay?" Ate Mariel's voice breaks like she's about to cry. She hugs Kitty and me again. "Be sure to always eat on time. Bart, don't forget to drink your vitamins. And text me as soon as you get there—"

"Okay, okay," Bart says, pushing Ate Mariel away as she attempts to hug him. "Stop fussing."

Ate Mariel gives us a gym bag full of spare clothes, energy drinks, potato chips, chocolate, and candy. She even packed us chicken adobo and rice.

"We're going on a rescue mission," Bart grumbles, carrying our bag of goodies. "Not a picnic."

"I got this," I say, taking the bag from Bart. Maybe it's because of my Salamangkero powers, or Bart just wanted to whine, but it really doesn't weigh a thing. "Where are we going, Tita Cecile? How do we find Anagolay?"

I throw one last look at Bads Bunny, where Ate Mariel is waving at us. She gives us a flying kiss before entering the store. I sigh. Why does it feel like I'll never see her again?

Kitty and I follow Tita Cecile and Bart down the sloped road. It's only ten in the evening, but we don't meet anyone on Inarawan Street. Tita Cecile must have told them to stay inside. Which is great—I really don't feel like having an audience right now.

Tita Cecile stops when we reach the street sign pole. "This is the end of Inarawan Street. Once we step out of it, I will lift the Balabal for the two of you. Your worlds will never be the same, and you won't be able to take back your decision." She looks at Kitty and me intently. "Will you be okay with that?"

Kitty and I exchange a look. Our answer is a no-brainer.

"We're sure," Kitty and I say at the same time. We *will* find our mother.

"As you wish." Tita Cecile whispers a spell, takes our hands, and together we step outside the safety of Inarawan Street.

CHAPTER SEVEN

The Army of Ugly Toddler Ghouls Says Hello

I HONESTLY DON'T KNOW WHAT TO EXPECT OUTSIDE THE BALABAL. BUT this is A-MAZ-ING!

There's Salamangka, like, literally *everywhere*. It's as if someone took the aurora borealis from the Arctic, turned it blue, then blanketed the whole world with it.

"Are you seeing this, Meow?" I can't believe all this has been around us all along.

"It's pretty!" says my sister. She touches the blue light. It moves like it's been pushed, creating a wavelike effect on the other floating lights nearby.

Tita Cecile waves her hand again, and the Salamangka slowly disappears. "The Balabal won't shroud reality for you anymore, but the rest of mankind won't know the magical world exists."

"How are we getting to the goddess of lost things, Tita Cecile?" Kitty asks, looking back at Inarawan Street. "Should we go back for your car?"

"It'll take us too long if we travel using non-magical human vehicles," Tita Cecile says, shaking her head. She cocks her head at the Sangang-Daan Tree. "Balete trees are pathways within the Realms. It requires a bit of Salamangka to use it as a portal, but I think I'm strong enough to open—"

Tita Cecile is interrupted by a bolt of lightning streaking across the night sky, along with loud, rumbling thunder. The leaves of the Sangang-Daan Tree shake violently.

All of a sudden we hear a toddler's cry. And then another baby wails loudly. And another. Before long, the sound of wailing babies drowns out the thunder—they're just *that* loud.

Then the wailing lessens. I pull out my balisong and buntot pagi as little toddler ghouls begin to emerge from behind the branches of the Sangang-Daan Tree and all four streets around it—north, south, east, and west.

"Stay behind me," Tita Cecile says. Kitty, Bart, and I don't need telling twice.

Tiyanaks. There are around a hundred of them, and more seem to be popping out of the shadows. Ugly, baby-sized ghouls with pointy fingers and fanged teeth.

The toddler ghouls make way for their leader, creating a path right in the middle of the tiyanak swarm. He towers over them. Like, *really* towers. None of the tiyanaks is tall enough to even reach his knee.

As the man gets near, I recognize him. Dressed in loose jeans and a basketball jersey topped with a garish tie-dyed cap, it's our giant neighbor who frequents Manong Sol's gym.

I point at him. "You're that guy who always tries to scam Manong Sol for free gym use and sari-sari store goods."

"I am not a scammer! Human money just confuses me," the tall man protests. His voice is strangely high and squeaky, like Mickey Mouse's. When he turns to Tita Cecile, he bows respectfully. "Sajangnim has been waiting for you, madam."

"Sajangnim?" I cock my head in his direction. "Who's that?"

The man shifts his feet. "Well . . ."

"Stop this nonsense at once, John Lloyd." Tita Cecile points at him. "I've been tolerating your presence for years. Get out of that suit if you wish to speak to me."

"Yes, madam," he mumbles.

John Lloyd touches his chest, and it expands. Like, literally expands. But instead of popping like a balloon, his expanded chest opens like wardrobe doors. Gears whir and steam escapes, revealing a tiyanak embedded in a nest of gold parts and wires. A tiyanak who's only as tall as a toddler steps forward. The metal parts and wires form a platform beneath him, depositing him safely on the ground.

"Oh wow, that is so cool, but really, really creepy," I say. I thought I'd seen the weirdest thing when Tannie became Bart, but here you go. This John Lloyd transformation tops the Weird List. "He's a tiyanak. A tiyanak in an automaton body."

Up close, the tiyanak looks like he can't be more than a year old. Like, a literal toddler. But he's standing up straight, walking around like a full-grown adult. And his face . . . well, there's no polite way of saying this, but it's really ugly. It's like taking the face of a rubber toad and squishing it, but it doesn't return to its original shape.

The tiyanak beams. "Deity Aman Sinaya's work is the best." He waves at his minions and points to the empty automaton suit. "Bring this back to Kasanaan. If I see any scratch on it, I'm going to cut off your heads. Deity Aman Sinaya's assistant charges so much for repairs."

"What do you want, John Lloyd?" Tita Cecile demands, impatience evident in her voice.

"I know you are busy, madam, but we need you in the Underworld." John Lloyd the tiyanak bows. "The Maligno used his spies to plant a device—"

"Don't!" one of the tiyanaks exclaims. "Master told us not to say anything!"

"Don't! Don't! Don't!" The murmuring spreads among the sea of toddler ghouls. They're like Minions from *Despicable Me*, but much, much uglier.

"SILENCE!" Tita Cecile beckons to John Lloyd. "Continue."

"The device destroyed the Hill of Despair, madam. Many corrupt souls escaped, including the Maligno—"

"The Maligno?" I feel like my insides are quivering. "Tita Cecile, is that the same evil spirit you told us about?"

"Yes." Tita Cecile nods. A worried frown creases her face as she looks at the tiyanak. "I have more reasons to stay here, then. These children need me."

"I understand, madam, but it is your father's wish that you return home." John Lloyd points at Bart and me. "The aswang can come, of course. And perhaps the Salamangkero, if she's strong enough." He then points at Kitty. "But not her. She's very human. She'll perish if she enters the Underworld."

"Hoy!" I put a protective arm around my sister, pulling her close to my side. "Very human? What am I, *less* human?"

"I will not abandon Kitty, nor will I put any of these kids in danger. Now move." Tita Cecile waves. The army of tiyanaks around the Sangang-Daan Tree get forcibly moved to the side, creating a path for us.

"But madam—"

The tiyanaks let out a simultaneous gasp. "He's coming!" They all drop to their knees. "Master's coming!"

The balete's vines form a gateway, and John Lloyd cowers in fear. "Sajangnim!" he says. "I tried to convince madam to come home—"

An imposing tall man with silver hair wearing a crisp black suit steps out of the portal. He glares at John Lloyd. "Be quiet."

Tita Cecile puts her arms around us and holds us tight, staring at the man. "Hello, Tatay."

Tatay. I look up at Tita Cecile. She called him father?

"Do you like this suit?" he asks. "I had it flown in from Italy. I heard this is what rich corporate South Korean heirs like to wear these days." The man adjusts his lapel and smiles down at us. It's so creepy. He looks like a pirate, even though he's wearing a black suit. A phone rings, and the man brings it out to answer it. "Hold on a second, anak. I need to take this."

We watch the man appease someone on the phone for a few minutes, then he hangs up. His phone rings again, and he says the exact same spiel: "We're working on it. Yes, I'll let you know more soon. Thank you for your patience."

This goes on for five more calls, until finally he orders his phone's voice recognition assistant to put itself on Do Not Disturb mode.

"These deities have been calling me all day!" he complains. "The Maligno's escape was not my fault— Oh, hello, children. I am Sitan, god of the Underworld and the guardian of the realm of Kasanaan."

Oh, great. Another deity. Well, not just any other deity—he's a god who's literally the big boss in his Realm. But with all that deity-appeasing he's been doing over the phone, he's more like an overdressed and overworked call center agent for Apple Support than a terrifying lord of the Underworld.

"Why do you need a mobile phone when you're already a god?" I ask. Beside me, Bart's shaking his head, but I ignore him. "How does that even work in the Underworld?"

"It's very convenient," Sitan says, showing off his phone. I notice he has the latest iPhone. Sitan must be rolling in a lot of money. How he got that rich while running a realm where souls of the dead go to be rewarded or punished . . . I'd rather not know. "Humans come up with great ideas every now and then. Add in some Salamangka, and you get an even better idea!"

"So you're essentially appropriating human ideas."

The tiyanaks let out a collective gasp. "Insolence!"

"Appropriating?" Sitan narrows his eyes. "How dare you—"

"*Oh-kay!*" Tita Cecile claps her hands, interrupting her father. "Why does John Lloyd keep calling you Sajangnim? Is that a new fad in the Underworld now?"

"Sajangnim means 'boss' or 'chief' in Korean," Kitty says.

Everyone stares at her in surprise.

"How did you know that?" I ask.

"Netflix."

John Lloyd nods in agreement. "Sajangnim is watching a lot of Korean dramas on Netflix lately."

"Ah," I say. That's interesting. "You have Netflix in hell?"

"Of course." Sitan preens. "Those snobs in the Upperworld finally granted my request for an internet connection. We have Wi-Fi in the whole Underworld now."

"Cool. Cool." I roll my eyes. "Souls get to stream K-dramas and update social media while suffering through eternal damnation."

Kitty perks up and steps forward. "Mom and I love K-dramas! Sir, have you seen *Extraordinary You* yet? It's about this girl who discovers she's in a comic book, and that she's just a lowly extra and not the main protagonist."

"I have not! But I will add that to my list." Sitan brings out his mobile phone and types it in. He nods at Tita Cecile. "Anak, we should bring this child along with us! Your siblings care nothing about these wonderful TV shows. It would be nice to have a companion who understands K-dramas. Of course, she will need to die first, since her mortal body will not survive the trip back home."

"No way!" I push Kitty behind me. "If you think you can take my sister to hell with you, think again, mister! You'll have to go through me."

Sitan looks at me from head to toe. "Turning you into

a tiny bulate is not worth the trouble it would create with Bathala and his family. Causing family issues is my daughter's expertise, not mine."

Kitty and I turn to Tita Cecile while Bart looks down. He obviously knows something, while my sister and I are left in the dark. *I'll deal with him later.*

"What does he mean, Tita Cecile?" I ask, narrowing my eyes.

Sitan seems genuinely surprised. "You did not tell them?"

"Tatay, don't." Tita Cecile crosses her arms over her chest. "We're in a rush. What do you want?"

"You know why I am here. Our obligation to the gods has been fulfilled—that child can protect herself now." His voice softens. "John Lloyd has told you what is happening in Kasanaan. I need you back. Come home with me."

Tita Cecile bites her lower lip. It reminds me of Kitty whenever she's uncomfortable. "After we find Jen, I'll go and help you, 'Tay."

"I did not want to have to do this, but you leave me no choice, anak." Sitan sighs. He squeezes his phone, and it turns into a cane with a huge black gemstone on top. As he points it at Tita Cecile, the jewel glows bright blue. "Mansisilat, goddess of broken homes, *agent* of Sitan . . . I summon you to Kasanaan with me."

Wisps of blue light appear around Tita Cecile's wrists. They grow bright, and Tita Cecile falls.

"Tita Cecile!"

"I'm okay, girls. The energy just caught me off-balance," she assures us, standing up. Tita Cecile turns to Sitan. "Can I at least give them a proper goodbye?"

"Very well, but do not take too long."

Wait. I'm not sure I heard right. "Did he call you goddess of *broken homes*?"

Instead of answering, Tita Cecile pulls me into a hug. "I'm sorry, kiddos. I have no choice. You'll have to continue the journey on your own from here onward. Anagolay is expecting you. Bart, protect the girls with your life."

"Yes, Lady Cecile."

"We can protect ourselves," I say, gently pushing her away. "*I* can protect us."

"You can't be the goddess of broken homes, Tita Cecile!" Kitty wails, burying her face in the goddess's chest. "You can't be the patron of such a mean thing. You're like a mom to us."

Cecile. Sisil. Mansisilat. I don't know . . . But it all makes sense. Tita Cecile's job as a family lawyer does break up families, and she's pretty great at it.

My heart sinks. I take a step away from her. Away from this woman who was like family to me. "What did you do, Tita Cecile? Were you trying to break our family apart?"

Kitty sobs.

"No, no. It's not what you think, kiddos." Tita Cecile's

voice breaks. "I didn't fake any of it. I really do care about you. And Jen. I love all of you."

She tries to reach out for Kitty and me, but my sister pushes her away and cries on my shoulder. The light bands on Tita Cecile's wrists glow bright again. She heaves a long sigh. "I'll explain everything, but I must go back to Kasanaan for now. I promise you, though, you will find your mother. I'll do everything I can to make sure you do."

"Don't make promises you can't keep." The words come out of my mouth before I can stop them.

Tita Cecile winces.

"What an insolent little girl." Sitan glares at me, but I don't care. He can turn me into a tiny worm if he wants—I won't care either. "Why do you let this child disrespect you, anak?"

"Tatay, stop it. It's fine." Tita Cecile squeezes my shoulders. I don't move or respond. "I will keep my promise. Stay strong, kiddos. Protect each other. You know who you need to see to tell you where you need to go. Bart knows the way and he will lead you there."

Bart nods. "Yes, ma'am."

"Do we have a choice?" I snap.

Kitty bawls louder.

"Watch your tongue, Salamangkero," Sitan warns. He turns around and heads for the Sangang-Daan Tree. He waves his hand, and the strangler fig's many thick vines rearrange themselves into a door. "Let's go home, my daughter."

Tita Cecile takes one last look at us before following her dad. "Bye, kiddos."

The toddler ghouls, led by John Lloyd, retreat to the balete tree gateway. One by one, the tiyanaks jump through the portal.

Soon Tita Cecile will join them in the Underworld, and we won't see her again.

I remember all the things Tita Cecile has done for us. How she laughed at my silliest jokes. How she gave Kitty and me anything we wanted. How she loved us like we're her daughters.

I can't let her go.

"Don't leave." I push aside the tiyanaks separating me from the goddess. "Tita Cecile, don't go!"

The goddess looks back and gives me a sad, tearful smile.

The gateway is closing. Tita Cecile is leaving.

"Tita Cecile!" I scream, but I can't get to her. The outermost ring of toddler ghouls forms a barricade and barrels right into the three of us. Some of them dissipate from the force of their own strength, while Kitty, Bart, and I are thrown a few meters away from the tree portal.

The tiyanaks are making sure we don't reach the goddess. "No. No. No. Don't go!"

We scramble to our feet and run to catch up, but we're

too late. Tita Cecile enters the portal, and so do the last of the surviving tiyanaks.

The vines return to their original shape. The Sangang-Daan Tree is now just a normal balete tree again.

The lightning disappears. The thunder falls silent.

I pick up Tita Cecile's kampilan. The sword is no longer glowing blue with the goddess's power. It vibrates in my hands, then dissipates with the wind.

Like Mom and the sword, Tita Cecile is gone.

CHAPTER EIGHT

The Pickup Truck from Hell

I CAN'T BELIEVE THIS IS HAPPENING AGAIN.

First Mom. Now Tita Cecile.

Why are gods like this? Why do they keep breaking my heart? My life was so peaceful not knowing about them.

I can't believe Tita Cecile just left us like that. How could she turn her back on us? Doesn't she love us?

We *need* her.

I hurry to the balete vines that formed the doorway, grabbing the last one that snapped into place, and I pull with all my might.

"Lu, that won't work. You'll only injure yourself," Bart

says gently. "Just tell me where Lady Cecile instructed us to go, and I'll do everything I can to get us there."

Kitty sobs louder.

I try prying the vines away even harder as my frustration builds.

My fists glow blue. As I keep pulling on the vines, the blue light spreads across my arms. I can feel sweat pour down my face, but I ignore it. I pull harder and harder, as hard as I can.

"It's opening!" Kitty exclaims.

Sure enough, the vine in my hands lifts ever so slightly. Blue light escapes from the space, and I feel a surge of hope. But just when I'm about to totally lift it up, the vine pries itself away from me. I release my hold, and the vine snaps the doorway shut.

"ARGH!" I pound my fists on the roots of the tree. It emits a low, gonglike sound. But the portal doesn't open.

I sob as hard as Kitty. In my frustration, I uproot a nearby banana tree. Unlike the balete's vines, I lift it off its roots without effort and tear the trunk apart.

"Please, Ate," Kitty begs, her voice shaking. "Stop destroying the banana trees."

Startled by my sister's tone, I put down the two halves of the banana tree and stare at her. Kitty sounds scared and angry at the same time.

Is Kitty angry at me? Or worse, is she *scared* of me?

"I'm sorry." I say. *I didn't mean to scare you. Don't leave me too, Kitty. Stay by my side.*

But I can't bring myself to say all that. I'm afraid of how Kitty will respond. What if she leaves me too?

"It's not a tree, it's a plant. Banana plants are basically weeds," Bart says. Really? He's giving us plant lessons *now*? "You probably did the owner a favor, uprooting it the way you did."

My eyes narrow. Bart has a lot of explaining to do, and none of it is related to banana trees. Or banana plants. Or whatever. "You knew Tita Cecile was the goddess of broken homes. Why didn't you tell me?"

"I know you're tired of hearing this . . . but I really couldn't tell you anything." Bart lowers his head, his eyes trained on his shoes.

Ha. Serves him right. He should feel ashamed.

"I thought you were my friend." I was ready to forgive him for not telling me he's an aswang. But not telling me which goddess Tita Cecile is? That's a different level of betrayal. I mean, she's the goddess of broken homes! With her around, our family was at risk of breaking up. For all I know, she might even be the reason we're a mess now. Bart could have at least warned us about her.

Kitty steps between Bart and me. "I know you're hurt, Ate. But we need to stay together. We'll figure things out, like we always have." She puts an arm around my shoulders and Bart's. "We'll find Mom, then Tita Cecile. We'll get them both back."

I'm certain Tita Cecile can take care of herself on her own. There might be some complications since the lord of the Underworld obviously has a hold on her. But she'll manage. Tita Cecile *is* a goddess.

Still, Kitty sounds so optimistic. And best of all, she doesn't seem angry or scared of me anymore.

I sigh, forcing myself to look at Bart. Not telling your best friend of eleven years that you're an aswang and that the tita who's like a second mom to you is a goddess are usually grounds for Friendship Over. But like Kitty said, we have to stick together. *For Mom.*

"How do we get to Anagolay?" I ask Bart, my eyes glaring at him like the repulsor rays fired from the palms of Iron Man's gauntlets. "Tita Cecile said the goddess of lost things can find anyone."

"I know someone who can help us," Bart says. Unlike me, he doesn't have the guts to meet my gaze. I guess it's hard to look into the eyes of the friend you've kept major secrets from. "Stay close."

I expected Bart to call a taxi. Or maybe ask some aswang cousin to drive us.

"Tell me," I say. "Why are we here again?" I stare at the closed gate of Silverio Auto Repair Shop. "What are we going to do, make a car out of scrap metal?"

"There's no need for sarcasm, Ate." Kitty shakes her head at me as Bart rings the doorbell.

Who needs an adult when there's Kitty? Come to think of it . . . I haven't even met an adult who nags as much as my sister does.

We hear metal crashing and a man cursing behind the gate. "We're closed! It's the middle of the night, for cryin' out loud. Come back tomorrow."

"Kuya Silverio!" Bart leans on the closed metal gate. "It's me. I'm with the Sinagtala sisters. We need your help."

"Oh." The gate slides open, and the owner pokes his ponytail-haired head out. "You should have called first! I'm still working on the upgrades you requested. Come in, come in!"

Every time Tita Cecile had car trouble, she always came to Silverio. "He's the only one who can fix my car problems," she always said. I was certain other auto repair shops in Caloocan City could do as well. But now that I can see what lies outside the Balabal, it's no wonder that magical beings prefer Silverio's.

At a glance, you'd think it was just your usual auto repair shop—an engine in the corner, a stray car part on the floor. But with a closer look you'll see that the radiator on the table is emitting bright-blue smoke. There's a seemingly normal toaster oven beside it, but it has springs and wires welded on its sides like crab claws. Instead of the usual see-through glass, its door is made from a material that resembles pearls. Kind of like the material on my pendant.

"Watch out, Lulu; that one bites," warns the man Bart referred to as Kuya Silverio.

Sure enough, the rusty toaster oven snaps its door at me threateningly, like an angry snapping turtle.

Kitty pulls me away before it tears my hand off. "Don't touch anything, Ate."

"Cute." I narrow my eyes at Bart. Don't tell me he's keeping another major secret from me? "I didn't know you had an older brother."

"Oh, I'm not an aswang." Silverio waves his hand in front of him. "We're totally not related. I'm just older—well, much older—than he is."

Bart beams at him. "He's a genius, and he's Deity Aman Sinaya's top assistant, which requires being a top-tier tinkerer and programmer. He made *Dambana Wars: Salamangka City.*"

"Ah. I see." I nod. No wonder Bart idolizes him. This guy is like the nerdiest of all nerdy nerds. "*Salamangka City*? Is that different from the game we played earlier?"

"Very, *very* different. And so much better." Bart pats the monitor beside him. "It's the best MMPORPG the three Realms have ever seen. That one is just Middleworld-wide. *Dambana Wars: Salamangka City* is universal."

"You've lost me at MM-what." I roll my eyes. Nerd talk. I don't know what that MM-thing means. And frankly, I don't care. I just know it's a kind of game that I'm not very good at.

Kitty holds out her hand. She nudges me to do the same. "We're so sorry to trouble you at such an hour, sir."

Silverio shakes our hands. I notice that his hand is

cold. Like, metallic cold. "Just call me Silverio. Or Kuya Silverio, if you're into honorifics."

I can't explain it, but there's something not quite right about Kuya Silverio. Like, he just doesn't feel like someone I'll get along with.

"You said you're not an aswang." I peer at the repair shop owner. "Are you a tiyanak in an automaton body too?"

"I'm not a tiyanak." The man shakes his head, yawning. "So, how may I help you kids?"

Bart explains our predicament. Thankfully, he leaves out the part about going on a quest to find Mom, just saying that we need a ride to Anagolay's temple—her dambana.

To Kuya Silverio's credit, he doesn't ask too many questions. "Lady Anagolay's dambana is in Mount Banahaw. Quezon Province is far from here. It's going to cost you."

"I know. Hold on." Bart brings out his cell phone. I wonder if it has some special magical feature. "Hello, Lolo? I need money. Yes. It's for Lulu. Yes. They're with me. Okay. Will do. Uh-huh."

I sigh. I really don't like the feeling of being Bart's duty. It seems that his grandfather is in on it too. He might even be the one who roped Bart into becoming my protector.

Bart says goodbye to his lolo and hangs up. "Can I Salamang-Cash you?" he asks Silverio.

"Of course. Step inside the crib, little pup." Kuya Silverio leads Bart to the cashier booth. "Let's do business!"

Thankfully, Bart doesn't take long. He walks back to us carrying a piece of paper, which he stuffs inside his backpack. I'm guessing it's the receipt.

"What's Salamang-Cash?" Kitty asks.

"Yeah." I glance at his phone. "It sounds like a salamander."

"It's a mobile wallet app for magical creatures." Bart checks the time on his phone. "We need to hurry. Lolo won't mind if we have to pay more. But it's getting late, and we must get there before sunrise. The queue gets pretty long."

"Thank you, Bart. Thank you too, Kuya Silverio." Kitty smiles at the man. "We really appreciate your help."

The pearly white pickup truck is already running in Kuya Silverio's garage. The smoke coming out of its exhaust is the same blue light that I see whenever I use my strength.

Kuya Silverio opens the pickup's door theatrically. "Ta-da! There's only room for one passenger inside. But an aswang in dog form doesn't count, as long as his feet don't touch the floor. I'm sorry, but you must be in puppy mode, my dude." He reaches inside and brings out a dog harness. "You can wear this harness, and I'll strap you to Katrina's seat belt."

Bart morphs into Tannie the shih tzu, complete with

his ugly candy cane sweater with golden ruffles. I make a mental note to ask him if wearing that ugly sweater is necessary. But for now—

"What about me? Where will I sit?" I ask.

Kuya Silverio points at the truck bed with his thumb. "You can stay in the back."

Argh. I'm liking this man less and less. "But why? Why can't I stay with you all inside?"

"The passenger seat was made for one person only. Puppy Bart doesn't count because he's . . . well . . . a puppy," says Silverio. "Magic is very particular about following its rules. If you say the seat is for one person, then only one person can sit on it. If you insist on sitting with someone on a seat made for one, magic will see you as a rule breaker and get rid of you."

"Get rid of me?"

The annoying smile vanishes from Silverio's equally annoying face. "You die."

Kitty and I exchange looks. Die? Yikes.

"I can stay with Ate at the back," says my loyal sister.

"Me too," says my equally loyal friend. I'm still upset with him, but I appreciate this show of loyalty nonetheless.

But Kuya Silverio shakes his head. "I'm sorry, but you can't. Only Lulu is strong enough to withstand the forces my truck will be subjected to."

"How do you know I can handle it?" I demand. Has this man been spying on us?

"Word gets around fast in the magical community," he says with a shrug. "Marites and Tolits spread gossip faster than a virus can spread in a dirty elevator. A little girl tossing the Underworld's scariest princess to the neighboring street using only her bare hands? Every nosy being in the universe knew about it before I could even finish my late-night snack."

"But how can you be sure I can take it? Is there, like, a measuring thing for my strength or something?" I don't like this. I don't like this *at all*. Even Silverio fanboy Bart looks skeptical.

"No, but I'm certain you can handle the ribbons. I made this truck myself."

I take a step back. Ribbons? I'm going to be strapped to the back of a pickup truck with *just* ribbons?

Kitty peeks inside the truck bed. "I don't know about this, Ate. Are they even seat belt grade?"

"They are not. They're like . . . Christmas gift ribbons!" I groan. If this truck has a habit of throwing extra people off it, these flimsy strips of fabric won't even last a kilometer.

"The ribbons are much sturdier than they look." Kuya Silverio sighs loudly. "Listen, I haven't got all night. If you don't want to hitch a ride with me, just go get yourselves a human taxi."

I pause. The map on my phone says that Mount Banahaw is 131.2 kilometers away from Caloocan City. That's, like, three hours, give or take, by car in light traffic. It's going to be superexpensive hiring a taxi to get there, if a driver even agrees to take the trip. It takes too long to ride the bus, so that's not an option either.

Silverio begins to cover the truck bed.

"Wait!" I pull on the cover. "I'll stay in the back. Meow, keep your seat belt on. Hold Puppy Bart tight."

Tannie the Puppy Bart snorts in annoyance.

Kitty throws her arms around me, squeezing me tight. "Be careful, Ate."

Kuya Silverio leads Kitty and Tannie to the passenger door. "You need to go inside while I get Lulu set up."

"I'll see you in a few," I promise my sister. I hope it's a promise I get to keep.

After I hop into the cargo hold, Kuya Silverio hands me the gold ribbons. As soon as they make contact with my skin, they wrap around my waist like a belt.

Kuya Silverio studies my bands. "The ribbons are strong, but they've never held anyone living before."

"WHAT?!" Is this guy for real? "Are you serious? You're telling me this now?"

"Here." Kuya Silverio gives me more shiny strips of fabric. This time they wind themselves around both my wrists. "Remain standing upright as much as you can—it may get uncomfortable if you don't. And use your strength to hold on. If the bands give way, your strength will keep you in the truck. Just be sure not to let go."

"This terrible idea is sounding terribler by the minute."

"You'll be okay." Kuya Silverio pauses. "I hope."

"Ugh. Just go drive already!"

The ride starts out okay . . . until the truck moves faster and faster, that is.

Everything around me is a blur. Lights, trees, road rails—all a blur.

My soul feels like it's about to be ripped from my body. Without ribbons holding my feet down, my legs lift up from behind like I'm flying as the truck moves even faster.

I hold on to the ribbons for dear life.

I close my eyes.

This truck is a speed demon spawned from the depths of the Underworld.

And then it stops. My legs drop to the floor of the truck bed. The ribbons around my waist and wrists release me.

Oh my gods. I'm still alive.

"Land!" I jump off the truck bed and embrace the ground.

"AHH-TEH!" Kitty bursts out from the passenger door. She grabs me in a tight hug. I hug her back. "You're okay."

"Barely okay." I glare at Kuya Silverio. "That thing almost killed me!"

"But it didn't," he says, shrugging. "I fulfilled my end of the deal."

"I've sent you the balance—did you get it?" Bart has morphed into human form once again.

Kuya Silverio's phone dings. "Yep. Got it. Enjoy your quest, little ones. Try not to die!" He jumps back into the driver's seat and waves farewell. Soon his demon truck from hell is zooming away, leaving a trail of glowing blue smoke in its wake.

CHAPTER NINE

We Scale the Mountain of Love and Fractured Friendships

"WHEN I GET MY HANDS ON THAT—"

Kitty gives me a warning look.

"—guy." I glare at Bart, balling my fists. They flicker with blue light. "I can't believe he did that to me! Even dogs get treated better. If he strapped Tannie to the back of a truck like that and an animal welfare group found out, he'd get sued for animal abuse."

"You just don't know him yet." Fanboy Bart is back to defending his idol again.

After that horrific ride, I'm not having any of it. "And you do?"

"Yes!"

"Dude, he was driving like a demon while I was barely

hanging on in the back of his demonic truck. I almost flew off in the middle of the South Luzon Expressway." I glare at Bart. "I could have died!"

"But you didn't!"

"I almost did!"

"Ate, Bart, please. Let's not fight. Mom needs our help, and we're the only ones Tita Cecile can count on." Kitty steps between us. "I wish you didn't have to suffer during the trip, Ate, but we're here now. And you're safe. That's what matters."

Kitty is too nice. She really is a lot like Mom.

The glowing blue light on my fists dissipates as my breathing slows down.

"Where are we, anyway?" Kitty asks, obviously eager to change the subject.

"Dolores, Quezon. That's Mount Banahaw." Bart gestures in some general, dark direction. "Lady Anagolay's dambana should be right about there."

"I can't see a thing." I squint my eyes. To my surprise, my vision adjusts to the dark automatically, like the high-tech camera on Sitan's iPhone. I can see what Bart is pointing at: a spot of silver at the summit.

"I can't see either, but it seems far," Kitty notes. I don't tell her how right she is, worried that it might scare her off the hike.

"I'll carry you if you get tired," I tell her, flexing my muscles. "I'm strong now."

Bart snorts.

I shoot him a dirty glance. Bart's chuckling dies down instantly. Call me petty, but I'm not letting him off the hook easily. "If we get lost or get killed, it'll be your fault."

"Ate . . ."

"We won't," Bart says as he tightens the straps of his backpack. "We have the goddess of broken homes's blessing to visit Lady Anagolay. Creatures tasked to challenge humans won't stand in our way."

"Being 'blessed' by the goddess of broken homes isn't exactly inspiring, you know," I snap. The words "broken homes" leave a bitter taste in my mouth.

Kitty puts a hand on my shoulder, but I step away from her.

I need to focus this anger elsewhere before I hurt Kitty. And yeah, Bart too. I don't want to harm him even though he lied to me.

Blue light appears on my hands, and the magic surges through me. I squeeze a boulder, crushing it to powder.

I wish getting rid of pain was that easy. But the sting of betrayal leaves a mark even when it's healed.

"Go ahead and hate me all you want," Bart says in a quiet voice. "But try to keep an open mind about Lady Cecile. She gave up a lot to protect you."

"So much drama! Who needs Netflix when I can just watch you three for free?"

A small orb of pink light the size of a saucer approaches us. As it gets nearer, I see the outline of a person. The outline gets bigger and bigger until it becomes a beautiful light-skinned girl with transparent, butterfly-like wings.

The girl is an engkantada—a fairy.

"Hi, Bart," the engkantada says, tucking a lock of her silky almost-blond hair behind her ear. "I haven't seen you since you learned to transform. It's been, what, five years?"

"Four years. Sorry, Mahal," Bart mumbles, shifting his feet in discomfort. "I've been busy."

"Mahal?!" I scowl. Who is this girl, and why is Bart referring to her as his "love"?

Bart clears his throat. "This is Mahal Makiling. Her family protects Mount Banahaw. They guided Lolo and me whenever Lolo needed to visit Lady Anagolay."

"Makiling?" I exchange a look with Kitty. The name sounds familiar. . . . Then I remember Maria Makiling.

Kitty and I both know it. It was even on a recent quiz we had before Christmas break. And it's a popular legend too.

They say that Maria Makiling is the guardian spirit of Mount Makiling in the province of Laguna. In one story, Maria had three suitors—a Spanish soldier, a rich mestizo, and a common Filipino farmer. Maria picked the farmer, despite his lowly status. The other two, who believed they were better than the farmer, couldn't accept defeat in love. So they framed the farmer for a crime he didn't commit. The poor man cried out Maria

Makiling's name as he faced the death penalty. Maria Makiling was heartbroken, retreating to her mountain. From then on, she never let anyone see her again.

Considering that they're both fairies and have the Makiling surname, I wouldn't be surprised if this Mahal girl is related to the actual Maria Makiling.

"Who's this?" Mahal's gaze travels up and down as she looks at me. Recognition eventually dawns in her face. "Oh. The Salamangkero."

"Hello. I'm her sister, Kitty. Nice to meet you." Kitty offers her hand, but Mahal just looks at it in disgust. "Oh-kay . . ."

"Hoy!" I scowl, putting a protective arm around my sister. Kitty was just being polite, and this brat acts like she's above us or something. I throw Bart a dirty look. This is *his* fault.

Bart avoids meeting my eyes as he tells Mahal that Tita Cecile's instructions included going to Anagolay's dambana. Since *he* is the one who is asking, the snobby engkantada agrees to help us.

"Don't trust the sounds you hear," Mahal says. "The magic of the mountain is meant to trick you to make it harder for you to reach Lady Anagolay's dambana. Because only those who deserve it will have the privilege to be granted a wish by the goddess of lost things."

I've read on a blog post somewhere that people typically climb Mount Banahaw as a religious experience or to prove something to themselves. "How come we hardly hear stories about people finding Anagolay?" I ask.

"Obviously, no one has been deserving of finding the goddess's dambana," says the engkantada, flipping her hair as she walks ahead with Bart. "Not even you. But there's nothing I can do when it's a deity who wants you to find it."

I ball my fists and make them glow in blue light. "Why, that little—"

"Ate, don't." Kitty grabs my left wrist. She holds on until the blue light disappears. "I know Mahal is very rude, but we need her help to find Mom."

I grit my teeth, but I listen to my sister. Good thing I do, because the deeper we get into the forest, the clearer it becomes that there's no way we can find our way on our own. There aren't any established trails—it feels like no human has been on this path for a very long time. The trees are densely packed; the moon and the stars barely light our way. If not for Mahal's engkantada glow, we'd be totally lost.

Mahal stops suddenly at a dead end. "We'll have to climb up these rocks."

"Are you serious?" I look up to where she's pointing. It's a literal wall of moss-covered rocks as high as a ten-story building. "That's like a hundred feet. Or more. And we don't have safety gear!"

"Isn't there any other path, Mahal?" Bart asks the

engkantada. The green monster inside me bristles every time he calls her by her name. "I can scale the wall easily in dog mode, but Lu and Kitty can't."

"Oops. I forgot we have humans with us." Mahal twirls her hair. The silky strands immediately fall back into place as soon as she releases them. I'm getting a sudden, violent urge to pull out those glorious locks of hers and turn them into a broomstick. "Sorry, Bart. This is the only way to Lady Anagolay's dambana. If they really want to find what they're looking for, they need to scale this wall."

"We'll climb the wall," I say, meeting my sister's terrified gaze. "We'll do it for her."

For Mom. This is for Mom.

"I'll go up first." Bart transforms into Tannie the shih tzu. "There are hidden vines you can hold on to. I'll find them for you."

"Yeah, yeah, whatever." I wave him away. "Just make sure nothing horrible is waiting for us up there. Go up after him, Meow."

My sister frowns. "What about you?"

"I'll be fine." I force myself to smile. "I got this."

I lied. I don't have this. Far from it.

Mahal flicks her wrist, and she turns back into a tiny fairy encased in glowing pink light. Bart and Kitty go up the wall. Just like Bart says, there are vines to hold on to. They're damp and muddy and they're hard to grip. But they're the only thing that keeps us tethered on the slippery rocks. I'd rather have burn marks on my hands than fall off this cliff.

"This isn't so bad—AHH!"

The vine I'm holding on to detaches from the rock, and I'm dangling on the side of the mountain. The gym bag with all the food that Ate Mariel gave us slips from my fingers, falling into the darkness below. My heartbeat is racing so loud and fast I feel like my chest is going to explode. "Help! Help me, please!"

Mahal, Bart, and Kitty aren't that high up yet. Why can't they hear me?

"HELP! Saklolo! Help!" I wind my arms tighter around the vine. Without my superstrength, my muscles are screaming in pain. But I don't want to risk crushing the vines or burning through them with my Salamangka's warm blue light. I just try to keep as still as possible, even if it hurts so bad and I'm extremely terrified. "Saklolo!"

The pink orb of light that is Mahal drifts down to where I'm hanging. I feel a surge of relief. "Mahal! Help me—"

"Oh, hey." As Mahal transforms to full-sized fairy, a knot forms in my stomach. Something's not right. The engkantada squats in front of me so I can have a full view of her face. "That's a long way down. It'll take a while to clean up your bloody mess once you fall and hit the rocks. Some of them are pretty sharp."

Against my better judgment, I look down. It's too dark

to see anything, but the movement causes me to spin like a top. Oh my gods. "Kitty . . . Bart . . . H-h-h-help!"

"They can't hear you. I made sure they can't." Mahal scowls. "You're like every human who's tried to get past me and my mountain—you're all too arrogant to listen. If they just followed my instructions, they wouldn't have disappeared trying to get to Lady Anagolay."

"Y-y-your mountain?"

"Yep. *My* mountain." Mahal flicks her wrists, and the rocks loosen around the vine I'm holding on to for dear life. "I control Mount Banahaw. But thanks to the Vengeful One's magic, Bart and your sister believe you're fine."

"But those people . . ." I gasp, trying to breathe. "The ones who wanted to find Anagolay . . ."

"They failed to find the goddess, obviously. I wouldn't bother looking for them if I were you. Unless you want to join them in the Underworld." Mahal giggles. "Lucky for you, the Vengeful One doesn't want you dead. . . . Not yet, anyway."

"Why are you doing this?" I whimper. I try to reach the rocks beneath my hanging legs, but they're too slippery.

"The Vengeful One wants me to delay you. He says I can play with you a little." Mahal lifts her hand, and I feel something touch the toes of my sneakers. But every time I think I can reach it, Mahal moves the rock away.

The engkantada lets out a gleeful laugh.

"But you're a Makiling!" I cry in desperation. "You're good fairies!"

"Good? I guess you can say that." Mahal's face contorts with a cruel smile. "I'm going to tell you a little secret."

Tears well up in my eyes. My only hope now is that she talks long enough for Bart or Kitty to notice.

"My lola Maria didn't retreat to a mountain like the brokenhearted maiden your human stories portray her as. Those evil men killed her beloved—Maria Makiling wanted vengeance. She hunted them down and made sure they met violent deaths." Mahal turns her wrist slowly and the vine drops another foot. "Humans like you don't deserve the powers you hold. *You* don't deserve to be the Salamangkero."

"But I didn't ask to be the Salamangkero!" If any of the gods out there can hear my prayer, please help me. Please, please, please. I can't do what you want me to do if I'm dead, can I?

I look up at the sky, concentrating hard to break free from the spell that's keeping Bart and Kitty from seeing what Mahal is doing. My pendant grows warm as it glows blue, and I see a star twinkle as if it heard me.

"It'll be so fun to see her when she realizes you're gone," Mahal says. "And Bart . . ." Her high-bridged nose flares. "Bart will finally be free of you. He won't need to degrade himself any longer being your guard dog— Ahhh!"

There's a flash of bright yellow light that comes out of

nowhere, making Mahal step back and cover her eyes in pain. Then there's another flash. This time, though, I can see where it came from—the light came from the stars.

"Hold on, Ate Lu, we're coming!"

Mahal and I see Bart in Tannie mode and Kitty coming down the mountain at the same time.

"MAHAL!" Bart bellows. Even from where I'm hanging, I can see his eyes flash red. He lets out an angry growl. "Leave my best friend alone!"

The harmless-looking Tannie starts transforming into the aswang of lore—wolflike snout, sharp teeth and claws, elongated arms and feet. A hair-raising, fearsome monster.

Frantic, Mahal meets my gaze.

"Once the Vengeful One succeeds, we'll overthrow the gods and take back the Realms." The engkantada flicks her wrist, breaking the vine. "Goodbye, Lulu Sinagtala."

A piece of broken rock falls on my head, and I black out as I fall into the dark abyss.

CHAPTER TEN

The Temple on the Disappearing Floor

People say our lives flash before our eyes when we die. Kind of like a highlight reel. But instead of a video montage with cheesy background music that shows my life's best moments, all I see is the underside of someone's dirty denim shorts.

"Wake up, Lulu Sinagtala," says the owner of the butt, gently tapping my arm with a talon. It's a wakwak. "We're landing!"

I expected to drop to the ground like Yoon Se-Ri did while parasailing in that K-drama *Crash Landing on You*. But the wakwak is surprisingly gentle, depositing me at the summit carefully.

"I have been following you since you arrived in Quezon on Lady Cecile's orders," says the creature. She shuffles her batlike wings. "But the engkantada shrouded your whereabouts on the mountain. Good thing Lady Tala was able to find you and shine light on your location in time. Or I would have been too late to catch you."

"Tala? As in the goddess of stars?"

"Yes."

Suddenly we hear the distant flapping of wings. Landing with a thud, Kitty and Bart arrive via Wakwak Airlines.

"Ate! Thank the gods you're safe." Kitty launches herself at me, hugging me tight. "I felt so helpless, seeing you fall, and I couldn't do anything."

"I'm fine." I breathe a long sigh. "But I lost our food. The bag fell when that brat—"

"It's all right, Ate." Kitty gives me a squeeze before releasing me. "I'm sure we'll find something to eat."

A smile touches my lips. I'm still shaken and upset, but I can't resist my sister's optimism—it's contagious.

"Your companions are here." The wakwak bows. "No danger lies on your path anymore, so we shall take our leave."

"Thank—" The three wakwaks fly away before I can finish. "Oh, whatever. Now what?"

Before Kitty can say anything, Bart steps forward. "I'm so sorry, Lu. I really wanted to tell you everything. I felt so bad every time I had to keep a secret from you," he croaks. "But being your friend . . . it's real."

I bite my lower lip as I stare back at him. Bart kept so many secrets from me, I really thought I doubted him. But deep down, I felt—I feel—our friendship is true.

"I get why you couldn't tell me about Tita Cecile. Her identity wasn't yours to share," I say to him. It's not just because magic doesn't allow it, but revealing someone's identity is something that should come from the person themself. You can't just out anyone—they need to be ready to tell people about it. After all, no one can tell us who we are but ourselves. "Let's just be honest with each other from now on, okay?"

"I promise," Bart says.

I wipe away my tears and grab Bart in a hug.

"Oh, I'm so glad you're friends again!" Kitty joins our hug, squeezing us both tight. "No more fighting. It's so hard to referee you two. Anyway, the nice wakwak who brought me here said the dambana is on the other side of this rock. Ate, I know you're iffy about climbing boulders after what just happened—"

"I got this." I ball my fists, making them glow blue. I lift the boulder Kitty is pointing at and toss it aside. "After you."

"Thanks, Ate." Kitty grins. "You should put it back, though."

"Why?"

Kitty throws Bart an uneasy glance. "Well . . ."

"The boulder is the only thing protecting Lady Anagolay's dambana," Bart explains. "I'm sure she'll find someone to replace Mahal, but there's no one right now."

I raise my eyebrows. "What happened to Evil Tinker Bell?"

"Bart sent her to the Underworld," Kitty says, chewing her nails. "I didn't see how he did it, though. It was very dark."

I peer at my sister. She's such a terrible liar. "It was pretty bright with starlight before I got thrown off," I say. "I thought we agreed, no more secrets?"

Kitty sighs. "I'm sorry, Ate, but it's Bart's—"

"It's okay. Lu's right," Bart says. "No more secrets. Besides, you'll find out one way or another." His eyes meet mine. "I went into aswang mode. Not the Tannie version—"

"The scary aswang version," I say, putting the boulder back in place and dusting off my hands. "I thought I saw a bit of you turning before Evil Tinker Bell tossed me off the mountain."

"Right." Bart takes off his glasses to clean them. His eyes are a familiar dark brown, but when the moon shines on them, they turn red. He's about to put his glasses back on when I stop him.

"Don't," I say.

"But these hide my aswang eyes." He avoids looking at Kitty and me. "I don't want to scare you."

Kitty gives him a reassuring smile. "You don't scare us."

"Yeah. You're an aswang, and you're our friend," I say firmly. "We'd rather you didn't hide who you are when you're with us. Just don't go aswang-ing to turn us into Kitty and Lulu stew or something."

"Don't worry, we haven't had a people-vore in the family for hundreds of years now," Bart tells us with a serious expression.

"People-vore?!" Kitty's brows shoot up on her forehead.

He's probably serious, but after all we've been through so far? I highly doubt Kitty and I are on the aswang menu. "People-vore sounds gross," I say.

Bart smirks. "Lulu stew sounds even grosser."

"Hoy!"

We burst out laughing. Once our giggles die down, we squeeze our way through a wall of bamboo trees. On the other side of this leafy barrier, we find a modern-looking house built around a giant balete tree.

"We're here!" Bart points at the top of the building. "Lady Anagolay receives guests on the fourth floor."

"There's only two floors, Bart." I frown. Exhaustion must be affecting his vision. I mean, we did go through a lot to get here. "Three, if you count the roof deck."

"It's there," Bart insists. "Trust me."

I take my sister's hand, and we follow Bart into the building. The house is empty, but all the lights are on. Carefully, we climb the stairs up to the roof deck.

We step out the doors, and I'm surprised by what I see. "Oh wow."

Kitty is speechless, and I don't blame her.

The entire roof deck is a well-lit, snazzy waiting area. In each corner is a vending machine full of a variety of drinks and snacks. Beside them are floating flat-screen TVs showing announcements and advertisements.

DID YOU LOSE SOMETHING?
OR SOMEONE?
THE GODDESS OF LOST THINGS WILL HELP YOU FIND THEM.
100% MONEY-BACK GUARANTEE!

Two seconds later, another announcement appears.

WE ASK ALL SEEKERS OF THE CITY TO BE PATIENT, PLEASE.
WE ARE EXPERIENCING AN UNUSUAL NUMBER OF REQUESTS.

In the middle of the floor, magical creatures of various kinds—tikbalangs, aswangs, manananggals, wakwaks, and the like—are seated on row upon row of comfortable modern benches.

I take a step forward to find us a seat, but my feet get stuck to the floor. There's a loud gonglike sound, then some invisible force pushes me away. I land on my butt a few steps from the stairs.

"Ate! Are you okay?"

Bart helps me up. "Lu, I think we should—"

"Excuse me, do you have a number?"

"A what?" I look up at the sound of the unfamiliar voice. Well, I have to look *way* up. The man wearing a security guard uniform is as tall as John Lloyd's automaton body. He smells like cigar smoke and wet trees, so I'm guessing he's kapre—a tree giant.

"A number." The guard repeats, pointing to the screen. "You go in when your number is called."

SERVICE BEGINS AT ~~DUSK~~ OR DAWN.
ONLY THOSE WITH NUMBER STUBS
BEFORE THE SUN ~~SETS~~ OR RISES
WILL BE ACCOMMODATED.
CURRENTLY SERVING: 555

"But we're in a hurry!" I stomp my feet. I know I'm acting like a spoiled brat, but we need to find Mom. "We can't wait all day—"

"Everyone can't wait all day, kid," the tree giant snaps. "Take a number or leave."

"Thank you, sir." Kitty takes the stub from the guard. "Come on, Ate. We can have a snack while we wait. You must be hungry by now. And it's almost time for your medicine."

"I'm not hungry!" My stomach growls, the traitor. "Fine."

Kitty, Bart, and I make our way to the empty seats on the other side of the roof deck, right in front of a vending machine. This place is like the waiting area of a hospital—the queue is so long, you can't help but wonder if you need to set up a tent and camp there for the night.

My sister brings out an energy bar, a water tumbler, and my epilepsy pill bottle from her messenger bag. "This is all we have at the moment, but we can buy some fish balls later after we see Lady Anagolay."

"Thanks." I stuff a bite of the energy bar into my mouth. "What's our number?"

Kitty shows me the stub.

"One thousand five hundred sixty-seven!" I groan. "Really?"

I pop the anti-seizure pill into my mouth as the three of us share the energy bar. But it's not enough to make up for our horrifying Mount Banahaw hike courtesy of Evil Tinker Bell. My stomach is still growling. "I'm so hungry!"

"Here, just read this, Ate." Kitty hands me a newspaper. "It'll keep your mind off the hunger. I'm gonna nap."

It looks like the usual daily, with the same news and all. Well, except for that familiar symbol on the upper-right corner of the page. It's the exact same symbol on my pendant, the silhouette of a man squatting. "What's this—"

As soon as my finger touches the symbol, the letters on the page shine blue. "Meow! Bart! Look at the letters. They're moving!"

Kitty glances at the paper and gives me a groggy smile. Although she's curious about the glowing letters, I can see she's exhausted, so I let her lean on my shoulder to sleep. Bart goes into dog mode and curls up in a ball. He barely lifts his doggy head in my direction. He's obviously seen this already and is too tired to bother.

Too bad for them, because the magical newspaper is doing something even cooler. The letters are now rearranging themselves into new articles. The headline is now "Realm-Wide Tremor from the Underworld; Mankind Forgets an Entire Hour and a Half!"

> A tremor struck the entire Middleworld yesterday, Friday, December 13. Our sources say it originated from the Underworld. We are yet to confirm what event could affect multiple Realms, as all Underworld creatures and human souls, from the heavenly Maca to the torturous fields of Kasanaan, are refusing to speak about it. Except for one, who agreed to be our anonymous Underworld source. "It is a coordinated attack," they said. "They wanted a certain corrupt soul to escape." When asked if they knew who that corrupt soul is, our source claimed to have no knowledge of it.

I bet that source is John Lloyd. Who else? He totally blabbered to Tita Cecile about the Maligno's escape while his fellow tiyanaks were beside themselves trying to keep him quiet. Even though the information in this article is nothing new, I still read on.

> Deities and creatures alike removed traces of the Realm incident. No human was harmed during the earthquake, evidence that the Balabal is still working. However, the deities had to come together to amplify the powers of Lady Anagolay, the goddess of lost things, in order to hide the memories of the past hour and a half from mankind. This story is currently developing.

Well, this paper got most things right—except for that part where "all" deities helped Anagolay out. From what I remember of what John Lloyd told Tita Cecile, the Underworld has its own problems, with the Maligno's breakout and all.

I skim through the other articles in the magical newspaper. There's a short piece about a bunch of corrupt souls possessing humans, and a feature about a tikbalang making scientific breakthroughs in the industry of navigation. By the time I get to the results of the latest wakwak fighting match, my eyes have begun to droop. Next thing I know, I'm fast asleep.

It's just a nap, but it's quite a deep sleep. So deep, in fact, that I have another weird dream where the sun falls from the sky while a snakelike shadow slithers across the dark clouds.

I dream about being Bernardo Carpio again. This time, though, I try to catch the falling sun. But I can't, and it hits the ground, exploding in a flash of blinding yellow light.

The force of the explosion jolts me wide-awake.

"You're sweating." Kitty dabs a face towel on my forehead. "Are you okay, Ate?"

I stretch my arms and crack my neck. "Never better."

"Okay," my sister says, but she doesn't look like she believes me. Kitty points at the sky. "It's dawn. Isn't the view just beautiful?"

It is. The sky is a dazzling gradient of dark blue and red-orange. In the distance, the sun is but a yellow dot rising from the horizon.

"This way, Lu." Bart ushers me to a new set of stairs that seems to have materialized in the middle of the roof deck while we slept. The handrails are yellow, while the steps are the same color as the morning sky. "Lady Anagolay's staff said they moved the waiting area to the second and first floors before the stairs appeared. They didn't want any impatient beings climbing up the steps before their turn. But we were sleeping, so they let us stay. We can go up now, though."

"Is that safe?"

"Yeah."

I hold Kitty's hand tight as we walk up the steps, which change color based on the color of the sky. Bart (now in human form) brings up the rear. At the top-most landing, we find a closed door. I deposit our ticket into the slot where the knob should be. It eats up the paper, and the door opens.

Anagolay's dambana is a huge, empty room with a bamboo sofa and a coffee table right smack in the middle.

"Over here, mga anak!" Anagolay beckons us from the bamboo sofa. She's a beautiful Tagalog lady with her hair pulled up in a messy bun. She looks like she's as old as Mom, but it's hard to know with gods. "Come sit with me."

Bart bows before taking a seat. "Lady Anagolay."

"Bartolome!" the goddess exclaims. Up close, I notice there's a plastic palanggana, a washbasin, in front of her on the table. It's filled with water. I wonder what she uses it for. "You're all grown up. The last I saw you, you were only a wee pup. How is your grandfather?"

"He is well, madam. Enjoying his retirement."

"As he should." Anagolay smiles at Bart, then at Kitty and me. "Luningning and Katrina Sinagtala. How may I help you, my children?"

There's no point in beating around the bush. "Will you really help us find *anything*? Or anyone?"

"Yes." The goddess purses her lips. "Anyone. Even your mother."

"How did you—ah, never mind." The gods know everything. I mean, they *are* gods. "Can you find Mom?"

"Yes, but you must give me a formal request. I'm sorry, anak, but rules are rules."

Ugh. No. Not more homework. "I have to write a request?"

To my relief, Anagolay shakes her head. "You can just say it out loud. But you must address me and clearly state what you are looking for. Be sure to be specific. Use your mother's name so the magic will have no doubt that she is the one you are looking for."

"Sounds easy enough." I squeeze Kitty's hand. Here goes nothing. "Anagolay, goddess of lost things, please find Jenalyn Sinagtala, my mother."

"As you wish, anak." Magical blue light leaves the goddess's fingers and swirls into the plastic basin in front of her.

The water surface stirs, and a projection of a shore appears, as if we're watching a video on the water. Then the vision fades, showing the place where Kuya Silverio dropped us off last night. It passes through roads, faster and faster, until all I can make out are random blurry colors. It stops at a fishing village, where letters on a boat show that it's at Catanduanes Island. The vision goes farther out to sea. Farther and farther, like there's no end in sight.

Then we see nothing but darkness. A burst of light, and we're back to an island. But this island is different. It *feels* different.

The vision brings us over the sea once again. I'm pretty sure it's not the same sea that I'm familiar with.

Our view stops in front of a different island. A city in the middle of nowhere, protected by a blue light bubble.

The vision enters the city. It's moving too fast, so I can't make out the buildings. Suddenly it spins around in a circle. It makes me dizzy, but I do my best to keep watching.

The spinning stops, and an image of a woman appears. She's shrouded in darkness, but I would recognize that silhouette even in my sleep.

"MOM!"

CHAPTER ELEVEN

Meet Apolaki, Patron God of Warriors and Horrible Puns

"THAT'S IT?" I PUSH THE BASIN AWAY FROM ME. "SOMEONE IS HOLDING Mom captive, and this thing doesn't show where she is!"

We got thrown off a mountain for *this*? We waited hours just to be shown vague locations but nothing concrete. What a waste of time.

"Let me try again, anak." Anagolay closes her eyes, and the scenes in the bowl play out once again. When she reaches the part where Mom is held captive, her brows furrow in intense concentration. The vision on the water blurs, and Anagolay herself starts flickering in and out. She's glitching like a BTS concert live stream on a really horrible internet connection, rapidly disappearing and reappearing. "Oh."

Kitty and I exchange troubled looks. I guess that's not what's supposed to happen. "What was that?"

Anagolay falls back on the sofa, breathing heavily.

Bart jumps to the goddess's side. "Lady Anagolay, are you all right?"

"I'm fine, Bartolome, thank you." The goddess clutches her chest. She frowns at the basin. "Your mother is in a magical place that's between worlds. It usually makes seeking harder, but on a good day, I'm easily able to overcome such a barrier. This . . . is . . . different."

"Can't you try again?" Kitty pleads. "Please, Miss Anagolay. Please help us."

Anagolay tries again and fails. But this time she glitches even more.

"I can't. I'm sorry." She bows her head. "The Maligno must be using Balabal magic to shroud your mother from me. I'm afraid casting that spell to make mankind forget the earthquake weakened me. If this flickering gets any worse, I might accidentally unleash my divine form. It would release so much magical energy, everything around me would burn to ashes."

"Oh." That does sound dangerous. A memory of Manong Sol and Tita Cecile talking at the beauty parlor flashes in my head. They must have helped Anagolay with the forgetting spell too. I mean, anyone would need backup if they had to misplace the memories of an entire Realm. "How do we get to that bubbled-up island?" I ask.

"My magic will show the way. I cannot pinpoint the exact location where your mother is being held, but I can bring you to the City." Anagolay holds out her hand. "Your agimat, please, Luningning."

"Agimat?"

"Your pendant."

"Oh. So that's what this is." I hand her my necklace. I don't even bother asking how Anagolay knows about it. The gods probably share everything they know about me through deity social media or something. A pitfall of being the Salamangkero, I guess.

Anagolay transfers the tendrils of magical light from the palanggana to the agimat.

"Release my magic into the water every time you need guidance," she says. "But remember, it is finite. You may only release it twice at most, so be wise."

"Okay. Thanks."

"Every being who seeks me out gets a wish. And they can use this wish to look for anything they've lost within the Realms." Anagolay looks straight at Kitty. "What is it that you want to find, my child?"

Kitty turns to me and Bart for help.

Bart just shrugs. "It's your wish."

I have a better idea. "Buried treasure that'll make us forever rich, maybe?"

Kitty shakes her head. "No, no. I think I'll save my wish for later. Would that be okay?"

I frown. No, it's not. I gave up my one and only wish while she gets to keep hers.

"A wise decision." Anagolay waves her hand. A tendril of blue light encircles Kitty's wrists and Anagolay's, and the light is absorbed by my agimat. "You can use my magic anytime you want to, Katrina. Like the map, just pour it into water."

"We can't thank you enough, ma'am," Kitty says.

"Doesn't Bart get a wish too?" I ask.

The goddess nods. "Of course."

"I . . ." Bart fidgets, then stares straight at me. "I would like to save my wish too, Lady Anagolay. It's not that I want to use it for something trivial, but I believe we might need it one day in a matter of life and death."

I study my shoes like they're the most interesting specimens in the whole three Realms. I honestly don't know what to say.

He's right. I shouldn't have thought such bad things of Kitty.

"I can do that," Anagolay says, smiling at Bart. "You are a true friend, Bartolome. Your grandfather will be proud of you."

Bart shrugs.

Anagolay stores Bart's wish inside my agimat.

As the glowing fades in the pendant, I stare at the image of the squatting man. I'm such a doofus. My sister and my best friend didn't think twice about entrusting their wishes to my care. And here I was thinking Kitty was keeping it for her own gain.

"Um, Miss Anagolay?"

Anagolay looks at my sister fondly. "Yes, anak?"

"Maybe I should just stay here with you and wait for Ate Lu and Bart." Kitty lowers her head. "I'm just a kid, and I don't have powers and—"

"What are you talking about?" I demand, taking my sister by the shoulders. "We're not leaving you behind!"

"But I don't want to hold you back." Kitty tells me she's just going to be a burden to us: "Magiging pabigat lang ako sa inyo."

"Hindi ka pabigat," I say firmly. "You are not a burden. We can't do this without you."

Bart nods in agreement. "Yeah!"

"I would be glad to have you as a guest, anak, but they need you," says Anagolay. "You might not have powers, but you have a lot of love in your heart. One day, you will find how important that is."

"Okay." Kitty gives us a small smile. "Can you come with us, Miss Anagolay?"

I guess my sister is still shaken from everything's that has happened to us in the past twenty-four hours. I'd be scared too if I were in her position. I mean, *I* don't know what I'm doing, and I have powers.

"Kitty, higher gods don't chaperone kids—" Bart begins.

"God levels are nonsense, Bartolome." Anagolay waves

away Bart's concerns. "I would love to accompany you, but as you may have noticed, a lot of beings need my help. However, I have already taken the liberty of asking my son to accompany you."

"Who's your son?" I ask.

"I know!" Kitty perks up. "Apolaki. We studied him in class."

"Oh." Unlike Kitty, I frequently forget a lot of things taught to us in school (it's not intentional, mind you), but Apolaki is one of those gods who's hard to forget. The great sun god, the patron god of warriors—he's frequently depicted in Tagalog fantasy TV shows as this really handsome being who's super buff and amazing. A true hero, the great love interest of romantic myths.

Kitty rolls her eyes at my dreamy expression, but I ignore her. The thought of actually meeting the Apolaki of lore in person makes my pulse quicken.

"I figure having a familiar face with you will make your journey enjoyable." Anagolay clears her throat. "It is time, my son."

I wonder whose likeness he'll use. I've read a theory on the internet that the patron god of warriors can shapeshift so he can spy on his enemies. For sure, Apolaki will be at least as old as Ate Mariel, and just as beautiful. "A familiar face" means he's probably an actor, right? Daniel Padilla? Amandla Stenberg? Or maybe a singer, like Jungkook? Or maybe—

The door opens.

There's that usual blue light. It glows for a bit, then it clears. Revealing . . .

Manong Sol?

It takes a minute for the fact that Manong Sol is Apolaki to sink in.

"You've got to be kidding me," I say.

Kitty's jaw drops. Bart looks like a dog with his tail between his legs—the god obviously scares him.

"Anak!" It's so weird hearing Anagolay, a seemingly youthful lady, call old man Manong Sol her child. "Come here. Give your mama a hug."

Old man Manong Sol awkwardly embraces his mama.

I guffaw while Kitty tries to hide her giggle with a cough. Bart morphs into a dog in an obvious effort to avoid laughing out loud. Cheater!

"What is so funny?" demands Manong Sol.

"Sorry po!" Kitty bows in apology. "You're just not . . . um . . . the Apolaki we expected."

Manong Sol puts his hands on his waist. He looks like an angry chicken scolding his little chicks. "What did you assume I'd look like?"

"Someone more *appealing*, definitely," I say with a snort. With my memories of the magical world slowly returning, I'm giving myself leeway to be a little disrespectful. He's been a huge part of my life, as much as Tita

Cecile was, and he's hidden this from me. "Well, at least no one's going to suspect us of loitering around without adult supervision. I mean, Manong Sol is as adult as anyone can be."

"Do not push your luck." The god wags a finger in warning. He uses that same finger to point in the direction of the sky. "I can barbecue you with my sunlight anytime I want."

"Yeah right." He's trained me all my life. I don't think he'll let those years go to waste by turning me into Lulu barbecue. Though admittedly, seeing the old man glow a bit is cool and, well . . . a bit scary.

"Stop this nonsense, children." Anagolay looks pointedly at Manong Sol, which means "children" also included him. It's quite amusing, really. The goddess then waves her hand, and food appears on the coffee table. "Have some bibingka! Fill your stomachs before your journey."

"Oh my gods." I gasp at the sight and smell of the mouthwatering apparition. It's almost too good to be true. "Food!"

We thank the goddess and dive right in. Bibingka is this yummy baked rice cake usually cooked in a clay pot lined with banana leaves. Pieces of cheese and salted duck egg are embedded in the rice cake, then it's topped with butter and dusted with sugar. We always have bibingka after night mass in the Christmas season. It's Mom's favorite.

I feel a stab of sadness at the thought of Mom. *Hold on, Mom, we're coming for you.*

Manong Sol doesn't seem to think food should be a priority, though. "Mama, we don't have time for this—"

"Nonsense." Anagolay stuffs the bibingka into his mouth.

Kitty takes a sip of water to wash down the rice cake and says, "Tita Cecile said you were somewhere important, Manong Sol."

"I was. And I am."

"That doesn't make any sense." I finish chewing, then swallow. "You can't be in two places at once."

"I can. I'm a god." Manong Sol puffs out his chest like a proud rooster. "We manifest differently to different cultures."

"Huh?"

"Mama, this is so good!" Manong Sol stuffs his mouth with bibingka. He waves his hand. A pen and paper appear in front of Bart. "Bartolome, explain it to them. I'm going to eat."

Anagolay beams at her son.

I roll my eyes. After all that drama about having no time to eat, Manong Sol looks like he could keep devouring bibingka forever.

"Yes, sir." Bart bows and takes the writing tools that have suddenly materialized in front of him like it's the most natural thing in the world. On the paper, he draws a triangle and two parallel lines across it.

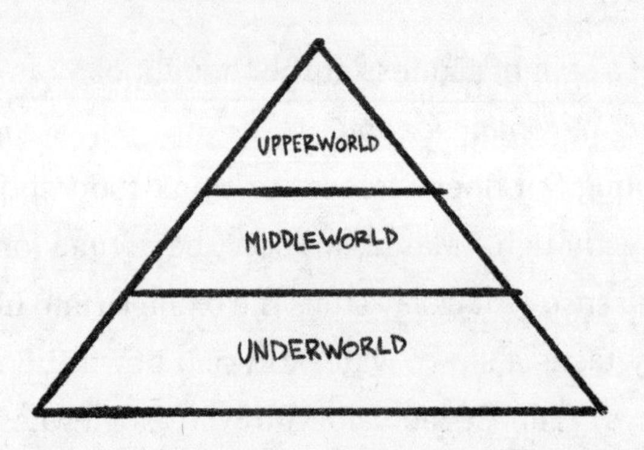

"Think of this pyramid as the entire universe. The Realms are independent from each other. You have the Underworld at the bottom, where humans' souls go when they die and where some creatures live," Bart says. "Above it is the Middleworld, where you and I are. At the highest point is the Upperworld, where the gods are."

"For humans and creatures, the universe is like this pyramid," Bart continues. "We can only go to one level at a time. But for gods, it's more like a diagram of overlapping circles."

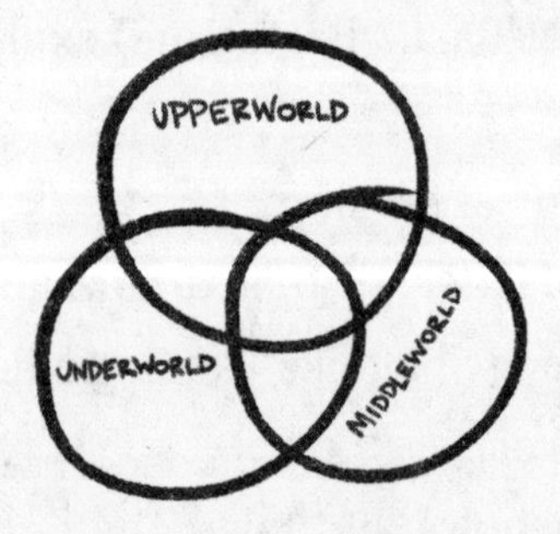

Manong Sol taps the paper. "Bartolome is correct. The Realms are kept as separate realities for non-deities like yourselves, so there is order and balance in the universe."

"Order and balance . . ." A frown creases my forehead as I rack my brain. "Manong Sol, do you remember that very tall man who's always at your gym and doesn't pay you correctly?"

"John Lloyd the tiyanak, the ugly bloke." The sun god scratches his chin. "Why?"

"He said something to Tita Cecile before Sitan took her."

"Ah, yes. Mansisilat already called me about the Maligno's escape." Manong Sol sighs. He pushes his empty plate across the table. "Thank you for the snack, Mother. We must go now and find Jenalyn."

Kitty stands up immediately. I do the same.

"Mom," she says. "We need to find Mom."

"You will find her," Anagolay promises. She waves her hand, and the door where Manong Sol entered reappears. "Use my magic wisely. Keep each other safe, my children."

Manong Sol reaches for his mother's hand and covers it with his own. "Take it easy, Mama. Don't exert yourself so much. You've barely had enough rest since you hid the memory of the tremor from the entire Middleworld."

"Pish." Anagolay dismisses his concerns. "I need to help the beings outside. Don't worry, my son; Aman Sinaya is working on an amplifier device for me. It will augment my magic once complete. Every time someone asks where the City is, I'll just press this button and it will show up in my palanggana. Now, go! The children's mother awaits their help."

"Yes, Mama." Manong Sol stands up, offering a hand to Kitty and me.

My other hand automatically takes Bart's. He looks surprised. Embarrassed, I wrench it back, but he doesn't let me.

A small smile plays on my lips. I clear my throat. It's totally not because of Bart that I'm feeling confident again. I mean, we have the sun god, the patron god of warriors, at our side. Nothing can stop us from succeeding.

Hold on, Mom. We're on our way.

CHAPTER TWELVE

The Island in the Middle of the Universe

GOING THROUGH MANONG SOL'S DOOR IS VERY MUCH LIKE WALKING through a long labyrinth. Anagolay's dambana was built around a strangler fig like the Sangang-Daan Tree back home, so I'm guessing we're inside a balete portal. The hallways are made up of intertwined vines branching out to different paths. Without the sun god leading the way, we could easily get lost inside this maze forever.

Every now and then there's an open door or two and we catch a glimpse of what's on the other side. We've seen a museum, a waterfall, and a forest. We've come across a staircase leading up to an upper floor that seems to be far away, and another that seems to lead to a dark basement.

“Don’t, Lu.” Bart stops me before I can peek down the steps.

Finally we step out of the portal, where we’re greeted by bright light. My toes touch sand, and my nose smells the salty sea. I cup my hand above my eyes as a visor, clearing my vision. Yep, we’re at a beach.

From where we’re standing, we have a perfect view of the Philippine Sea. At least, what looks like the Philippine Sea. It’s hard to know for sure when dealing with gods and magic. The view is breathtaking, though. Against the backdrop of the clear blue sky, blue and green waters push waves gently to shore, wetting our feet.

“Wow!”

“It’s beautiful,” Kitty agrees.

“My lolo told me about this place,” Bart says, pointing over my shoulder.

I look behind us. The beings here live in houses designed like the traditional bahay kubo, bamboo huts on stilts, with dried grass roofs and bamboo mat walls. These houses appear every few feet, lined up behind a paved road that leads to town. But this seaside settlement is surrounded by limestone cliffs, forming a crescent moon shape. I can’t help but wonder what’s beyond it.

“I am unsurprised your grandfather spoke of it.” Manong Sol gets this look old people get when they reminisce. “He traveled often with me, back in the day.”

Manong Sol is a god, so "back in the day" must be really far back.

"Wait. How old is your lolo, Bart?" I ask.

"Very old."

I laugh. That's one of the things I love about Bart. You ask a question, he answers. He doesn't overthink it, just says the first thing that comes to mind. It's not very helpful during a crisis (as I've found out the hard way), but it's funny in chill times like this.

"This is so nice." Kitty buries her toes in the sand, watching the particles slip between them. "Where are we, Manong Sol?"

"Sagitna Island. It is the only port in the In-Between—the place between Realms—that allows inter-Realm travel for non-deities like yourselves."

As if by coincidence, I notice a discarded sign propped up against a coconut tree. "Welcome to Sagitna Island, Your Gateway to the Universe," it says. Beside it are street signs pointing to the town proper and four ports—Station 1, Station 2, Station 3, and Station 4.

"This is like Boracay Island, except that Boracay only has three ports," I say, even though I've never been to Boracay. We can't afford to go there by plane, and going by boat takes too long. But once we find Mom, I'm going to ask Manong Sol to take us there by balete portal. We deserve a vacation after this whole Salamangka business. "Where do those ports lead to?"

"The three Realms and places around the In-Between." The old man doesn't follow any of the road signs. He leads us all the way to the end of the beach, where the sea meets the limestone cliffs. We stop and enter a bahay kubo, which has a huge open-air lanai up front. The lanai looks like it was carved from the limestone cliffs. Kind of like a slice of cake, but you only eat the top layer and leave the lower half.

"I remember this!" I run to the middle of the lanai, where I get a full blast of the sun, the limestone floor reflecting the light. Memories of sparring with Manong Sol under the sweltering heat replay in my head. "You sometimes bring me here to train."

Manong Sol shrugs, but he's obviously pleased with himself. "It's good to have a bit of sunlight near the open sea every now and then. We needed the break."

"Easy for you to say. You're a god," I grumble. I remember the training sessions here very differently. "I almost died of dehydration and sunburn!"

Manong Sol rolls his eyes. "I won't burn you. You're the Salamangkero."

Manong Sol won't ever understand sunburns. I mean, he's the *sun god.* But I don't answer back. He did say he *won't* burn me, which basically means he *can,* but he just chooses not to. There's a difference.

"Let's go." But as Manong Sol takes a step forward, he flickers in and out like the flames on a lit candelabra.

Except he's emitting light and heat, the way the sun does when radiating solar flares.

"Ouch!" I rub my arm on the spot where Manong Sol's light ray stung. I check on Kitty and Bart. Thankfully, they're unharmed. Still, I'm getting a sick feeling in my stomach. "Manong Sol, you're not going to explode, are you?"

The expression on the sun god's face tells us that he actually might. Oh no. "Step away from me, children."

We do as he says.

Manong Sol glitches again. This time, little flames appear on his skin.

My pulse quickens. I push Kitty and Bart behind me. I know I'm not indestructible, but his divine form might be more forgiving to me since I'm the Salamangkero. Maybe the Anito will protect me.

"I can't control it, Luningning." Sweat falls from Manong Sol's forehead. Deity or not, sweating usually isn't a good sign. "Listen to me carefully. You need to get to Maharlika City. That is the only place where the Maligno could have taken your mother. He wants you there—I don't know why yet, but I will search for answers. Look for the Omen-Bringer and his allies. I will find a way to tell him to expect you. Don't trust anyone else."

"Manong Sol, are you okay?" Kitty tries to touch him, but he waves her away. I pull my sister closer to me.

"Don't," he says. "I might burn you." He is breathing

heavily now. "Use my mother's map. Be wary of the petty god of the— CLOSE YOUR EYES, CHILDREN!"

In a burst of very bright and warm light, Manong Sol is gone.

I'm never going to say this out loud, but ugh, I wish Manong Sol hadn't disappeared. Without the patron god of warriors on our side, the task of rescuing Mom just leveled up from "easy" to "next to impossible." And yeah, I'm worried about him too.

I hope he's okay. I know we'll have to talk about this eventually, but I don't want to worry Kitty about it yet. Because right now, we have a bigger problem to solve.

We've scoured the entire port, but no one wants to sell their boat for the money from Bart's mobile wallet app. Some of the sellers have no idea what it is or how to use it, but most just refuse on principle. "Barter only," they say.

"It's not like we can barter our souls with them or something," I grumble, massaging my legs. Walking on beach sand is like trudging in a pool of Jell-O. You can't lift your foot without tripping or sinking into the sand. And we've been doing that all day. "This is so frustrating!"

I've always believed that every problem has a solution, no matter how unpredictable it is. But magic has proved otherwise.

"Bartering a soul is illegal," Bart says matter-of-factly,

sipping coconut juice straight from the fruit. "Once you trade it, you can't ever get it back."

There goes another idea down the drain.

"ARGH!" I grab the biggest rock near me and crush it between my hands. The rock crumbles to dust. "That feels good."

"Ate, if you keep doing that, all the limestone rocks on this island will disappear," Kitty says, putting a hand on my shoulder. As usual, her touch calms me the way Mom's does. She rummages through her messenger bag for her tumbler of water and my meds. That bag is roomier than it looks. "Drink up," she says. "I got this tumbler from Ate Mariel at the sari-sari store. It just keeps giving me fresh cold water, so I'm guessing it's enchanted too."

I pop the anti-seizure pill and wash it down with water. "I wonder how much we'd get for this tumbler."

"Practically nothing," a squeaky voice says.

I turn around and find a duwende, a dwarf, in a white shirt, red tie, and high-waisted brown shorts. He's wearing yellow sunglasses and smoking a cigar. He's like a mean version of SpongeBob SquarePants. Behind him are two kapres in tropical shirts.

"I can help you," says the duwende.

"Who're you?" I say. If he thinks he's scaring me with his mafia SpongeBob look, he's totally failing at it.

The kapre in the red shirt growls. "Why, you disrespectful little—"

“Oh, be quiet, SpongeBob minion!” I ball my fists, and they glow blue. “I don’t know who he is. I don’t know who either of you are. We’re minding our own business here, and you butted in.”

Kitty takes hold of my shirt. “Ate . . . please don’t.”

“She is right,” the duwende says. “We should be welcoming to our guests!” He waves at his goons and holds out his hand to me. “The name’s Gavino, young explorers.”

Kitty is the only one who takes the duwende’s hand and introduces us. I simply nod at him in acknowledgment.

Gavino the mafia SpongeBob duwende laughs. “You’re just like your headstrong brother!”

“I don’t have a brother.”

“They really did a number on you, didn’t they?” The duwende grins as though amused. “That’s why I don’t trust the gods. They believe themselves to be above everyone and everything in the Realms, running around and messing up the lives of those they think are beneath them.”

“There are good gods too, you know,” Kitty says. “Tita Cecile—”

Gavino scoffs. “Mansisilat, the goddess of broken homes? You are so naive.”

While I agree with what he said about the gods, I don’t like him calling Kitty names. “Leave my sister alone. Are you gonna help us or not?”

Gavino's kapre goons take a step forward.

"Ate . . ." Kitty says. "Let's not bother Mister Gavino and his friends." She bows to the rude duwende. "Thank you for the offer, sir. But I'm afraid we don't have anything to give you in return."

"It's free."

That stops me in my tracks. "Is that so?"

"Yep." The duwende pushes his ugly yellow sunglasses up his nose. "Just follow me!"

I narrow my eyes. This feels like a trap. In myths and legends, every time a suspicious magical character says that exact same phrase, the protagonist ends up either imprisoned, injured, or turned into a tree.

"Aw, come on! What do you have to lose?"

Nothing, actually. We've lost Mom, we've lost Tita Cecile and Manong Sol. We have absolutely nothing else to lose.

"I got this," I say, giving Kitty and Bart a reassuring pat each. "Lead the way, SpongeBob. If you ever try anything that will hurt my sister or best friend, you're going to have to answer to my fists."

"Whatever you say, kid. But I'm telling you, you won't be able to pass this up."

CHAPTER THIRTEEN

Desperados Pawnshop for the Broke and Hopeless

I REFUSE TO RIDE IN GAVINO'S HORSE-DRAWN WAGON. I'M STILL TRAUMAtized from Silverio's demon truck from hell and that parachute-less free fall off Mount Banahaw. The duwende is so up-front about his sleaziness. Who knows what he'll do to us once our backs are turned?

So, we end up walking all the way to the center of town. It's okay. It gives us a chance to see a little bit of the port island. The roads are paved with limestone bricks and compacted sand, branching out to smaller paths that lead to the island folks' bahay kubos.

Gavino has appointed himself our tour guide. "It's value-added service," he says. "My customers get the best deals."

"Really now." I highly doubt that. Every time we pass someone who recognizes him, they either scowl angrily or scuttle away in fear. I'm going to have to be extra cautious when I deal with this dwarf. He's giving me serious scammer vibes.

"Ate, let's just leave," Kitty whispers from behind me. I can feel the warmth of her breath on my neck. "I'm sure we'll find another way."

"I told you, I got this. I know what I'm doing, Meow. Just trust me."

Unfortunately, my confidence dampens when we reach our destination.

"Welcome to my shop!" says the duwende, theatrically presenting his sign. "The shop that gives hope to the hopeless like yourselves."

"Desperados Pawnshop for the Broke and Hopeless" is a business name that doesn't really inspire hopefulness, if you ask me. Gavino isn't even hiding the fact that he's taking advantage of his customers' desperation. Still, I keep my cool. I have a plan.

We follow Gavino and his goons into the pawnshop. Its interior looks too big for the actual space it occupies. The tiny hut with the offensive sign is actually a huge, three-story warehouse inside. Every storage rack is full of random stuff, so I'm guessing business must be booming for Desperados Pawnshop.

Gavino's kapre cronies climb the huge mango tree

that sits in the middle of the warehouse. They settle on opposite branches, both lighting up cigars while keeping a close eye on us. It's the perfect vantage point to make sure that none of Gavino's customers can even attempt to cheat.

Well, I'm not planning to cheat Gavino per se. But if my plan goes well, we'll come out of this place getting the better end of the deal.

"Hay, ang gulo," Gavino says, complaining about the mess. He puts a gold tumbler back in place on his table. "Magic has become unstable in the entire In-Between realm, all because of the mess these gods and spirits are making. It's bad for trade. The last transaction I had was with that nervous wakwak last week!"

Kitty, Bart, and I exchange a look. The duwende can't mean what I think he means.

"Do you have something here that can . . . I don't know . . . smuggle someone into Maharlika City?" I ask the question as casually as I can, pretending not to notice Kitty chewing her fingernails nervously and Bart turning into Tannie so he won't need to keep a straight face.

"Why would you need that? Your aswang friend's backpack is spacious enough to carry two human adults." The duwende raises an eyebrow. "I'd trade for it, but aswang bags are tricky things—they can only be inherited. If your aswang friend dies without appointing an inheritor, the bag's free for anyone to take. I'd be more than happy for you to come back to my shop and trade for it when he's dead."

Tannie growls. I grab him off the floor and restrain him before he goes into monster mode. "Dude. Chill."

"Anyway, I can't get you a magical bag. That well-dressed wakwak already got it," says Gavino. The hairs at the back of my neck stand up. This is the wakwak who took Mom, I'm sure of it!

"Is there a way for us to contact him? Maybe we can do a side trade." I try to keep my voice even and as uninterested as possible. But inside, I'm screaming. This is, like, *huge*. "You'd get a commission, of course."

"Side trade already? We haven't had a deal yet. But I like it." Gavino scratches his chin. "What's his name again? Ah. Warren. He has the prettiest voice—I tried to trade for it, but I guess he loves singing too much—and he hangs out at karaoke bars a lot. Said he needed to bring some wares in, so of course I delivered."

"You didn't ask him what he was bringing in with the bag?" my sister exclaims.

The duwende shrugs. "The less I know, the less trouble I get into."

Tannie leaps out of my arms and transforms into Bart before he reaches the ground. Thankfully, he walks over to Kitty and ushers her to a seat before my sister's outburst can ruin my plan.

"You're sure he's in the City?" I ask Gavino, throwing

Kitty a warning look. I want to strangle this dwarf too. He basically helped the wakwak kidnap Mom. But we need to keep our focus. "This Warren guy?"

"Yes, yes. Enough about that. I like side trades and all, but I want something that's worth my time. Let's talk business," the duwende says, sitting on a stool behind his desk that makes him look taller than he really is. "If I'm going to lend you my boat, I'll need collateral."

"Collateral?" Kitty's brows shoot up on her forehead.

"Of course it isn't free," I say. "Well, we don't have anything of value for you to hold on to until we return your boat." I put on my most dramatic, disappointed tone. "Let's go, Meow."

"Oh, you do." As expected, Gavino points to my agimat. "I want that."

"My agimat?" I touch my pendant. "I don't know . . ."

"Not your agimat. The magic inside it."

"Anagolay's map?" I ask innocently. Okay, I'll admit it. I knew he was going to ask for it. When Kitty, Bart, and I were at the docks looking for a boat, I overheard an aswang say that Anagolay's maps to the City are of high value in the magical world lately. Which makes sense, considering that superlong queue at Anagolay's dambana. Many creatures seem really eager to go to the City.

While it seems like holding on to this magic is probably best, there's one other thing that a boat seller mentioned. There are boats that can be operated manually or automatically. The automatic ones have a fancy built-in magical GPS thing preprogrammed to bring you to the City. Considering how huge Gavino's warehouse is (and how shrewd he is), I'm pretty sure he has one of those fancy automatic boats lying around.

"In exchange for Anagolay's map," he says, "I'll lend you my best boat. It's the latest model. The engine is so silent you'd forget it was there. It will bring you to the City as long as it has fuel." He rubs his hands together. I don't know how he stays in business—this greedy dwarf has no idea how to hide his intentions. "Using my boat, you technically don't need the map."

I knew it. He *does* have the automatic boat that we need. I make a huge act of pretending to consider his offer, then reach out to shake Gavino's hand as slowly and dramatically as I can.

"Oh, by the way," the dwarf says. "The boat doesn't have fuel yet."

"That's not fair. What's the point of having a boat if it won't run?" My heart sinks. Okay, I totally didn't consider that. This duwende is shrewder than I thought. I pull back my hand. At least he unknowingly gave us a lead to Mom's kidnapper. "We can't make a deal, then."

"Wait!" the dwarf exclaims. "I sense two more threads of magic inside your agimat. If you pawn them both, I can throw in enough fuel to bring you to the City."

"No. We can't do that—"

"Let's do it," Kitty and Bart say at the same time. Both have determined expressions.

"No way!" This is definitely not part of the plan. "Those are your wishes."

"Nothing is more important to me than you and Mom, Ate," Kitty says firmly. "Not even magic."

"I'm a dog," Bart says, morphing into a black shih tzu and back to human again. "We have the best sense of smell. I don't need a wish to help me find something I've lost."

"If you're sure . . ."

"We are!"

But as I'm about to take the dwarf's hand to seal the deal, I withdraw again. I remember what Anagolay said about the power of words.

Gavino sighs loudly. "What do you want now?"

"You said 'pawn.' That means you'll return our magic when we return your boat in one piece, right?"

"Yes. That is, if you *do* return." Gavino chuckles, his kapre minions giggling along with him. "I doubt you will."

"What do you mean?"

"Nothing, nothing." The duwende hops off his stool to dance with glee. He runs to my side, holding out his hand. "Deal?"

"Ate, I'm starting to think this isn't a good idea." Kitty doesn't miss a beat. Doubt must be written all over my face.

"I agree," Bart croaks.

"I know what I'm doing." Well, I really don't. But we've got no choice. "Okay, so you take our magic hostage—"

"Collateral," Gavino corrects me. "The term is 'collateral.' I run a legitimate business, and I don't want people to think I'm a bandit taking advantage of young people!"

The duwende certainly acts like a bandit, but I keep this thought to myself. I need to make him agree to our deal.

"Okay, then. Collateral," I say. "You take our magic as collateral while we make full use of your boat, fuel included. We get the magical map and Kitty's and Bart's seeking wishes back once we return your boat to you in *one piece*."

"That sounds right." Gavino rubs his chin thoughtfully, then grins. "I'll even throw in the freebie of helping you with your travel documents."

"*Clean* and *legal* travel documents." I shake my finger at him in warning. "No fishy deals, no paying off corrupt officials to acquire them."

"Of course!" Gavino brandishes a contract and shows it to me. From the looks of it, magic has recorded everything I've said, including the terms of the freebie, even those two words I emphasized. So far, so good.

"It's a deal, then," I say.

The dwarf and I shake hands.

Almost instantly I feel the magic of our contract. A

tendril of blue light appears, winding around our clasped hands. It glows for a bit, then dissipates.

"Oh!" My agimat grows warm. Three tendrils of blue light come out of it, snaking their way into the open flask in the duwende's other hand.

Gavino puts a cap on the bottle. "Perfect!"

The kapre in a red shirt comes down from the tree. He brings out three oars from the storage rack behind Gavino and gives one to each of us.

"Pleasure to do business with you young and naive people." Gavino grins. "Enjoy your voyage. I doubt you'll survive, considering how petty the sea god is. But try not to die. I am very fond of that boat!"

CHAPTER FOURTEEN

Never Argue with the Petty God Who Has a Hundreds-Year-Old Grudge

It's almost sunset when we finally set sail. Gavino grumbled about how much faster we could have gotten our documents if we'd just let him pay someone off. But I insisted he stick to our deal. For one, I don't feel comfortable condoning corruption. And for another, I'm pretty sure the illegal stuff would bite us in the end.

The duwende's boat looks like the typical paraw. It has a banana-shaped hull and two outriggers propelled forward by a big sail shaped like a crab claw and a smaller, triangular sail up front.

I expected an actual control panel for the GPS system the duwende bragged about. But like most things in the

In-Between, it operates with magic. We tell the boat our destination, it glows blue. Gavino assures us it's a sign that the paraw understands and is ready for the journey.

I don't trust this duwende, so I keep an eye on him from boarding to actual sailing.

Gavino and his goons wave to us from the beach until they're just tiny little dots in the distance. Once I'm sure the duwende won't send projectiles our way or pull some last-minute shenanigans, I swap places with Bart, so I'm facing forward and he and Kitty are facing the disappearing shoreline.

Kitty is the first to break the silence. "He doesn't think we'll survive. What do you think he meant, Ate?"

Bart heaves a long sigh. "Loan sharks only make deals that are favorable to them. I hope we did right on this deal, Lu."

"Yeah. Same." Looking back now, I was pretty obvious. Yet Gavino agreed so easily to my proposal. He's a shrewd duwende, and I'm sure he saw right through me. I feel like I missed something. "Well, at least we have a boat. I was afraid we'd be stuck in Sagitna Island forever and never find Mom. And he gave us that info about the wakwak without realizing that he was helping us with it for free."

"Exactly!" Kitty says brightly, trying to lighten the mood. "I feel like Moana. Our boats look similar, but ours has that extra sail in front."

"I guess so. You and Bart should sit facing front, like

me," I tell them. "We don't see a view this pretty every day."

I help Kitty and Bart resettle on their seats. It's hard to have privacy in such a cramped space. But with all of us facing forward and not looking at each other, I'm able to relax a bit.

It's almost nighttime. The sea turns violet as the sun gets lower and lower on the horizon. It's not like in my dream where the great ball of light falls from the heavens. The sky is gradually changing from blue and white to a pretty gradient of purple, pink, and orange.

There's another thing that keeps bothering me.

I turn in my seat to face Kitty and Bart. "I'm getting a vibe that this glitching we've seen is related to that thing I read in the newspaper. Something about corrupt souls leaving the Underworld and going on a possession spree. The gods are weak. The borders between Realms are blurring—that Underworld quake affected even our Middleworld. Gavino said that magic in the island is getting messed up. There's got to be a link between all these events."

Kitty tilts her head to the side. "Glitch?"

"The flickering thing the gods are doing."

Kitty bites her lower lip. "Hopefully, it's just a coincidence."

Bart and I exchange a look. Nothing in the magical world happens by coincidence. "Yeah. Hopefully."

"Manong Sol glitched worse than Anagolay, Tita Cecile, and Sitan," I say under my breath. "Actually, I don't remember even seeing Tita Cecile or Sitan glitch at all."

"It might have something to do with how and how often they use magic," Bart says, his brows furrowing. "Lord Sitan didn't need to use his power; he had John Lloyd Tiyanak open the portal for him, most likely with pre-stored Salamangka. And Lady Cecile intentionally doesn't use her magic around you."

Bart is staring at me with an intense look in his eyes. I know what he's thinking—he said it before Evil Tinker Bell showed up. He wants me to give Tita Cecile a chance, to trust her even though she could have single-handedly destroyed our family.

I turn away from his gaze. I'm not ready to forgive Tita Cecile yet.

"As creatures of the Underworld, our family is bound to serve Lady Cecile," Bart says, sighing. "But she's always been kind to us. We've also seen how much she cared for you. She loves you and Kitty a lot, you know. And your mom too. I have never seen her use her powers as the goddess of broken homes around you. Not even once."

"Yeah, well, she's in the Underworld now." I shrug, but I still can't meet his gaze. Bart has this way of looking at me that makes me feel he's seeing straight into my soul. I don't like it. "We'll probably never see her again."

"Let's focus on one thing at a time, Ate," Kitty says.

"It's no use worrying about things we don't really understand. Our main goal for now is to go to that city where Mom is, rescue her, and leave. Then we'll find a way to get Tita Cecile back somehow."

"Right. And we'll just worry about the end of the worlds later."

It's a joke, but, well . . . I'm just *partly* kidding. The thought of the three Realms falling into chaos continues to trouble me. I mean, I'm the one who's supposed to protect them, after all. How I'm supposed to do that, I have absolutely no idea.

Our boat continues to move forward. Its lights turn on automatically, but they didn't need to. The moon is up, and there are so many stars in the sky lighting our way.

The sound of the waves is starting to get to me, though. And the cold. And the irritating, noisy flapping of the outriggers on the water's surface, which sounds like someone slapping their belly. It was funny at first, but I've been hearing it over and over again for hours, and it's totally lost its funniness.

"Doesn't this thing have a music player or something?" I touch the sides of the boat. Nope. Nothing. With a sigh, I bring out my phone. It probably won't work but— "Oh great! My phone still works."

"It should." Bart nods. "We *are* in the middle of the universe. There's a bit of the Middleworld in here too."

"Awesome." I'm so glad I loaded up my phone with the entire *Love Yourself: Answer* compilation album last week.

I may be in the middle of nowhere floating in an endless sea between Realms, but at least I'll have BTS songs to listen to. With all the weird stuff going on around me, it's nice to have a little bit of normalcy.

"How about some music?" I swipe through my phone, opening the music player app. "I'm so tired of hearing nothing but the water."

Bart looks up. "Bad idea. We might disturb—"

But the first verse of "Anpanman" is already playing before he can finish his sentence. I crank up the volume, drowning out any of Bart's attempts to complain.

"Anpanman" is my most favorite BTS song *ever.* I read on a website somewhere that it was based on a cartoon character, a superhero named Anpanman.

I lean back on the boat bench, moving my head in time to the music. As always, the stars twinkle brighter when I look at them.

Anpanman doesn't have powers—he's literally just a man made of red bean bread. He gives pieces of himself to the needy, like a true symbol of self-sacrifice. He's super weak and I'm superstrong.

But am I a hero?

It was only yesterday when I found out about my superstrength, but I've already made so many bad decisions. Will I ever be a fraction of the hero Anpanman is?

"WHAT IS THAT NOISE?" an unfamiliar male voice bellows.

"Noise?" My eyes narrow.

"Turn it off, Lu!" A panicked Bart points at my phone. "Turn it off!"

The boat suddenly jerks. The docile waves have somehow awakened from their sleep and are now hitting our paraw. It's like they're playing volleyball, and our boat is the ball.

"Ate Lu!"

I hug my sister close. Bart huddles on my other side. I take his hand in mine. Awkward or not, I'm not about to lose my best friend if the boat breaks apart in the middle of an endless sea.

"We'll get through this." I say it, but I don't mean it. I *can't* mean it. I don't know if any of us will even emerge whole from this ordeal—the sea seems to be bent on shredding our boat and us apart.

Every time the waves hit our poor boat, we hear a hollow, gonglike sound. I can see creepy, humanlike forms appear on the waves, like the waves are alive.

A pair of glowing blue ropes pop out from the sides of the boat. Bart grabs them and hands them to me, saying, "The boat's on manual mode! Grab the ropes, Lu! Use your strength!"

I wind the glowing ropes around my hands, then stand up for more leverage. Kitty and Bart remain on the floor, holding me in place and helping me keep my balance.

A surge of energy suddenly radiates from the paraw, flowing from the ropes into me. The magical boat has shared its essence with me and is now dependent on me for survival. I squeeze the ropes tighter. "Hold on, boat. We got this!"

"YOU DARE MAKE NOISE IN MY DOMAIN?" A deep masculine voice reverberates from the sea. I can see the vibrations in the water. "I have warned you about trespassing on my domain, Sun Warrior!"

Amanikable, the god of the sea, rises out of the water. He doesn't have a shirt and is just wearing a bahag—a loincloth—while brandishing a golden trident. He has long hair and huge muscles. He's every bit as strong, as imposing, and as scary as the sea god depicted in my textbooks. My superstrength will be no match for him. I hold the ropes tighter.

"Okay! Okay! You don't like the music." I guess the sea god isn't a fan of BTS. "We've turned it off. Now please stop killing us!"

Amanikable blasts a jet of water into our boat. My muscles scream in pain and exhaustion.

I have to hold on. For Kitty. For Bart.

"You arrogant Salamangkero." The god blasts us with his current. "How dare you cross my seas so disrespectfully!"

"I'm sorry, I'm sorry, I'm sorry! I didn't know you disliked K-pop." I'm in so much pain, and my strength is getting stretched to its limits. "Just stop it already!"

The god responds by hitting our boat even harder.

"I'M ONLY ELEVEN!"

"The power inside you is old. You Salamangkeros only

care about yourselves. Maganda was my only love," says Amanikable. I'd feel sorry for him if he weren't trying to kill me and my sister and my best friend. "Your predecessor didn't even ask about her when she died in battle after he won his war. He just reveled in victory and didn't care about anything else!"

Our boat gets hit by another superstrong wave. I scream in pain.

"ATE!" Kitty cries. She almost loses her balance, but she holds on to my waist.

I gasp. I'm getting tired. But I can't let my sister and Bart die. This is a fight I can't win, so the most logical thing to do is to yield. "Please, Mister Sea God. I don't know what the old Salamangkero did to you, but whatever it is, I'm sorry on his behalf. I'm so, so super-duper sorry."

The god punches our boat with his wave. It's not as strong as his earlier blasts, but it still hurts. "No amount of apology can save you—"

"Then please spare my sister and my friend. Let them go, and you can do whatever you want to do with me!"

"Huh?" Amanikable's waves stop assaulting our boat. Without the flurry of the sea, I can see that the god is accompanied by two giant sea horses that are probably two feet tall.

"I'm the one you have a problem with," I say. "Well, not really me. I honestly have no idea what the other Salamangkero did. I mean, I'm not him." I gasp for breath. "But it's me you have a problem with, not Kitty or Bart. Please, sir, just let them through, and you can have me."

"Wait. Let me get this straight." Amanikable frowns. "You mean to tell me you're willing to lay your life down for these two? You're not going to trade their lives to save yours?"

Sacrifice others to save my own neck? "That's ridiculous. I'm not *that* selfish."

Amanikable exchanges a look with his two pet sea horses. He sighs, twirling his trident. "My waters will keep your boat together, so you can let go of the ropes now. I'm not going to kill you today."

I loosen my grip on the glowing ropes, but I don't release them. Still, I feel the paraw's energy leave me. Our connection's gone, and the boat is back to automatic mode. I guess the boat trusts the god more than I do.

Kitty releases my waist and looks at Amanikable. "Thank you for sparing us, sir."

Bart continues to hang on to me from the boat's floor, frozen in place.

"Who are you—oh." The odd look the god gives my sister makes me wary of him. But it might be best not to annoy him by asking about it. The important thing is to get to the City alive and to save Mom. The god looks at Bart and spits into the water. "You."

Kitty squeezes my hand. I grit my teeth but heed my sister's warning. I feel icky for not sticking up for my best friend. But really, what can I do? This temperamental god hates me. It's a terrible idea to set him off again. I throw Bart a look of apology and hope he gets it.

"I'm Lulu Sinagtala, and this is my sister, Kitty." I pat Bart's shoulder. "My best friend, Bart. He's an aswang."

"A dog." Amanikable wrinkles his nose. "You stink of were-dog."

"Hey—" I catch Bart's gaze. He shakes his head. I back down and keep my tone steady. "You don't like dogs?"

Maybe if I can keep Amanikable talking, we'll eventually reach the City.

"I hate dogs!" he says. The sea horses grunt in agreement.

Bart lowers his head. Still, he keeps quiet.

I give his hand a squeeze. "But dogs are loyal and cute—"

"They are loyal to a fault." The god pats his sea horses. "They hurt my babies."

"Oh, I know that story." Kitty frowns. "We read about it last quarter in class. Remember, Ate?"

"I don't— Oh yeah."

According to legend, Amanikable had two pet horses who lived on land. One day, while grazing on the beach, they came upon a group of men and their dogs. The dogs and these awful men hunted the two poor horses to exhaustion across the land, cornering them on the shore. As the hunters and their canine companions closed in, the horses prayed to Amanikable for help.

The god of the sea heard his pets' pleas. He sent a wave inland to carry the horses out to sea. Since they couldn't breathe underwater, Amanikable turned them into sea horses.

"I'm sorry your babies went through that. They're very beautiful." I mean it. Before continuing, I take a quick look at our boat. Thank the gods we're still moving. "You know, Mom once told us about helping treat a patient who got bitten by a dog. The patient was a dog trainer. He said that there aren't any bad dogs—only bad owners. Those dogs who chased your pets were trained by horrible people. The poor animals probably even lived in awful conditions, and that's why they ended up that way."

Thinking about Mom makes my heart ache.

"That's a good point." Amanikable stares at me. "I was wrong about you, Luningning Sinagtala. Apolaki was right—it was a good thing you grew up away from it all. You'd have been as insufferable as that little Salamangkero upstart, had you been raised with the knowledge of the power you hold. You may share his powers—and some of his traits, sad to say—but you *are* a different person."

Of course I am. There's no one like me. But I keep this thought to myself.

"Be careful around those eels, my loves," Amanikable tells his sea horses, pointing at the elongated fish breaking out from the water's surface. "Unlike these mortals here, you'll survive the electric current, but you'll get knocked out from the shock. Remember what happened to Apolaki? I warned him that these fish are not like the freshwater electric eels in the Middleworld, but he wouldn't listen. The powerful sun god slept all day!"

Ohh. I didn't know that! I grin. "Manong Sol got electrocuted?"

"Is that what you call him now? Why, yes. I took photos of him too. Look!" Amanikable shows me his phone. Sure enough, it's a photo of Manong Sol—and an unflattering one at that. The old man is sprawled on the seabed, his arms spread wide and his mouth slightly open.

I don't bother thinking about the science of a mobile phone working in the deep sea. Like everything else pertaining to the gods, it's magic.

Bart tries to stand up in the rocking boat so he can look at the photo too. I don't believe he's interested in seeing the sun god in an embarrassing position. He just doesn't want to offend Amanikable.

"Just stay where you are, dog," the god orders. Bart falls back to his seat immediately. "I'll come to your side."

I'm still miffed he almost demolished our paraw, but I'm glad the god is so much friendlier to Bart now. I mean, just look at that. He even made an effort to swim to Bart's side of the boat so my friend can see his phone.

Bart must sense my gaze. He looks in my direction as Amanikable talks into his ear. Bart doesn't say or do anything, but I can see in his eyes that he's grateful. I wink at him, and a ghost of a smile plays on his lips.

Bart's smile lifts my spirits—because he's my friend, duh.

Amanikable's sea horses approach the god to tell him something. He nods in confirmation.

"I am needed at my dambana. Climate change is really messing up a lot of my reefs. So many poor creatures are getting displaced." He shakes his head. "Your destination is near. My waters will see to it that your boat makes it to port."

"Thank you so much, sir," Kitty says.

Bart bows really low. "Lord Amanikable, you are merciful."

What a suck-up. I can't blame him, though. Before today, Amanikable would have gladly fed him to a shark.

Amanikable nods, undisturbed. "I have learned something from you today, Luningning Sinagtala, so I shall give you a gift in return."

"Okay . . ."

"Don't let the City's shine distract you from the truth," he continues. "The Maligno's knowledge of the Balabal allows him to hide in plain sight. Trust no one but your sister and your friends."

I'm not sure what to make of this "gift." It sounds more like a warning than a gift, to be honest. "Bart is my only friend," I say. Amanikable doesn't acknowledge or refute me. "Okay, then," I add. "Thanks?"

"You're welcome." He gives us a nod. Gosh, deities are so terrible at detecting sarcasm. "I take my leave. Good-bye!"

With a spin of his trident, Amanikable and his sea horses disappear in a swirl of bubbles.

Kitty heaves a huge sigh of relief. She touches her heart as her legs buckle into the hull.

"Phew," I say. "That was intense!"

Bart doesn't say anything. He's probably afraid Amanikable will hear. After all, we *are* still on water.

"Ate, look!"

My eyes follow Kitty's outstretched finger to where she's pointing. It's the City.

Maharlika City is an island city like Sagitna. Except that it's perfectly round and has a lot more buildings and fewer limestone cliffs. And it's encased in a bubble of bright blue light. Kind of like that force field thing around the country of Wakanda in *Black Panther.*

Amanikable's waters deposit us onshore. Kitty, Bart, and I hurry off the boat.

I drop to my knees as soon as my feet touch the sand. "Oh my gods, we're alive!"

Our boat—our exhausted, heroic boat—shudders and breaks apart into a million pieces.

CHAPTER FIFTEEN

Beware the Formidable Gills of Amanikable

Kitty, Bart, and I mourn and salute the remains of our paraw. I know it sounds so melodramatic. But the torture this boat went through under the apocalyptic temper tantrum of the sea god was just horrible. It totally deserves a proper send-off.

"That's that. So long, boat!" I take a tiny piece of it—about the size of my thumb—and tuck it inside my pocket.

Bart raises an eyebrow. "What is that?"

"My backup plan." I give him and Kitty a tiny piece each. "Try not to lose it. Because if I lose my piece, we'll use one of yours."

"Okay. I'll keep this safe," Kitty says, putting the piece

in her bag. I'm glad my sister trusts me enough to do it without question. She knows that whatever it is I'm doing is for our own good.

Bart does the same, hiding the little piece in his backpack. Like Kitty, he trusts me, though he obviously doubts some of my ideas. "Sana di tayo mapahamak dito," he says.

"When have my plans ever gotten us into trouble?" I demand.

Kitty and Bart answer me at the same time. "All the time!"

"Whatever," I say, rolling my eyes. "You two underestimate me so—"

Suddenly the water recedes from the shore we're standing on, exposing the seafloor. Fish caught in the sudden low tide are bouncing on the surface like popcorn. A crab widens its eyes, then hurriedly buries itself in the sand.

We turn to look behind us. Hearing the loud ocean roar, we don't need to guess who's the culprit.

"Now what?" I hiss. The sea god just won't leave us alone.

Amanikable pops up over the tsunami-like wave. I grab Kitty and Bart, shielding them from the impending crash.

The sea god releases the wave on my head. But instead of the full force of a huge tsunami, I feel only the impact of a pail of water.

"Don't flatter yourself," says the sea god's voice. "You

aren't *that* special for me to kill personally. See you around, Salamangkero. Don't litter on the beach!"

After drenching us from head to toe, the sea takes the remains of our paraw.

"I really, *really* do not like this god," I grumble, sputtering as I try to wipe water off my face with the front of my shirt. But it's no use—I'm totally drenched. We're *all* totally drenched, and my phone is ruined, no thanks to the petty god of the sea.

"Shh! He'll hear you," warns Bart. He holds out his hand. "Give me your phone. I'm not a whiz at combining tech with Salamangka like Kuya Silverio is, but I'll give it a shot. I can repair it, at least."

"Thanks," I say, pretending not to hear him praise the man who strapped me in the back of his vehicle with flimsy gift ribbons. After I got pushed off a mountain by Evil Tinker Bell and almost drowned at the hands of a grouchy sea god, Kuya Silverio's pickup truck from hell seems tame in comparison.

"Where to now, Ate?" Kitty frowns at the blue barrier of light. "I don't think we'll be able to get through that."

"Manong Sol said that someone's expecting us." I turn to face the sea. Since I'm no longer distracted by the island's light barrier and the terror of drowning, I notice tiny pinpricks of light above the dark water. I remember seeing something similar when Mom and Tita Cecile brought us to Baywalk. The boats of Manila Bay lit up the horizon like stars on the water. "Maybe we can ask the people on the boats for directions."

"We can't swim to those boats, if that's what you're suggesting," Bart says, dusting beach sand off his cargo pants. "The stuff you see from here is farther than you think. Distance over water is misleading."

"Well, I was actually thinking of *shouting* at them for directions. I don't want Amanikable—"

"HOY!"

We turn around and find a row of girls in front of the blue light barrier. They're all wearing tight jeans and blue shirts with the same print—a golden silhouette of a trident. They're like members of a club or a cult of some sort, except they're also carrying long golden spears. And they're pointing those sharp things right at our faces.

The tallest and eldest girl steps forward. "Who are you and how did you get special treatment from Lord Amanikable?"

"You call that 'special treatment'?" I retort. Unbelievable. "He nearly killed us!"

"Deities speak only to the Supremo's family and the Omen-Bringer," the leader says, putting her hands on her hips as the other girls egg her on. "We saw how the Handsome One ushered your paraw to shore personally. He never does that!"

Handsome One? Is this girl for real? Kitty, Bart, and I exchange incredulous looks.

"He only did that because he felt bad for trying to tear our boat apart!" I ball my fists. I'm about to will them to glow blue when—

"TRAINEES! What's going on here?" A girl about my age breaks the group's formation. Even in the dark, her beauty shines through. Her long black curly hair is like miniature corkscrews dancing on her shoulders. Her eyes stare fiercely at the leader, making her cower as she should. "It's after dark. Go back to the barracks before I report you to the commander. Speak of this incident to anyone, and I will personally cut off your tongues."

The blue shirts scurry away like cockroaches as the new girl and her companion approach us. Unlike the group they dispersed, the two girls are wearing tight-fitting tank tops and cargo pants. Their clothes have centipede and typhoon patterns similar to the fabric patterns that indigenous Filipino tribes use.

As they come even closer, I notice that they're carrying sheathed swords on their belts, and canisters of arrows hang on their backs.

More soldiers. And from the looks of it, *highly skilled* soldiers.

Bart and I exchange a look. I nod, and he brings out his weapon, a sibat—a spear. I ball my fists and they immediately glow blue.

"Whoa, whoa. Power down, Salamangkero. Tell your aswang friend not to skewer us," the shorter girl says from behind the curly-haired one. Up close, I see she's wearing a Muslim hijab. "We come in peace."

Bart lowers his spear, and I unclench my fists. Kitty takes my hand, and the blue light instantly disappears.

"We've been expecting you," the pretty soldier says.

Oh. So they're the ones Manong Sol told us about. "Which one of you is the Omen-Bringer?" I ask.

"Neither, but you'll meet him soon. He told us to look for a tiny noisy girl accompanied by a tall Chinese Filipina and a nerdy aswang with a backpack." The pretty soldier looks around. "We must hurry before anyone else sees you. I'm afraid I can't threaten everyone to silence."

I'm a bit miffed that the pretty girl called me a tiny noisy girl, but she's able to get us through the magical barrier using a device on her wrist. "I doubt the latest Apple Watch can do that!"

"Not the ones you have in the Middleworld, but our smartwatches here are all Salamangka-ready. You get the usual features like fitness tracking and GPS along with the magical stuff. We'll get you one later," the hijabi soldier says, leading us to a lighted cement path flanked by coconut trees. "Hay! Those Gills are always hanging around the shoreline, even at night. They'll risk a reprimand just to catch a glimpse of the sea god."

"Gills?" Kitty's eyes widen.

"Gills. That's what Lord Amanikable's die-hard fan group calls themselves. They are the most organized god fandom in the island. Not to mention the most *intense*. Unlike us Sunbeams. We're harmless."

"Sunbeams?" Bart raises an eyebrow.

"Lord Apolaki's fandom."

I shake my head. "Oh wow. You people are *so* weird."

"Don't be judgy, Ate," Kitty says, giving me her Mommiest Mom look. Gosh, I really miss Mom. "Remember, you're ARMY."

"Army? Lord Apolaki didn't say you're military." The curly-haired soldier finally joins the conversation. If she weren't so pretty, I would have forgotten she was there. Actually, I think it'll be very hard not to notice her because she smells very nice too—like sea salt and caramel. Not that I find that attractive or anything.

"A.R.M.Y., or Adorable Representative M.C. for Youth," I say proudly. "It's the bestest fan group for the bestest South Korean boy band in the world, BTS!"

"That's cool," says the soldier wearing a hijab. "You have fandoms in Middleworld too!"

"Tsk, tsk." The pretty soldier shakes her head. "Idolatry knows no bounds."

"Paloma doesn't like this form of god worship," the Muslim girl says wryly. "I'm Gamila, by the way."

We quickly introduce ourselves.

"Idolatry is an extreme form of worship," Paloma huffs. I was thinking of introducing her to BTS music. But I value my tongue and I don't want it cut off, so maybe it's best not to. “It makes you do things your sensible mind usually wouldn’t do.”

Wow. She’s gorgeous *and* smart.

“Do you have travel documents?” Gamila asks. We show her the papers Gavino gave us. “Looks all good. No one’s going to question you since you’re with us, but it’s best to have them ready.”

We follow the two girls to a heavily guarded tollbooth under an archway that reads “Welcome to Maharlika City.” As Gamila said, no one asks for our documentation. They simply let us through, saluting her and Paloma as we walk by.

At the end of the wooden path is a cobblestone road where a black SUV is waiting for us. Paloma enters first, beckoning us to follow her. The light inside the car is so bright it nearly hurts my eyes.

“Get comfy,” the hijabi soldier says as she closes the car door. “The Balay Dayao compound is still thirty minutes away. Maharlika City isn’t a big island, but we’ll have to go around some mountains to get there.” She taps her smartwatch, and a wall of blue light appears between us and the driver. “He can’t hear us. You can talk freely now. And of course, fasten your seat belts!”

The vehicle lurches forward, and off we go. Before long, we’re near the town proper. The light barrier protecting the island subtly illuminates our surroundings, giving us our first glimpse of Maharlika City.

"Wow." I stick my face to the window. "Look at that, Meow! It's like we're in a history book."

Unlike the islandy vibes in Sagitna Island, the buildings in Maharlika City look like they came straight from the nineteenth-century Philippines, totally preserved and as good as new. They're bahay na bato, an architectural style popular during the Spanish colonial era.

Bahay na bato translates directly to "house of stone," but the odd thing is, it's not entirely made of stone. It's more like an updated version of the nipa hut. The ground floor has adobe stone walls, while the upper floor (or floors) is made of wood. The roof is thatched with dry cogon grass and the walls have lattice windows embedded with capiz shells.

"It's more beautiful in daylight," Gamila says, pride evident in her voice. "Anyway, sorry about the less-than-happy welcome. The City's been on red alert since the Underworld incident. Corrupt souls have been attempting to get in."

"It's all right," says my sister. She gives the soldier a warm smile. "We understand."

Bart nods. "Yeah."

"We've had worse," I say dryly. It's true. Evil Tinker Bell's welcome push off Mount Banahaw makes the encounter with the Gills seem like a huge group hug. I'm curious about one thing, though. "How are they doing that? The corrupt souls, I mean."

"Human possession," Paloma answers, her expression grim. "It's the corrupt souls' favorite mode of transport."

Paloma talks like she's not human herself. I'd like to ask, but I don't want to offend her. She seems like the type of person who'll impale you with her sword if you do.

Gamila heaves a sigh. "It used to be so easy to detect the possessed, but they're somehow able to get past our security now."

"Wait. I just remembered something. . . ." I feel the hairs at the back of my head stand up. "Can corrupt souls possess people in the Middleworld, too?"

"Of course." Paloma throws Gamila a glance. "Why? Have you encountered them?"

"I did." I tell them about the incident at the inihaw stand yesterday, about how the customers and the vendor suddenly got all weird. "Then black smoke came out of them, and their eyes became normal. They didn't seem to know what had happened."

"I was with you that time, Ate." Kitty frowns. "I didn't see anything."

I shrug. "It happened while you were getting our drinks."

"They might have been using Balabal magic too," Bart says. "It seemed normal everywhere except for the inihaw stand."

Kitty doesn't seem to hear what Bart said, though, as she's too busy glaring at me. "Why didn't you say anything?"

"I thought I imagined it," I say. Why is Kitty being like this? It's not like I intentionally forgot to tell her about it. "We didn't know about the whole magical thing at that time."

"You still didn't tell me, even after we found out about that 'whole magical thing'!"

"Well, I was too busy getting attacked by a wakwak, getting strapped into the cargo hold of the pickup truck from hell with flimsy-looking ribbons, and being thrown off a mountain." I can't believe I need to say this. "Do you honestly think I'd remember those weird people reciting bad poetry?"

"We promised no more secrets." My sister pouts, crossing her arms over her chest. "You can't just leave me—"

Kitty doesn't finish what she's saying, as Bart suddenly transforms into Tannie and jumps onto her lap.

"Hey, hey," he says. "That's enough. You two are making our hosts uncomfortable with your arguing." The dog returns to his seat and morphs back to Bart. "Anyway! We saw some lights over the water when we got here. Are they from boats?"

Gamila seems relieved by the sudden change of subject. "Some of them. Floating houses, mostly. The ones farther out are Maharlikan settlements in the islets—small islands."

"Oh. Wow," I say, smirking. She might be glad for the interruption, but I'm not. "So you're not only soldiers, but colonizers too?"

"No, we are not," Paloma says. "They're also part of Maharlika City . . . they're just outside the border of the main island."

"It doesn't seem right that you're keeping them out on boats like that." Kitty purses her lips. I'm glad she's annoyed at something else instead of me.

"I'm not sure we're the ones who should tell you about this. . . ." Gamila pauses, looking at Paloma. She only continues when the other girl gives her an approving nod. "All right. Maharlika City is a haven in the In-Between that Lord Bathala, the god of gods, made for all beings in the three Realms. To make it a refuge, he enlisted the help of Lady Anagolay and Lord Apolaki to secure its borders. The only way you can find it is through Lady Anagolay's magic. Anyone who knows of the City can leave, of course, but you must have conscious knowledge of it in order to go back."

My pulse quickens. This story sounds very familiar, but I have to know more to be sure. "So if you take a baby out of the City—"

"The baby can't return," Gamila finishes for me. Her eyes are filled with pity, and I don't like it. "Families who have left with their toddlers can only stay outside the border. The parents wait to return until their children are around three or four years old, the age when they are able to have accurate memories and can remember the City using Lady Anagolay's magic. Some stay in Sagitna

Island, some even move to the Middleworld. But there are those who prefer to stay around the Maharlikan main island."

I feel my stomach turn. "So, if the baby was taken outside the City by someone who isn't their parent, or was kidnapped, they won't be able to return."

"Yes." Paloma stares straight at me with her piercing brown eyes. "Yes. They can't."

It doesn't take a genius to realize that she's referring to me.

That's exactly what happened to me. That's my life story.

Me. A child born with epilepsy and the gift of the Anito. A child taken from her family in a city she couldn't return to until now.

The Maligno did all this. It's because of him my life got all messed up.

I glance at my sister. I wait for her to say something about how unfair it is for a baby not to be able to return to their home just because they and their parents need to leave the island. Or something about Anagolay being mean to families who simply wanted to travel. Or just . . . I don't know . . . ask if I'm feeling okay. Because I'm totally not.

But she doesn't. Instead, Kitty's transfixed by the car window, watching the structures and greenery go by. I'm sure she also managed to put two and two together about

Maharlika City being the place of my birth, and what this knowledge might mean for our quest.

No, Kitty. I won't forget about Mom. I know why we're here. Let me prove it to you.

"Where's the nearest karaoke place?" I ask as loudly and as nonchalantly as possible. Like before, Kitty and Bart can't hide their discomfort. Good thing the soldiers don't notice.

Or not.

Paloma raises a perfectly arched brow. "That's very random."

"Oh, you like singing? Cool," says Gamila. "There's one—"

Paloma shakes her head. "She can karaoke all she wants tomorrow, but not now." Lucky for me, she doesn't question why I asked about karaoke. Maybe she thinks it's normal for me to just randomly blurt things out. "We're about to approach the gate to the Balay Dayao compound," she says. "The Omen-Bringer said that Lord Apolaki wanted us to go straight to the main house. It's important that you meet the royal family first."

Kitty, Bart, and I exchange a worried look.

"Why?" I ask.

"Because they're *your* family," Paloma says, a serious look on her face as she stares at me. "You're our long-lost dayang—our princess."

CHAPTER SIXTEEN

The Awkwardest Reunion of All Awkward Family Reunions

A PRINCESS. ME. SERIOUSLY? FIRST I GET TOLD I'M THE SALAMANGKERO, the one who's supposed to protect the Realms. Now they're saying my biological family is alive and I'm the princess of a city inside a literal bubble. Why can't I just be simple, not-worth-killing, plain old Lulu?

"Gosh." I massage my temples. Two days. I've learned all these things in just two days. "When Tita Cecile said my life is going to change, she wasn't kidding."

Kitty tears her gaze away from the window and looks at me. "Are you okay, Ate?"

"I'm fine." Finally! It's about time she asks me if I'm all right. I'm on the verge of an identity crisis and all she's been concerned about is how I forgot to mention a bunch of forgettable possessed people.

"You sure, Lu?" Bart asks, his forehead wrinkling. "Maybe if the car slows down, you can have a bit more time—"

"No, really. I'm good."

I feel Paloma's eyes on me, but she doesn't say anything.

"Don't get us wrong—Lord Apolaki knows best," Gamila says in a soft voice, her gaze lowered. "But gods sometimes forget that we're mortals, unlike them. It's not fair that you're forced to meet your biological family this way. Meeting them should have been your choice and at your own time."

"Yeah. I know." I ball my fists and will them to glow with blue light, showing them to Gamila. "But I have this . . . this power. So it's not like I have a choice, do I? If the gods believe meeting my biological family now will help me protect the Realms, then I should meet them."

That's a total lie. Honestly, I agree with Gamila. Meeting my biological family for the first time is such a huge moment in my life as an adoptee. I should have been able to decide when and *if* I wanted to meet them. At the very least, I should have been given time to prepare for it. Or even just have a moment to process the fact that they aren't dead . . . which I found out only minutes ago.

Still, I get it.

Thing is, I can put off princess-ing and the emotional processing for a little while. Mia Thermopolis in the old *Princess Diaries* movie found out she was a princess in high school. *I'm* only eleven—I'll catch up. But as the one chosen to protect the Realms from whatever danger lies ahead, I don't really have the luxury of time to wait for the perfect moment.

Besides, meeting my bio-fam is just a side trip. The main thing is still finding Mom. I never really looked for them anyway—all my life I thought they were dead. Come to think of it, Tita Cecile (or even Mom) never mentioned anything specific about my birth parents passing away. They've always said that my biological family "couldn't be with me in the same Realm." I'm the only one who assumed that Mom and Tita Cecile were referring to the Underworld.

But I have no idea what I'm going to do at this meeting. If I had more time, I would have read through blog posts and articles on the internet. Like, what to wear. What to say. How to show them that even if they don't know me, they won't be disappointed to learn that I'm their daughter—their *biological* daughter.

I take a deep breath and exhale slowly. I can do this. I've already survived so many dangerous situations. Meeting my bio-fam is just a tiny bump on the road to finding Mom, the loving mother who took care of me for all my eleven years.

Suddenly, I feel a warm weight on my hand. Kitty has covered it with hers. She avoids looking at me and keeps her eyes fixed on the scenery outside, but she gives my hand a squeeze.

Yep. I can definitely do this. And even if I can't, I'll have my sister with me.

"We're here," Paloma says, tapping her smartwatch. The wall of light separating us from the driver disappears. She orders the driver to park the SUV. Once we get out, Paloma leads us through a labyrinth of hallways until we finally stop in front of a huge room with double doors.

"Don't talk unless you're asked a question. Answer politely and honestly," Paloma whispers in my ear. Her breath smells like peppermint. "You'll be okay. The Omen-Bringer has this all planned."

Every time she talks about the Omen-Bringer, a picture of a scheming old man pops into my head. I hope this Omen-Bringer isn't a shrewd one like Gavino the duwende. My head is buzzing with so many thoughts, I worry that I won't be able to think on my feet.

We step inside the double doors, following Paloma and Gamila. It's like being in a throne room, but bahay na bato style. The ceiling is decorated with ornate arches, and in the center is a crystal chandelier. At the back of the room is a floor-to-ceiling painting of three stars and a stylized sun, with the figure of a squatting man in the middle of it—a figure very much like the one on my agimat.

Right in front of the painting is a cushioned chair. There sits a dark-skinned, middle-aged man with a goatee and wavy black hair. The waviness of his hair isn't like what you see on shampoo commercials. It's wavy like mine—unwieldy and wild.

Standing beside the seated man is a guy who looks like a college-aged version of him, but the younger guy sports a buzz cut like Bart's.

These two men are my father and my brother. I gulp. They look very strict and not easily impressed. And they're flanked by soldiers who look like they won't hesitate to stab us with their swords if we say the wrong thing.

"Good evening, Supremo and Komandante Yani," Paloma says, bowing as she stops two feet away from the throne. "The human girls and the aswang boy are guests of the Omen-Bringer, who requested that we present them to you first."

Yani. My brother's name is Yani.

The Supremo continues to drink coffee but looks at Paloma. Komandante Yani is the one who takes an interest in us. "Why must you trouble Papa with a bunch of kids? I'm disappointed in you, Paloma."

My heart drops straight to the Underworld. *My father and brother don't know who I am.*

I try to meet Paloma's gaze and Gamila's, but they keep their heads bowed.

The Supremo finally puts his cup down and studies us. "What are your names, children?"

Seriously? I can't believe he's asking who I am.

Bart and Kitty introduce themselves. Somehow I manage to croak out that my name is Lulu. The Supremo's expression remains the same—stern and barely interested.

I sigh. I shouldn't have made fun of Manong Sol when he revealed to us that he is Apolaki. It feels awful when you fall short of people's expectation of who they think you should be. I guess that's why the Supremo can't seem to recognize me.

Kitty takes my hand and gives me a reassuring squeeze. She lets go, but I hold on.

Gamila gestures for us to bow. My pendant slides out of my shirt as I do, but I ignore it, keeping my grip on Kitty's hand.

That's when the Supremo gasps. And, for the first time, loses his composure. "Where did you get that agimat?"

"Tita Cecile gave it to me." I let go of Kitty as I meet his eyes. I feel like my chest is about to explode from my heart pounding so fast and loud. "Tita Cecile . . . as in, Mansisilat, the goddess of broken homes."

"Broken ho— Luningning? Lulu, as in Luningning?" The Supremo continues to stare at me. He doesn't look scary or intimidating anymore. I'm seeing something else in his eyes—pain and longing. "Can it be?"

Komandante Yani unsheathes his sword. "You lie!"

Paloma and Gamila immediately close ranks around me as the other soldiers draw their swords. Bart brings out his sibat, pushing me and Kitty behind him.

I stare at my fists. If I will them to power up, I'll be stronger than everyone in this room put together. But I can't.

It's as if something inside me broke when Komandante Yani said the words "you" and "lie." I've often used them together myself. But now I know it's a totally different thing when you're the one on the receiving end. It hurts a lot.

I shake my head sadly. Even though I've always thought my bio-parents were dead, there were times I imagined they were alive and well and eager to see me. But this isn't how I pictured our first meeting.

"Stop!" a woman cries out. The door opens, and someone enters the room—a woman in a motorized wheelchair. The soldiers, Paloma, and Gamila bow low, referring to her as "Lakambini." I guess she's their queen, since they're using the old Tagalog styling for a lady ruler of the kingdom.

"Hello, brother." The lakambini bows to the Supremo and frowns at the grumpy commander. "My dear nephew, I'm disappointed in you. Haven't I taught you not to make hasty decisions? A good Maharlikan supremo meticulously investigates all the evidence first before deeming a suspect guilty."

The lakambini called the Supremo her brother and the commander her nephew. So I guess that means she's my aunt. I wonder where my biological mother is?

Komandante Yani, to his credit, has the decency to look ashamed. He bows to the queen and steps back.

I'm scared to hope, but I'm getting positive vibes from the lakambini. Real positive vibes, unlike the pretentious "Good Vibes Only" shirt of the wakwak that threatened to torture me. I feel like she'll be a kind aunt whether or not my father and brother accept me.

The queen beckons to the soldiers. "Open the door and let the Omen-Bringer enter."

My bio-mother is still a no-show, but at least we'll finally get to meet this mysterious Omen-Bringer everyone, including Manong Sol, keeps talking about. I hope he'll be ready for some singing, because I plan to visit each and every karaoke place until I find Mom's kidnapper. If my so-not-welcoming bio-brother doesn't throw us into prison, that is.

The door opens, and everyone in the room bows. But I don't see anyone.

Plak! Plak! Plak!

"Oh, that's so cute," Kitty says under her breath. "It's a duck, Ate!"

It *is* a duck.

Said duck lets out a raspy quack—it's a boy duck with brownish-black plumage. He has an iridescent green head and white markings above his eyes that make it look like he's wearing eyeliner. His chest and the tips of his wings are white as well.

The duck stops in front of me, preening his too-heavy stomach. He must feel my gaze because he immediately stops grooming. He looks at me and shakes his fluffy duck butt in excitement.

Then the duck opens his bill to speak. "Welcome, Lulu! It's been quite a while."

I'm still trying to wrap my head around the fact that this duck can talk, when said waterfowl struts up to me, spreads his wings, and bows.

The Supremo nods at the soldiers and his son. "Yani, Kawagad Paloma, Kagawad Gamila, stay. The rest of you, leave us."

Once the last of the soldiers are out of earshot, the Supremo's expression softens. My hope for a better (at least without screaming or bloodshed) bio-family reunion might actually come true. "Are you really my Luningning?"

"Well, I don't belong to anyone. But as far as I know, yes, that's my name." I frown. I'm starting to get annoyed. Is it so hard to believe I could be his daughter? Does he think I'm not good enough?

The duck—I mean, the Omen-Bringer—flaps his wings. "She can easily prove her identity, Supremo. It is but a simple test."

Kitty, Bart, and I exchange a startled look. "A test?"

"Yes. The dayang of Maharlika has powers no human possesses." The duck looks at me with a beady eye. It's unnerving, but somehow I know I can trust him. "If you really are who you say you are, show us your strength."

Hmm. This is one smart duck. A very smart talking duck.

It's annoying that I must do something to prove I'm related to these people by blood. Sure, I was hurt and a bit sad when they couldn't recognize me. But Kitty's presence is a great reminder that I already have a family.

And right now, I need to play along for Mom's sake. Even if they can't help me, at least they won't get in my way.

I look around the room for the heaviest object I can find. Something a single person couldn't carry, preferably one that needs special equipment to move.

"Aha," I say under my breath. On the side of the room is a decorative terra-cotta pot that's taller than a man. I go and pick it up with one hand, one hand that's glowing blue. See if you can top that, Komandante Yani!

The duck looks at me proudly. I like this duck.

"Well done!" he says, tilting his head in the direction of my doubting biological family. "Do you now believe she truly is your daughter, Supremo?"

The Supremo is staring at me too intently to answer. Then, finally, he speaks. "You look so much like her. My Lumen. Your mother."

Ooh-kay. Maybe I'll make an exception for my bio-dad. I'm still miffed he didn't immediately recognize me. To his credit, though, it didn't seem like he knew we were going to meet. Paloma and Gamila had been kind enough to warn me on the way here. Considering how my bio-brother reacted, I can see why they couldn't tell my bio-family about my arrival.

But I'll admit that seeing my father get all emotional like this softens my heart a bit. *Just a bit.*

The Supremo continues to stare at me. If he doesn't close his mouth, flies might enter it. Which is super gross. Unless they don't have flies here in Maharlika City?

"Forgive my brother." The lakambini brings out a hanky and daintily wipes away her tears.

I was right about her being a kind aunt. Like I said, I'm getting good vibes from her. I feel like I can ask her about this topic no one is bringing up. "Where's my biological mother? Isn't she coming out to meet me?"

"I'm afraid not, anak," the lakambini says with a sigh. "Your mother . . . she passed away when you were still a baby. I'm sorry."

I don't know how to feel about this news. Part of me is disappointed. I really wanted to meet the woman who gave birth to me. I mean, I did live in her womb for nine months. I don't remember any of my baby memories, but I'm pretty sure she cared about me.

But I'm also relieved she's no longer here. Because that means I don't have to feel guilty about possibly liking my birth mother when Mom herself is locked up in a magical dungeon somewhere.

"Don't worry about my sister. She has me," Kitty says. "And we already have a mom." She puts an arm around my shoulders. It reminds me of the time when we were fighting over the blue teddy bear Tita Cecile bought for us. Kitty hugged it and told me not to worry about the bear since she'd be there to take care of it. I feel like I'm that teddy bear right now.

"I'm glad." The lakambini smiles. Her smile doesn't light up the room like Mom's, but it's pleasant. "We would be honored to make your mother's acquaintance one day."

Kitty beams at my aunt, then formally introduces herself and Bart. I guess my sister can sense the good vibes from the lakambini too.

"Luningning." The Supremo looks at me again. I wish he'd stop looking like a sad puppy so I could get back to being annoyed at him . . . and so that I won't hope for a chance to see what it's like to have a dad. "My daughter. When the gods assured us you'd return, I couldn't believe it. But you're here. You're really here."

"Yeah, I am." What else can I say? He and my bio-mother seem to have cared about teeny tiny Lulu a lot. But the Maligno took me away from them, and I grew up thinking they were dead. I'm eleven now. I've changed a lot. I'm not the same little baby he knew back then.

"Oh, Luningning! My little shiny star!" The Supremo holds out his arms, as if expecting me to hug him.

Er . . . no.

I take a huge step back, pulling Kitty and Bart along. This is getting weird.

"It's too soon for that, Kuya." The lakambini gently pushes down the Supremo's arms. "Yani? Bayani!"

Komandante Yani blinks, tearing his gaze away from me. "Yes, Tita."

"Can you show your sister to her room? Kitty can stay with her. I'll have the kitchen send them food." She gives me an apologetic smile. "I promise to treat you to a proper Maharlikan meal tomorrow. But for now, you must rest."

"Wait, Tita."

We all turn to look at the commander, the duck included.

Komandante Yani clears his throat. "She might be our dayang physically, but how can we be certain that she isn't possessed?"

"No way. I'm not being inhabited by an evil spirit!" I say. I *can't* be possessed. Can I?

"We shall see." Komandante Yani studies me intently. His gaze is even more unnerving than the duck's beady-eyed look. At least the duck's cute. "What do you think, Omen-Bringer? Shouldn't we at least make sure she isn't carrying a maligno?"

I know he's referring to a maligno as in the Tagalog term for an evil spirit. But *the* Maligno has done so many awful things to me that the mere thought that I'm hosting him is super gross and very, very offensive.

The duck throws me a glance and sighs. "Show her the vault tomorrow. But tonight she must rest."

"It's not—"

"It's settled, then," the Supremo says. "The Omen-Bringer has spoken. You shall escort your sister to the vault in the morning." The Supremo has finally come to his senses, thank the gods. I don't think I can bear anymore staring. His expression softens. "I'm very happy to see you, my starlight. My heart tells me you do not carry a maligno. But I am also Maharlika City's supremo—their leader. I must abide by the rules I myself set to ensure the safety of our people."

"I'm pretty sure I'm not possessed." I glance at Kitty and Bart, who both shake their heads. "But whatever. I'll prove it to you."

"Get some rest. I will see you at breakfast tomorrow."

Komandante Yani is asked—or rather, ordered—by his father and aunt to escort us to our rooms. I can't say who's unhappier about the whole thing, him or me.

Thankfully, the duck is waddling along with us.

"You might not remember me, since you were still a baby when we first met, so . . ." he says, flapping his wings to fall into step with me. "My name is Haribon."

I introduce my sister and Bart. "Haribon?" I raise my eyebrows. "As in—"

"Haring ibon, yes."

"Haring ibon means 'bird king,'" I point out, wriggling my raised eyebrows.

The duck shakes his feathers. I can see he's getting irritated. "Yes. I'm a tigmamanukan, an augural bird. I make prophecies and auguries. I deserve my name!"

"Yes, definitely. It suits you," Kitty tells the duck, giving me a warning look.

"I know it does!"

I stifle a giggle. "Okay . . . but did you name yourself?"

"It's always been my name."

Before you tell me off like Kitty for teasing the duck, you first need to know that "Haribon" is also what the great Philippine eagle is called locally. Like, you know, the Philippines' national bird that's about three feet tall. It's so big, in fact, it eats monkeys. I *think* it eats monkeys. After all, it wouldn't be called "monkey-eating eagle" if it couldn't. "Aren't you a bit too small for your name?"

Haribon the duck just gives me the side-eye and wags his tail in annoyance. I hope he doesn't poop. This family reunion is awkward enough as it is.

"Ate, I think you've offended him."

I'm not paying attention to my sister, though. I can't help but notice how Paloma's smile makes her prettier than ever.

Bart clears his throat. "Hey, Lu. The door. Watch where you're—"

"I know, I know. I see it." I tear my gaze away from Paloma and follow Komandante Yani through the revolving door.

We enter a room that looks like a lobby, with two glass doors that open to a grassland. We step out, and I see it's not an empty field but a huge manicured lawn with brick pathways. This "palace" is not really a palace, but more like a compound.

We stop in front of the biggest house in the square.

"Kagawad Paloma and Kagawad Gamila," Komandante Yani says in an authoritative voice.

Paloma and Gamila straighten up and salute him. "Sir, yes, sir!"

I snicker loud enough for both of them to hear. Paloma acts like she didn't hear anything, while Gamila's face twitches. Still, the hijabi soldier keeps her cool. I've got to admire these girls. I would have dissolved into giggles if I'd been in their place.

"Show the aswang to one of our guest rooms on your way to your quarters. He is our guest, after all," says Komandante Yani. "I'll bring Luningning to hers. There's some . . . explanation needed when she sees it."

Who cares about my room? I'm sure it'll look old-fashioned, like everything else in this city. The green monster inside of me is more concerned about the fact that Bart and Paloma are going off together. They're with Gamila and surrounded by guards, sure, but I don't like the idea of the two being someplace where I'm not included. Bart's *my* best friend, after all.

"I stay with Lu," Bart says firmly, frowning. "I have orders to protect her."

"You do?" Komandante Yani raises an eyebrow. "From who?"

Even though his show of loyalty makes the little green monster in my tummy dance with glee, I still shake my head at Bart. This man already doubts me. If Bart says he's under orders from the goddess of *broken homes*, Komandante Yani will doubt me even more.

"If you do not have a valid reason, you stay in the male side of the barracks," the commander says sternly. "We have enough problems to deal with. I do not want to add rumors of the dayang having boys in her room."

"Geez, I'm only eleven." I roll my eyes.

"The Supremo will not allow it, I assure you."

"Fine. Whatever." I purse my lips. You'd expect them to be open-minded by now, but nope. "Just go with them, Bart."

"Don't worry, she'll be safe," Haribon assures my friend. Worry leaves Bart's face as he murmurs his thanks.

He's okay with it, but I'm not. I hope Bart remembers that *I'm* his best friend.

I glare at Paloma's and Bart's retreating backs. But left with no choice, I take Kitty's hand and follow Komandante Yani and the duck to the other side of the garden.

CHAPTER SEVENTEEN

Duck Butts Are the Grossest Hiding Places

The first thing I notice about "my" room is that it's huge. It's probably even bigger than our dining room and living room put together. "Wow. Is this really mine?"

There's a four-poster bed in the middle of the room, flanked by ornate bedside tables. The wide lattice windows with embedded capiz shells slide open to reveal the yard outside. A lamp hangs from the middle of a glass ceiling, while colorful floral patterns decorate the walls. Across from the bed is a dark wooden chest of drawers and shelves, and beside it, a door that leads to a walk-in closet and a bathroom. Near the balcony is a large, elaborately carved desk and a coffee table for two.

It's like staying at a five-star heritage hotel that would cost Mom's salary for an entire year just for a single night.

Komandante Yani nods. "I suppose you like it?"

"Of course!" I mean, duh, what else can I say? It's not like I can say no, I hate it. Feeling conscious of Kitty's gaze, I look up at the skylight. The moon is full, and the night sky is dotted with bright, twinkling stars. Mom always said that if the stars are out, it means there won't be rain in the evening.

Kitty walks over to the desk, lifting a framed photograph. "Look at this, Ate! Are these all yours?"

Curious, I join my sister.

On the desk is a laptop, a bunch of fifth-grade textbooks, and an opened journal. Nothing's written on it, but it's positioned on the desk in such a way that it looks like someone is working on their homework or something. There's even a half-filled bottle of epilepsy medicine beside the pen jar. It's like the room is in use and not abandoned.

Also, how and where did they get *my* pictures? They have photos of me during my every milestone—moving up day, seventh birthday, first Holy Communion. This is super weird. I turn to Komandante Yani. "Were you stalking me?"

He makes a fuss of fixing his collar before clearing his throat. "This is why I needed to show you your room personally. We've always believed you'd be back home with us. So Papa and Tita Ligaya thought it was best to decorate your room as if you'd lived here all this time."

"Oh. Okay. That's nice." I avoid Kitty's gaze. For some reason, it's making me uncomfortable. "Tita Ligaya?"

"The lakambini."

"I see. So where did you get my pictures? Wait. Let me guess." I roll my eyes. "The gods?"

"Yes."

"Lord Apolaki kept us updated about you," Haribon says, staring at me with his beady duck eyes. "It's like we were watching you grow up, but not really, you know?"

"Not exactly, but okay." It's a really messed up way of watching someone grow up. "If you wanted it so badly, why didn't any of you come to see me?"

"It was for your safety and that of the people around you," Komandante Yani says coldly. "Surely the gods have told you about the being who took you away from us?"

"Of course."

"Then you know that visiting you would have been like sending a flare into the sky and giving your location to every corrupt soul who supports the Maligno. Your lack of knowledge of our world and our family protected you." Komandante Yani clicks his tongue. "A true Salamangkero trained by the god of warriors should understand that."

"I do," I say to the commander, glaring at him. He could have just said it's for our safety and left it at that. He didn't need to remind me how totally unqualified I am to be the protector of Realms. I already know that.

Before I can say anything else, there's a knock on the door. It's the food being delivered.

"Come in." Komandante Yani waves the servers through. "Just let the guards outside your room know if you want more," he tells me. "They will get you anything you want. Kitty, you can take the room adjacent to Lulu's—"

I put an arm around my sister, giving her shoulders a squeeze. "We stay together. The bed is super huge. We'll be comfortable."

Actually, the bed could even fit ten more of me.

"Where does Haribon sleep?" Kitty asks.

"Here!" Haribon waddles to the bedside table. He pokes a button with his beak and the cabinet door opens, revealing a dog bed. "Don't worry, unlike regular ducks, I can hold my poop until I reach my litter box on the balcony."

I can't help but smile. The duck must be super loyal to me for him to sleep in this creepy Lulu room alone. I hope I'm worth it. I wouldn't want to disappoint the poor guy. "That still sounds gross, but okay."

Komandante Yani chuckles, which I find weird. He's been so grouchy since we've met, it's odd seeing him laugh like that. "I suppose you're good now. I'll take my leave. Tomorrow I'll give you and Kitty and your aswang friend a tour of the City."

"Okay."

"If you're not possessed by a maligno, that is," he adds.

"I am not— Never mind." I'll prove him wrong tomorrow, and he'll regret being so rude to me.

The Supremo's son bids us good night and leaves the room. Good riddance.

I watch him close the door, then exchange a look with Kitty. It's so hard to ignore the yummy smells of the food. My sister is warily eyeing the spread, but the loud grumble of her stomach betrays her.

"It's not poisoned. You can eat it," Haribon says. He stares me straight in the eye without blinking. Do ducks even blink? "With so many eyes on you, you're going to get caught."

"How did you . . . What do you mean?"

"Lord Apolaki visits me often. More often than your family—I mean, biological family—are aware of," the duck reveals. "He told me about your quest to save your mother."

Kitty's tummy grumbles again. "Are you sure it's okay to eat this? I'm really hungry."

"Yes. Throw me a cucumber slice, and I'll prove it to you."

Kitty does, and Haribon gobbles it up. "Yum. Can I have another one?"

"You can have them all." Kitty picks the cucumbers off the plates and gives them to the duck. "Ate and I don't really like cucumbers."

"More for me, then!" The duck swallows a cucumber slice whole.

"Yes. They're all yours." Kitty giggles. She spoons rice and binagoongan into her plate and pushes the serving platters closer to me. "Have some, Ate. You still need to take your epilepsy medicine."

Haribon stops pecking at his food. "Yani is epileptic too."

I pretend not to hear him, spearing a piece of roasted eggplant. I have better things to think about than my colder-than-a-freezer bio-brother. "Okay, so you mean to tell me . . . Manong—I mean, Apolaki—already told you our mom's here, but you didn't start looking for her yourself?"

"Couldn't. For one thing, I'm a duck. For another, your mother is in a magical prison shrouded in Balabal magic." Haribon exhales loudly. "The goddess of lost things herself is too weak to find it—what can a mere tigmamanukan like me do?"

"That's a good point." I'm seriously impressed. "Never mind that you're the only duck I've met who can talk . . . you're actually *way* smarter than the average duck. Like, a thousand times smarter."

Haribon swallows the last cucumber slice whole before answering. Amazing. He demolished the cucumbers in seconds. "Of course I am. I'm an *augural bird.* I can tell people if they're going to have good or bad luck. I've always been the smartest of my kind."

"There are more of you?" I imagine a cute island full of cute ducks eating cucumbers while making auguries. "Cool."

"Why aren't you with your kind?" Kitty asks. "Don't get me wrong, I like having you around. But you should be able to live with your fellow augural birds."

"That's not relevant at the moment." The duck shakes his head, showering us with cucumber water. "What you should know is that ever since Lulu was taken, I've been on alert. It took a while and many lives before the Maligno could be imprisoned back in Kasanaan. Still, he had many supporters. Some bravely came forward, loyal to their master. But others . . . they stayed hidden among us, perhaps biding their time. That is why the gods ordered me to stay here and wait."

Imagine having eleven years of anxiety and looking over your shoulder. Sounds very tiring. Still—"How can we be sure we can trust you?"

"Ate—"

"Don't worry," Haribon says. "Lord Apolaki warned me that this would happen. Regardless of what Yani said, the sun god taught you well. With everything going on, you really shouldn't trust just anybody. Wait. Let me get it. . . ."

I expect him to get something from inside his bedside table "room," but he doesn't. Haribon quacks as he waddles in a circle, looking mighty uncomfortable. He then wags his tail and lets it rip.

"Eww!" Kitty and I exclaim.

"Do you mind?" I pinch my nose. "We're eating!"

"Sorry. This is the only way I can hide it." Haribon uses his bill to roll a glowing blue marble to me. "Put that in a bowl of water."

I make a face. "No way! It has your poop on it."

"That's just water. And probably some bits of the kang-kong I ate an hour ago."

"*Still.* It's gross."

Kitty uses a napkin to pick up the marble. She takes an empty bowl from the dinner cart and places it on the dining table. I move my plate away from it. "How much water?" she asks the duck.

"Just deep enough to submerge the marble." Haribon tilts his head to one side so his beady eye stares straight at Kitty. "I like you. You're nice."

I beam at my sister. "She's the best."

Kitty drops the marble into the bowl. It glows blue, and soon we see a projection of Manong Sol on the surface, kind of like the vision of Mom in Anagolay's water-filled plastic basin.

"Are we live?" The image of Manong Sol taps the surface of the water, causing it to ripple. We get a close-up view of his wrinkly finger, kind of like what cats do when they want to embarrass you during a video call. "Hello, children."

Haribon bows, his wings spread wide. "My lord."

"Manong Sol!" Kitty exclaims. "We're so glad you're okay."

"What happened?" I ask. He better have a good explanation for going glitchy and all. "Were you hurt?"

"Goodness, no. A great god such as I cannot be destroyed simply with that." Manong Sol yawns and stretches. I try hard not to roll my eyes at this. "I am still trying to recover my strength. I . . . er . . . got very tired after using the portal."

"Gosh." This doesn't sound good. Gods influence everything, which means they affect *everything*. "Is that why you can't be here in person right now?"

"It's very dangerous for me to be around mortals at the moment. You almost saw my divine form, which would have been devastating. Aman Sinaya's technology is a great help," he says. Oh. Aman Sinaya again. No wonder Bart idolizes Aman Sinaya's assistant so much. Aman Sinaya is like the Tony Stark of the deities. "But do not worry about us gods. We are all just very tired. Everything will turn out fine in the end."

"Okay." Thing is, that's not the case with the myths I've learned in school. But whatever. "Guess what, Manong Sol? We found out stuff about the wakwak who took Mom."

Kitty and I tell the sun god about how I wheedled the info out of Gavino.

"Very good. That duwende is tricky, but my student is shrewder than a seasoned scammer!" Manong Sol gives us a grin, revealing that he has a few teeth missing. "The wakwak doesn't know you're aware of his habits. He will likely be at his usual haunts, which is, in this case, a karaoke place. He will want to appear as if nothing has changed, so as not to arouse suspicion."

"You seem to know a lot about deceiving people," I remark, totally miffed at being likened to a scammer. I mean, *he* was the one who trained *me*. If I'm shrewd and scammy, he's shrewder and scammier.

"Of course." Manong Sol puffs out his chest proudly. "Spying is part of warfare, and I'm the god of warriors."

"Manong Sol, there's something else." Kitty leans closer to the bowl. "Komandante Yani wants to check whether Ate is hosting an evil spirit. Haribon said something about a vault—"

"The vault is perfectly safe, do not worry about it, Katrina." Manong Sol frowns at Haribon. "Did you not ask Luningning to demonstrate her strength? That should have been enough proof of her identity."

"I did, my lord." The duck bows. "But the Supremo's son still insisted on ensuring that Lulu isn't possessed."

Manong Sol's frown deepens. "Bayani is a cautious young man. But for him to be suspicious of his own sister hosting a maligno . . . there must be a great number of corrupt souls trying to enter—or that have already entered—the City."

"What do we do now, Manong Sol?"

"I . . ." The old man suddenly becomes very busy with something beside him. "I . . . I do not know, my child. My fellow gods and I have expended our magic putting everything back to the way it was before the earthquake. Then we had to empower my mother's spell that made the Middleworld forget the earthquake. We are all weakened. It's difficult to see situations the way I usually do."

"Oh." Well, that's just great. The Maligno that's after me apparently has the genius of all the smarty-pants in the Marvel Cinematic Universe put together. Shuri, Tony Stark, Bruce Banner, Hank Pym, and Rocket Raccoon in one brain. The Maligno not only escaped the Underworld, he also managed to incapacitate the gods so they can't find him while he's doing all these evil deeds. Evil deeds that, unfortunately, have me as the main target.

"I will try my best to gain back my strength as soon as possible so I can help you." Manong Sol continues to avoid eye contact. "It pains me to say this, but I must leave it up to you to find Jenalyn. Your aswang friend will help you. Paloma and Gamila—those two are good warriors to have on your side. Trust the duck. He would rather become roast duck than betray you." The god laughs at his own joke.

"That's not a nice thing to say," Kitty tells Manong Sol, patting Haribon's head sympathetically.

"I'm okay," Haribon says. "Lord Apolaki always had an interesting sense of humor."

“Your family—your *biological* family—knows about your powers. However, it would be prudent not to use them except to protect yourself or others. The politics in this island . . . ay, I do not want to bore you with that!”

“Keep a low profile,” I say, giving him a thumbs-up. “Okay. Got it.”

Manong Sol’s expression softens as he meets my gaze. “I have trained you well, but be careful, Luningning. The Maligno that took your mother—”

The water in the bowl momentarily turns white. He’s glitching again. Thankfully, Manong Sol isn’t here in person. I don’t want to be burned again.

“Hay naku!” Manong Sol says. “This glitching is impossible. Just be careful. Watch your back. And do your best not to die. I believe in both of you, Luningning and Katrina. You will save your mother.” He waves his hand in front of him, and the image on the water disappears.

I push my plate away. “I think I’ve lost my appetite.”

Kitty does the same. “Me too.” She hands me my epilepsy medicine, which I down with a glass of water. “Manong Sol said it. We’ll save Mom.”

I cross my arms over my chest. “He really didn’t give us anything useful. He just gave us some vague advice.”

“You know, it takes a lot more courage to admit you need help than to pretend you can do everything on your own.” Haribon sighs audibly (I didn’t know ducks could sigh). “Lord Apolaki is one of the Realms’ most powerful deities. It must have been very difficult for him to accept that he cannot assist you on your quest and that you, the human child he's been protecting, are the only one who can help him."

I fall silent. That makes a lot of sense. But Manong Sol, the sun god, patron of warriors, asking *me* for help? Granted, I do have the gift of the Anito . . . but I'm still a kid.

"Okay! I'll wash up now," Kitty says, pushing away the dining cart and heading for the bathroom with her bag.

Haribon stretches his legs. "Phew. What an exciting day. I'm exhausted! Good night, children."

As I watch the duck waddle to his bed, I have so many thoughts whirling around in my mind. I look up at the skylight, where I see a star and an even brighter star shining together. Kind of like a mommy star and a baby star.

I long to see my own mother. *Mom, just hang in there for a bit. We'll find you, I promise.*

"G'night," I whisper into the darkness.

CHAPTER EIGHTEEN

Start the Day with a Blood Test, Bloodlines, and a Bloody Sword

We wake up to a loud pounding on our door.

"Don't Maharlikans sleep?" I grumble as I swing the door open.

"We do, but we've yet to know if you truly *are* one of us." It's Komandante Yani, my grumpy older brother. Paloma and Gamila are with him, plus a bunch of equally grumpy soldiers, all wide-awake. And Bart, who's as sleepy as I am, but is now dressed up in Maharlikan fashion—black shirt and cargo pants with the native Tagalog centipede pattern. "Please get ready and come with me," the commander says.

"I'm sorry," Gamila mouths from behind him.

"What's going on here?" Haribon pokes his feathery head between my ankles. "Let your sister sleep in. She's been on a long journey."

"My apologies, Omen-Bringer." Komandante Yani bows. "But time is of the essence. The possessed—"

The duck sighs noisily. "I know, I know."

"What is it?" I ask as I follow the duck inside, closing the door behind me. To my relief, my brother and his soldiers don't protest.

"Wake your sister up," Haribon says. "Let us just get this over with." He flaps his wings in annoyance. "If he wants a blood test, then he'll get it. Besides, you need to learn about your biological family's history, one way or another."

"A blood test?!" My jaw drops. "I thought I was just going to see a vault!"

"It won't hurt. I promise."

That's what nurses say about stuff they claim won't hurt but actually does. I should know—my own mother is a health-care practitioner.

But, whatever. As the duck says . . . the sooner we get this over and done with, the better.

Komandante Yani leads us to the main house's basement and through a maze of tunnels, kind of like a labyrinth. It's a bit similar to that portal travel we did with Manong Sol. Except here, it's all gross walls everywhere.

I know Haribon said the "blood test" won't hurt. But the icky, sewagey walls aren't inspiring any confidence. "I have a bad feeling this test is going to be super unhygienic," I say.

Gamila snorts. A touch of a smile reaches Paloma's lips even though she tries not to react. Yani remains cold. What a grouch.

Thank the gods I grew up with Kitty and Bart instead of this sourpuss. My childhood would have been very, very boring with a sibling like him.

"It's not that kind of test," Haribon repeats for the nth time.

"If you're really who you say you are, you shouldn't have a problem with this," the commander says, finally stopping in front of a huge golden door. I wonder if it's made of the real precious metal. "This is the Maharlikan Vault. Only direct descendants of our first Supremo can open it. You need to have his blood running through your veins to do so. Interestingly, it doesn't recognize only his blood, but also the souls of his direct descendants. If you're carrying a maligno, the door will expel the evil spirit inside you."

"Lulu has been chosen by the Anito," Haribon says firmly. "You are fully aware that a maligno wouldn't survive in the same body as her soul. But by all means, let's have your test."

Well, if you can't trust the duck, it's hard to trust

anyone else. I'm pretty sure there's no creepy soul with me in this Lulu bodysuit. But having an antagonistic older brother who also happens to be the commander of the Maharlikan army is going to be a problem when I search for Mom. So let's just play along.

I take a deep breath and reach for the door handle. I don't feel any different, but the handle starts to glow with blue light. The light then spreads to the door, tracing the frame. It glows really bright, then dissipates.

The lock clicks open.

Gamila and Kitty cheer. Bart and Paloma look relieved.

Haribon flaps his wings proudly. "I told you so," he says.

I roll my eyes. "That's it? That's the test?"

"Yes, that's it." Komandante Yani opens the door for me and smiles. "You coming, bunso?"

Being called bunso, or "younger sibling," by someone who's accused me of carrying a maligno doesn't sit well with me. It feels awkward and not genuine.

I mean, look at Haribon. He just accepted me for who I am. It's not because he's a magical creature, but because he has faith. He believes in Manong Sol. He believes, without question, that I am the Salamangkero . . . even though I don't feel like I deserve this powerful gift.

Anyway, I step inside the vault. There is so much cool, totally random stuff in here. There's a sibat that looks like Bart's weapon, except this one is made entirely of stone. There's a kampilan on a sword stand on the edge of a table. Whoever put it there has absolutely no regard for safety. If someone trips near it, they might find themselves on an unplanned trip to the Underworld.

Next to that dangerously displayed sword is another odd thing. This one is enclosed in a display case. "What's this? It looks like a piece of coconut husk."

"It is a piece of coconut husk." Komandante Yani comes up behind me. "You can touch it if you want, but be careful with the glass case."

I lift the glass case slowly and place it over the kampilan. "There. No one's going to get accidentally stabbed anymore."

"Good thinking."

I pick up the coconut husk and study it. Komandante Yani's right—it's nothing special. I hand it to him. "Well, that was disappointing. I guess it has sentimental value for someone."

"You might be right." He gives me a big smile.

"Ate, look!" Kitty exclaims, pointing at a relic in a display case. "It's like the pendant you have."

"The one you have is a typical agimat, carved from the Sacred Batumbakal and blessed by the gods," the commander explains. Well, he's wrong—my pendant isn't just "typical," it's a gift from a goddess. But I don't want to get into which goddess gave me this agimat, so I just let him continue. Komandante Yani takes the other agimat from the box. "This one, on the other hand . . . this belonged to a powerful sorcerer who obtained it the traditional way."

"Traditional way?" I raise an eyebrow.

"There are two traditional methods. The first one is waiting for it to drop at midnight, under a moonless sky, from the heart of a banana flower that's pointing upward," Gamila says. Phew. That's a mouthful; I gasped for air just listening to Gamila say it. "The other method is . . . disturbing."

Gamila exchanges a troubled look with Paloma before continuing. "The stone is formed from the offering of fresh blood to an evil spirit bound to a place of despair and suffering."

"The blood of what?" I shudder at the thought of someone taking a life just to acquire a magical rock. "You don't mean it's from a human. . . ."

Kitty and Bart look like they're going to be sick.

"It requires human blood. The wicked act of murder is part of the magic that forms the agimat," Paloma answers, her expression grim. "This disgusting method is likely how that stone was obtained. Its first and last owner was a sorcerer who betrayed not only his people, but all humankind."

I notice that Komandante Yani isn't saying anything. He simply continues to study the agimat in his hand. It's weird. If I were the one holding that agimat and I heard what Gamila and Paloma said, I would have dropped it like a hot potato. Instead, my brother is studying it like it's mildly interesting.

Well, I have my curious moments too. I guess he just has weird tastes.

"This was also the agimat that defeated Bernardo Carpio," says Komandante Yani. "Bernardo Carpio, the great hero favored by the gods, falling into the hands of a humble sorcerer."

Haribon lets out an angry, raspy quack. "'Humble' isn't a word I would use to describe that vile man. 'Greedy' would be more appropriate."

"You knew the sorcerer?" I ask, my eyes growing big. "And Bernardo Carpio?"

"The sorcerer was called Restituto." The duck quacks and shakes his feathers like he's trying to get rid of filth. "Your ancestors could have been free from the iron hold of the Spanish colonizers—we were making a huge dent with the freedom campaign. But that sorcerer colluded with the Spaniards to magically entrap Bernardo between two boulders, where the hero eventually met his doom. I found out later that the sorcerer was betrayed by his Spanish contacts—surprise, surprise—and had to go into hiding."

I notice Haribon didn't say whether or not he knew Bernardo Carpio. But I guess he did. After all, Haribon seems to have inside knowledge of what went down during that time period.

Anyway, now it makes total sense why a particular tale of Bernardo Carpio was considered accurate by some historians. Because everything, even the magical part, really happened. "How did he die? Restituto, I mean?"

"I don't know. I was . . . already somewhere else at that time. I never heard what became of him," Haribon says in a hard voice. This is amazing. If Haribon witnessed all this, he must be a very, very old duck. "But I am certain that being a traitor to his people earned him a front-row seat in the torture chambers of Kasanaan in the Underworld."

Komandante Yani gives Haribon a small smile. "Listen to the Omen-Bringer. He knows everything."

"Oh wow. Have you seen this, Lu?" Bart says, pointing at the wall behind the sword.

It's a framed set of pants and a white camisa de chino—a collarless shirt with a three-button opening on the chest and sleeves without cuffs. I've seen these clothes as the usual getup of lower-class Tagalogs in historical movies. I can totally understand why someone from my birth family would want to preserve that for some sentimental reason, but this keepsake is far from ordinary.

It's covered in blood. Dried blood, definitely, but still blood.

"Ay! That's so creepy." Kitty turns away. This is why she's not the best companion if you're going to a museum.

She doesn't really like looking at relics—especially bloody ones like this. "Don't look, Ate."

I look anyway. "It's creepy . . . but cool." With that amount of blood, whoever was wearing it died for sure. "It looks like the remnants of a crime scene in the nineteenth century."

"You are correct. It is the remnant of a crime scene," a man's voice carries from across the vault. We turn around and find that the Supremo has joined us. "The Omen-Bringer said you like learning about Philippine history. I suppose you've heard about how Ka Andrés died?"

"Of course!"

It was pretty nasty how he died, actually. Andrés Bonifacio—also called Ka Andrés—was the founder of the Katipunan, a society with the goal of freeing the Philippines from its Spanish colonizers through a revolution. He was betrayed, murdered, and left in the mountains of Maragondon by his own comrades. So tragic, really. It kind of makes you wonder what the Philippines would have been like had he lived long enough to see his goal succeed.

"Good." The Supremo looks up at the bloodied clothes. "What you won't find in the history books, though, is that Ka Andrés was favored by Apolaki."

"That makes sense." I've known the sun god long enough to know that he'd definitely approve of someone as brave as Ka Andrés. "He's the god of warriors, after all."

"Correct." The Supremo nods. "When Apolaki saw what happened to Ka Andrés, he pleaded with Bathala to save the Katipunero. The Supreme Deity agreed, and he resurrected the wronged Ka Andrés and his most loyal comrades, who were also killed with him."

"Sounds like *Dawn of the Dead*." I wriggle my brows. "Did they become zombies?"

"No." The Supremo doesn't even crack a smile. Thank goodness I didn't inherit his obvious lack of humor. "The lives of Ka Andrés and his loyal Katipuneros came with a cost—they and their descendants are to protect the Realms when chaos threatens them. Bathala brought the Katipuneros to this island in the In-Between, a haven for all beings, protected by Apolaki and hidden by Anagolay. Since the word 'Katipunan' became a reminder of betrayal for them, they decided to call themselves the Maharlika, after the caste of noble warriors of the precolonial Tagalogs."

"So you mean to say that those bloody clothes on the wall belonged to Ka Andrés himself?" I can't keep the excitement out of my voice. This is amazing. I'm in the presence of an actual, probably unhygienic, historical relic.

"I'm glad you're pleased." The Supremo gives me a smile. "There's more that you'll want to know."

"What?" I ask eagerly, like an excited puppy.

"As you may have already noticed, Ka Andrés retained

the Katipunero tradition of the Supremo as the leader of the Maharlikan army. And he passed this title to his descendants, who also carried his surname, Bonifacio—"

My eyes widen. "You don't mean—"

"Yes. We're the descendants of Ka Andrés." The Supremo nods. "I am Artemio Bonifacio, and your name was once Luningning Bonifacio."

"No way! That's so cool." I turn to face Kitty. "Meow, can you believe it?"

"Yes, Ate. But you're a Sinagtala now." My sister purses her lips, her voice cold. "I'm sure Mom will find your bloodline fascinating too."

"Yeah." I throw her a warning look. I know what Kitty's doing. She's trying to remind me about Mom. Which she doesn't have to do, of course.

Komandante Yani clears his throat, looking at his watch. "We'll have to hurry if we want to make it in time for lunch, Papa. Tita will have my head if she finds out I've been starving our bunso."

"Ah yes," the Supremo says. He tilts his head in Kitty's direction. "Would you and your aswang friend join us?"

Kitty's stomach grumbles.

"I think that's a yes." I grin. Kitty gives my father a look that's a cross between a grin and a grimace, making him chuckle.

A small smile appears on the komandante's lips. This time it feels like a genuine smile.

Maybe I judged my brother too harshly. And maybe, just maybe, there will come a time when we can be more than just blood relatives . . . but something that resembles a family too.

Don't get me wrong. That doesn't mean Kitty and Mom and Tita Cecile aren't my family anymore. They still are, and they always will be.

But I just want to know what my life with my birth family would have been like if the Maligno hadn't taken me away from them. Is that too much to ask?

CHAPTER NINETEEN

When in Maharlika, Do as the Maharlikans Do

I'll never admit this to Kitty unless I really want to pick a fight . . . but sometimes I've daydreamed about having Sunday lunch with my biological family.

Nothing superspecial. Kind of like those "happy family" get-togethers on TV, where the dad oversees the carving of the roast chicken, the older brother gives up the best part of the bird to his younger sister, and the mom-like figure makes sure everyone at the table is able to get their gazillionth serving.

The funny thing is, I'm right smack in the middle of this exact scene in real life, yet it's not as fulfilling as I thought it would be. I mean, Kitty's with me. Even Haribon, the pet duck I didn't know I had, is on a toddler's high chair across the table beside Bart. We're eating at a fancy restaurant where the dishes are so expensive, Mom would have had to pay the bill with her entire salary for a month.

It should have been the perfect lunch scene, but it's not. Because it lacks two very important characters: Mom and Tita Cecile.

I want to say I wish Manong Sol were in this scene too, but I'd be lying if I did. The faces of Manong Sol, Amanikable, and other popular deities are all over the ads and merchandise in the City, even inside the business establishments. They're literally everywhere, and it's disturbing. God fandoms are really thriving in Maharlika City.

"Can you pass me a paper napkin, please?" I say, reaching across the table. Bart hands me one from a dispenser that has a photo of Manong Sol in a muscle shirt, his arms crossed over his chest. Thankfully, the Maharlikans make such great food that even this gross picture of the sun god can't ruin my appetite. "That was, like, the most delicious sinigang I've ever had."

Sinigang is my comfort food. I love to slurp its tangy, slightly spicy tamarind broth, then pour the soup onto steamed rice mixed with water spinach, bangus fish belly, and mashed taro. The swanky local Maharlikan restaurant where we had lunch makes sinigang cooking seem like art.

“I’m glad you enjoyed it,” my brother says with a smile. He’s actually much nicer now that he’s sure I’m not carrying around an evil spirit. In fact, he even asked us to refer to him as Kuya Yani instead of using his military rank.

After our meal, my father takes us for a walk in the nearby park. Tita Ligaya, the lakambini, buys Kitty, Bart, and me ice cream from a dessert kiosk. She gets Haribon an unflavored cucumber slushie (apparently sugar is bad for ducks).

There’s a huge variety of trees in this park. I’ve only seen Central Park in pictures, but this is probably how it would look—except that the plants and animals are tropical, of course.

Kuya Yani says this park is called Bonifacio Park, after the national hero *and* our ancestor, Andrés Bonifacio (I’m totally still not over finding out I’m related to such an important person in Philippine history).

As I said, there’s a lot of trees here, but nothing beats the one in the center. It’s massive. Like, *huge* huge. Its trunk reminds me of those trees in California that I read about on the internet—sequoia trees. Except this one has the trademark predator vines of a balete tree.

“We call this Bathala’s Tree. It’s the only tree of its kind in Maharlika City,” my father says as he pushes his sister’s wheelchair. “Unlike the ones you have in the Middleworld, Bathala’s Tree can’t be used as a gateway, even by gods, because of the City’s protective magic.”

"Like, never?"

"Well, the effort can really drain them," Tita Ligaya answers for her brother. "If they're not strong enough, they could be drained so much that they cease to exist in this Realm."

"Wow." Kitty's eyes widen. "Let's make sure to remind Tita Cecile and Manong Sol never to use that tree."

"Oh, they know," my father says, his lips forming a grim line. "They know better than anyone."

Ring! Ring! Ring! Kuya Yani's phone chimes. "Excuse me, I have to take this."

As the Supremo and the lakambini continue their walk, Kitty, Bart, and I settle on a bench, where we eat our desserts. That's when a group of grandmas and grandpas walks by. They're holding signs that say "We need help too!" or "We are people. We are not disposable!"

Kitty bites her lower lip. "That's so sad."

Haribon hops on the bench and sits between us. "As your father told you while we were inside the vault, Maharlikans are warriors bred from birth. They're supposed to answer the gods' call to protect the Realms as needed," he explains. "It was an idea born from almost-indestructible immortals, beings whose concept of time is very different from yours and mine."

"Wait. But you're immortal too."

"My spirit is." He nods in agreement. It's adorable how he nods. His long neck bends like a licorice stick.

"However, my physical body cannot live perpetually. Every time my body dies, my spirit must wait to be incarnated in another form. Gods do not worry about things like that. So when warriors get old or become no longer needed—"

"They get discarded," I finish for him.

You'd think that being shielded from colonization, Maharlika City would be spared from this awful thinking—discarding people when they're no longer of use to you.

I study the huge picture of Manong Sol's face on a stand near the parking area. Now I think I understand why the sun god chose the likeness of an old man instead of the expected "handsome young man" manifestation of Apolaki. It was a statement, a reminder that old people should be honored and supported, not discarded.

"Looks like the commander is going to take a while on the phone, Ate," Kitty says as she continues to devour her strawberry ice cream. "We can run while he's not looking."

I stop in the middle of licking my mango drumstick. "You're kidding, right?"

"No. Why not?"

"Do you see that man near Bathala's Tree? Those three near the lake and those four at your right?" I point with my waffle cone. "Soldiers. They're all here to guard my bio-family, Haribon, me, you, and Bart. We can't escape."

"Hay naku! Buti nga may nai-suggest pa ko eh." Kitty

says at least she was able to suggest something. "If we just sit here, we won't find Mom in time. You aren't even trying to do anything."

Seriously? "I am trying!"

"Hey, hey." Bart swallows the last of his dessert and transforms into Tannie. As a little dog, he wedges himself between my sister and me. "We're all doing what we can. Let's just calm down and—"

Kitty angrily chews the last of her cone. "I'm not the one with powers. And I'm not an aswang."

"Well, I can't teleport, and neither can Bart." I scowl. Kitty thinks I have the solution for everything just because I have powers. I'm a Salamangkero, not Google. "I can't visit every single karaoke restaurant in this city at the snap of my fingers."

"The snap of your fingers can't bring us there, but a vehicle can."

Kitty, Bart, and I look at the duck.

Haribon shakes cucumber slush from his bill, splashing us a bit. "There's only one restaurant that has a karaoke room in all of Maharlika. We'll be there in fifteen minutes, tops."

"Okay, cool." There's just one problem, though— "How can we go there without my family noticing?"

"Family. Huh," Kitty grumbles. "*I'm* her family."

I pretend I didn't hear her. I'm honestly starting to grow weary of Kitty and her sour mood. I'm doing the best I can to find Mom. But is it so wrong to get to know my biological family while we're at it?

Kitty just doesn't understand. Throughout my life, I've always felt like a part of me has been missing. And now that I'm finally getting answers, Kitty is being selfish and thinking only about herself.

"No more fighting!" The duck bobs his head. "Just leave it to me."

We watch Haribon jump and flap his wings to catch up with my father and Tita Ligaya by the lake. As he talks, we notice that he's got both the Supremo's and the lakambini's attention. Then Kuya Yani finishes his call and joins them. I can't hear what they're saying, but it seems like our father is telling him something that makes him back away.

Haribon returns to our bench, waddling happily. "Let's go. Your father will give us a ride, and he'll wait for us at the nearby café. He doesn't find karaoke appealing, apparently."

"WHAT?" I nearly fall off the bench. "Why did you tell him—"

"I didn't tell him about your mother." The duck's head feathers stand up in irritation. "I just said you wanted to sing karaoke."

I feel a stab of guilt. "Sorry. What about Kuya Yani?"

"He's not coming." Haribon quacks in what seems like an amused manner. "Your father tried to make him accompany you, but he would rather be eaten alive by one of Lord Amanikable's giant sharks than risk being forced to sing karaoke."

I laugh. "Brilliant!"

Bart and even sourpuss Kitty applaud Haribon too.

I love this duck so much. He's like one of the giant eagles in that old fantasy movie *Lord of the Rings: The Return of the King*. The ones that appeared out of nowhere to save the good guys every time they were in deep trouble and had no way out. Well, I have a smarty-pants duck that talks, which is loads better.

Soon, black SUVs arrive in front of the park's entrance. Tita Ligaya bids us goodbye and gets into one of the cars. She's going to the temple, which she promises me I'll visit with her soon. Kuya Yani joins Gamila and Paloma in their vehicle, while Kitty, Bart, Haribon, and I go on a ride with the Supremo.

Our convoy splits into three as we reach the intersection. From the window, I catch a glimpse of the temple on the eastern horizon.

"The east is also where the sun rises here in the In-Between. It is the best place for the temple so our katalonans—our priestesses—will be the first ones to welcome Lord Apolaki's light every morning. Ate Ligaya is the head katalonan of our city," Papa, as he insisted I call him, explains.

I feel a bit weird calling the Supremo "Papa." But it's

not like I have anyone else to refer to that way. Besides, there are times I call elderly men whose names I don't know "Tatay" as a sign of respect. "Tatay" is basically the Tagalog for "Papa." So it's fine. "Papa" it is.

"Could my brother become a katalonan too?" I ask, pretending not to see Kitty bristling at my mention of "brother."

Papa nods. "Yes, but he would need to choose to become a woman. Katalonans are all priestesses—we regard women highly here in Maharlika, just like our Tagalog ancestors did. The Spanish colonizers subjugated women as secondary to men, and we Maharlikans want to unlearn that."

I remember something I've always wanted to ask about. "Is that why you're a Supremo and Kuya Yani is a komandante while I'm a dayang and Tita Ligaya is a lakambini?"

"That is correct. You and your aunt are royalty and can hold the sacred role of katalonan, while males such as myself and your brother serve under your authority."

"Cool." I wonder how different Manila would be if we also thought like Maharlikans. I haven't seen enough of Maharlika to judge, but I'm pretty sure it won't be as bad. After all, our ancestors had been okay even before the Spanish came to our shores.

We get to see more of Maharlika City on our way to the karaoke place—there's a plaza, a grocery, and a school.

There's even a hospital and a pharmacy, where the nurses, doctors, and pharmacists are just hanging out in the lobby or crowding around a taho vendor. "Mom would probably get bored working at a pharmacy like that. They don't look like they have patients," I remark. "Mom loves helping people too much."

It's only when I see Kitty blink fast that I realize what I just said. Bart shifts in his seat in discomfort. My sister looks like she's trying not to cry. "Meow—" I say.

Kitty squares her shoulders. "Yes, Ate. I agree. Mom would get bored there."

"You should bring your adoptive mother to visit Maharlika City," Papa says warmly. "Our lack of patients in need will be a good way for her to relax."

"I think you mean 'our mom,' sir," says Kitty. "Ate Lulu and I might not share the same blood, but we *are* sisters."

"Indeed you are."

I give Kitty a nudge. What's gotten into her?

Papa seems to be watching us closely. He looks like he's about to say something, but the duck quacks loudly. Or at least as loud as his raspy quack lets him.

"We're here!"

Sure enough, the SUV stops in front of a white building. It's designed like most bahay na bato, except the entire ground floor has glass walls, like most restaurants. There's also an inihaw stand right beside the entrance, the smell of the barbecue making my mouth water.

The duck jumps out of the vehicle, flapping his wings as he lands. Show-off!

Papa alights from the SUV last. "Don't forget. At any sign of trouble—"

"Papa, we'll be fine," I say, rolling my eyes. So this is what it feels like to have an overprotective dad. "I was trained by the god of warriors himself, remember?"

"I know." Papa pats my head. "You might be the Salamangkero who will protect us, but you are also my daughter."

I stare at my sneakers, feeling Papa's and Kitty's gazes upon me. I feel awful that I still can't bring myself to trust my father fully, when it's obvious he's doing his best to make up for the time we've lost together. At the same time, I feel like I'm betraying Mom for enjoying time with my biological family while she's trapped and scared in that magical prison.

Thankfully, Papa doesn't wait for my answer and leaves to go to a nearby café with his bodyguards. They're far but near enough to come running at the sign of trouble.

"Here we go." I hold Kitty's and Bart's hands. Together with our supersmart duck, we enter the restaurant, where we're greeted by the sound of a moaning, dying animal.

"What is that noise?" Haribon demands as he shakes his feathery head.

One of the staff hurries to meet us, bowing apologetically to the duck. "We are sorry for this, Omen-Bringer.

We try to limit our customers' singing within the confines of the karaoke room, but sometimes they're just . . . er . . . too loud."

"You call *that* singing?" I can't carry a tune the way Kitty does, but gosh. I'm like Jungkook compared to this customer. "Your restaurant should give earplug freebies for situations like this."

"I'm sorry."

Ugh. The idea of having to endure this wailing all day is pure torture. Because we're not leaving the restaurant until Warren the wakwak shows up. We'll keep returning to this place until he finally does, even if it means listening to the sound of despairing souls in Kasanaan on repeat. Let's just hope the scammy duwende didn't lie to us about the wakwak.

"Mister Gavino said the wakwak is supposed to be a great singer," Kitty says. She's obviously trying not to grin.

Bart points his thumb in the direction of where the noise is coming from. "Guess that's not who we're looking for."

"Definitely not."

It's nice to see Kitty in better spirits. Can't blame her—I am too. I'm getting this lighthearted feeling that we'll find Mom's kidnapper soon. Which means we're a step closer to getting her back.

"Can we have a table near the karaoke machine?"

Haribon asks the server who welcomed us. "The children would like to sing."

"Of course, Omen-Bringer." The server nods and leads the way to the back of the restaurant.

We enter another room, and the ugly singing intensifies. Kitty winces; Bart transforms into a dog and covers his ears with his paws. I shamelessly cover my ears. Haribon ruffles his feathers in annoyance and shakes his head. I make a mental note to ask him later where his ears are—I've never seen duck ears before.

"Oh wow, it's extra awful inside this room. No wonder they keep the door shut," I say as I study the menu. I raise my eyebrows at Haribon. "Do you have money?"

"I have an open tab in every establishment in this city—the perks of being the Omen-Bringer," the duck brags. He peers at me. "Don't tell me you're hungry again?"

"Lunch was so long ago! It's time for merienda."

"It's only half past two, Lu." Bart transforms back to a boy. "We had lunch just an hour ago."

I shrug. "I'm a growing girl."

"Your stomach is like a pit so deep it leads all the way to the Underworld," Haribon says. Regardless, he still gives the server my order of calamari, dirty nachos, and sweet pineapple juice.

Unlike the karaoke place I've been to with Kitty, Mom, and Manong Sol in the Middleworld, which is totally soundproof and has fancy lights and all, this room is just an area separated from the main restaurant by a glass wall and a sliding door. The karaoke machine is on an elevated platform at the back of the tiny room, with huge sliding glass windows on the right side.

But the walls . . . wow. There is an unusually high number of posters plastered on the adobe walls. The prints feature a pretty girl around my age in different poses and backgrounds, overlaid with text that reads "Twinkle on, my Starlight."

Bart bursts out laughing. "Lu, this looks like your side of the bedroom that you and Kitty share!"

I stick my tongue out at him. That's all I can do, because I can't deny it—half of the bedroom I share with Kitty is covered with photos of Jungkook and Rosé.

When the screamy customer finally leaves, the server looks relieved too and keeps the sliding door open as her colleague brings in our food. Our server places a thick book in the middle of our table as the other waitress leaves.

"This is the list of songs we have," she says. "You can pick any, except for song number 7777."

"Why?"

"It's dangerous." Haribon answers my question. "That's the reason Lord Apolaki doesn't like karaoke. It is not that he cannot sing. I'm certain the patron god of warriors has the voice of an angel—"

I let out a loud snort. "He does not have the voice of an angel. Trust me."

"Anyway, karaoke use around magical creatures needs to be highly regulated."

"Everything we've encountered in this city so far has been dangerous," Kitty points out.

"You should just remove the song from the system," Bart suggests.

"Yes, that would be ideal," the server agrees. "But karaoke is not our crafters' top priority. We've been trying to get our system updated and the songs digitized, but they are always busy. A combination of electronics and magic is involved, so we can't just open the machine by ourselves." She gives us a notepad and a pencil. "You can write your choices while you wait for your turn."

I frown. "We're not next?"

"Ate, we don't really need to sing—"

Our server looks very apologetic. "I'm sorry. He already made a reservation last night. But if he's not here in ten minutes, I'll let you take his slot— Oh! He's here. Welcome back, sir."

Kitty lets out a gasp and grabs my arm.

The customer who enters the karaoke room is none other than the well-dressed wakwak who kidnapped our mother.

CHAPTER TWENTY

"My Way" or the Alleyway

Unbelievable. Warren the wakwak is ordering food from the menu like he didn't just kidnap Mom a few days ago.

"Lu, stop it. Someone might see." Bart holds my hands under the table. I'm so startled, I lose control of the Salamangka—the blue light—and it dissipates from my fists.

"Do something, Ate." Kitty's voice cracks. "Mom—"

"I will, Meow. Shh." I put my arm around my sister and give her shoulders a squeeze. From the corner of my eye, I watch the wakwak. Well-dressed in a white polo shirt, black pants, and custom-sneakered talons.

The server brings Warren's order and sets down

another copy of the thick list of songs. He leafs through the pages forlornly while eating his grilled cheese sandwich.

As soon as the waitress leaves the room, I march up to the wakwak's table before Bart or Haribon can stop me. He's chewing his sandwich so thoughtfully that he doesn't seem to notice me taking a seat in front of him.

I clear my throat. Bart, Kitty, and Haribon join me at the table, sitting on the empty chairs beside me.

The wakwak continues to chew slowly, still lost in thought.

I clear my throat louder. But again, he doesn't hear me.

"HOY!" I shout at the wakwak, snapping my fingers inches from his face.

He finally looks up. "Lulu Sinagtala."

"Hello, Warren," I say coolly. It's nice to see him squirm. "Yes, that's right. I know your name. Our 'dear friend' Gavino told us all about you. Where's my mother?"

The wakwak looks at me, then at Kitty.

I ball my fists under the table until they glow with Salamangka. I'm ready for battle. "If you put even a single claw on my sister, I'm going to—"

The wakwak suddenly bursts out crying. "I'm sorry, I didn't mean to. The Vengeful One made me do it!"

I look at my companions for help. Bart and Haribon are at a loss for words as well. We were all expecting to do battle, not this.

Only Kitty seems to know what to do.

"Just let it all out, Mister Warren," she says, handing the wakwak a tissue. "We're here to listen, if you need to talk."

"What?" I say. "No, we're not. We're here to find Mom." I point at the wakwak's bag. Gavino said that the easiest way to smuggle somebody into the City is by using an enchanted bag. I swallow hard. The possibility is disturbing, but I have to know. "Did you put our mother in there?"

"No. It's a different bag." Warren sobs. "I'm so sorry!"

I feel my anger build. He talks as if my mother is some kind of an object he can carry around. "Where did you put her?"

Instead of answering, the wakwak bawls even harder.

"Ugh!" I bury my face in my arms on the table. "We're going to get nowhere with this one."

Kitty frowns at me and shakes her head.

Really? She's been whiny and grumpy all day about finding Mom, and now she wants me to go easy on our mother's kidnapper?

"Let him calm down first, Ate. Not everything can be solved by punching your way through," she says, giving me a pointed look. "Sir, I know you feel terrible about what happened. I would too. But we need our mother, and you're the only one who can help us."

"Hay naku!" Haribon lets out an annoyed, raspy quack.

"We've wasted so much time already. Just bonk him on the head or something."

"Or we can zap him with a jolt of electric current," Bart suggests. He looks around the room. "I can work with that stand fan. If we can borrow it—"

Kitty frowns. "Absolutely not. No one is bonking or electrocuting anybody. He just needs to calm down a bit. Let's see . . . Mister Warren, you should sing us a song. Mister Gavino said you're a wonderful singer."

The wakwak stops bawling. "He did?"

Kitty nods, smiling at him in encouragement. "Uh-huh."

Hmm . . . Kitty might be onto something. I push the list of songs over to the wakwak and hand him the remote control for the karaoke machine. Maybe this could actually work.

"Okay, let me see. . . ." The wakwak leafs through the book, stopping when he finds what he likes. "I'll pick song number 7–7–7—"

I reach over the table to stop him. "NOT 7777!"

Of course, the last button the wakwak presses is 7. He lets out a terrified screech. "Oh no! Look what you made me do."

"Hoy." I point at him. "You're the one who pressed it!"

"I wouldn't have if you didn't scare me! I was going to pick 7778, not 7777!" Warren tosses the remote and grabs his bag. "We need to go—"

The doors slide shut, and metal bars barricade the

glass windows. From the restaurant side, the waiters are struggling to pry the door open. But every time they're close, the door frame glows with blue light, strengthening the barrier even more.

"7777" appears in large, bold letters on the screen of the karaoke machine. The numbers fade out, and the opening notes of Frank Sinatra's "My Way" belts out from the speakers.

The restaurant staff gives up on opening the door.

"There's nothing we can do anymore," our server says. She reminds me of doctors delivering news of fatal diseases to patients in the K-dramas Kitty and Mom love to watch. "He must finish the song, or he will die. Please help him if you can, and watch out for your nonhuman companions—"

"I'm fine. Just a bit . . ." Haribon shakes his head, then closes his eyes. "Kitty, come here and carry me. We need to help the wakwak finish the song. Stay away from Bart."

"Why?" The hairs at the back of my head stand up as my pulse quickens. Kind of like Spider-Man's "Peter-Tingle," which forewarns him of dangerous events. And right now, I feel like something very, very bad is about to happen. "Dude, what's wrong?"

Bart grabs my hand, pulling me away from Kitty and Haribon. "The song. It's enchanted. Hold me down, Lu. I can't control it—GRRRRRRRRR!" A low, guttural sound escapes Bart's throat as he transforms into a dog. Not into the cute, adorable shih tzu Tannie—Bart goes into full were-dog mode this time. The scary, snarling, will-bite-your-head-off aswang kind.

I will Salamangka to course through me. The magic obliges, and my arms emit blue light as I hold on to Bart from behind. Weredog Bart is no match for the power of the Anito, but he struggles violently nonetheless.

Suddenly one of were-dog Bart's claws escapes. He scratches my arm, leaving long, bloody lines of damage on my skin. I yelp in pain, but I still don't let go.

Warren isn't faring well on the karaoke either. He keeps making mistakes with the lyrics. It gets even worse when the screen of the karaoke machine blinks red in warning.

"You can do it, Mister Warren!" Kitty joins the wakwak on the platform. She takes the secondary microphone while carrying Haribon with her other arm. "Just focus on the words and timing. Sing louder! I'll fill in the words you miss."

With my sister providing backup for the wakwak, the karaoke screen stops blinking red. They're on track with the song again.

Still, I can feel chaos building inside the room. There's rage, fear, confusion, and panic—like everything is just going to start falling apart.

Were-dog Bart is getting more and more violent as "My Way" progresses. Haribon shakes his head to fight off the effects of the song every now and then, but he's able to keep his wits and not go into a full-on zombie rage in my sister's arms.

"HAH-REE-BON!" I call to the duck. "What are we going to do?"

"Destroy the machine—it's the only way," Haribon gasps. "Kitty, hold me tighter. The spell is getting harder and harder to overcome!"

I take an arm off were-dog Bart to bring out the buntot pagi from my pouch. His claws dig into my skin as I do. I gasp in pain, but somehow I still manage to wind the stingray's tail around the aswang, taking great care not to squeeze him too tight. The buntot pagi glows every time Bart struggles. I sit him on a chair. "Stay!"

Warren is singing his soul out. Sweat pours down Kitty's face as she provides backup vocals while carrying a heavy duck with one arm.

"Be careful, Lulu!" Haribon croaks.

I tell my sister and the wakwak to move away from the karaoke machine. I unplug it, but the song continues to play. Haribon's right. I have no other choice—I must destroy it.

I throw my balisong at the machine's screen, and the glass shatters. Still, "My Way" keeps on playing. With my entire upper body glowing like a half-powered Captain Marvel, I lift the machine off the ground. I slam it hard against the adobe wall, breaking it into pieces. The karaoke ruins glow blue, dissipating as the music finally fades to silence.

Warren drops to the floor in relief. Bart morphs back to his normal self again. Haribon buries his feathered head in Kitty's hair.

We're safe.

I pull my balisong from the broken screen. "Bart, can you get my buntot pagi—"

"We must leave!" Warren gasps at the sight of restaurant staff trying to pry the enchanted glass door of the karaoke room open.

"Go," Haribon says as Kitty gently deposits him on top of a table. "Find a safe place where you can interrogate the wakwak. Meet me at the coffee shop when you're done. I will take care of this."

I survey the mess. I not only broke the karaoke machine, I destroyed a few tables and chairs too. I really hope Haribon can negotiate us out of this. The damage I've caused looks pretty expensive. "What about Papa and his soldiers—"

"I'll come up with something. They will believe anything I say. I am the Omen-Bringer, you know." Haribon turns to glare at Warren the wakwak. "You've seen what Lulu can do. Make sure you tell her what she needs to know. We will protect you as a witness for agreeing to help us."

The wakwak nods weakly.

Without magic protecting the windows, I easily punch through the glass. Kitty, Bart, the wakwak, and I escape into an alleyway, hiding behind the trash bins near a dead end.

Kitty gasps at the sight of my wounds. "Ate, you're hurt!"

"I'm fine." I stare pointedly at Bart, who's totally horrified. "Stop. I'm going to get mad at you if you say sorry. *It wasn't your fault.* You were enchanted."

I watch Bart throw his backpack to the ground and bring out a first aid kit. He cleans my wounds and patches them up without a word.

"Let's talk later," I promise my friend. "We don't have time—the soldiers will be here soon. Tell us what you know," I say to the wakwak.

For the first time, Warren doesn't resort to bawling and actually gives us his side of the story. As it turns out, the Maligno threatened to harm Warren's mother if he didn't kidnap Mom and smuggle her into Maharlika City. Warren was too afraid to ask the Maligno why he had to bring Mom here. But luckily he overheard a couple of the Maligno's supporters discussing it.

"The Vengeful One wants you to do something for him, and it can only be accomplished in the City," the wakwak tells me. "They don't know what it is exactly, but it's related to his plan of conquering the Realms."

"How is that possible?" I ask. That plan sounds so unrealistically ambitious. "A single evil spirit can't conquer the universe!"

"He can, if he causes enough chaos," Bart says, his expression grim. "You felt the chaos in the karaoke room.

Now imagine that feeling multiplied Realms-wide. The humans in the Middleworld will experience wars, famine, and disease. The Underworld will then be overrun by the influx of souls. The chaos will snake its way between those two Realms, including the In-Between. The Salamangka then becomes unstable. Sooner or later, the gods in the Upperworld will be thrown into panic when the magic that keeps them alive slowly disappears."

Considering how smart the Maligno is, I'm pretty sure he's figured out how to cause such a horrible chain of events. But right now, the most important thing is finding Mom. "So, where's our mother?"

"I'm sorry, I really have no idea." The wakwak hangs his head, staring down at his sneakered talons. "All I know is, they put her in a magical prison that only the Vengeful One can open. That's when he sent my own mother to the Underworld . . . just because he no longer needed us."

"That's terrible!" Kitty says, biting her lower lip. "I'm so sorry to hear that."

"Can't you at least tell us who he is?" Bart prods.

Warren takes a step back from Bart, terrified. I guess were-dog Bart is still very fresh in his memory. "I . . . I can't!"

Kitty puts a hand on his arm. "Mister Warren, I know you're scared—I'd be scared too—but please, think of your mother and how she would have been proud to see you do the right thing."

"All right." The wakwak heaves a long sigh. He takes my hands in his. Bart tries to intervene, but I give him a nod to assure him it's okay. "The duck gave me his word," Warren says, "but I need to hear it from you too, Lulu Sinagtala. Promise me you'll protect me."

"I promise."

"Even from your relatives—your biological relatives."

That gives me pause. "My bio relatives? But why?"

"Just promise me."

"Okay. I promise to protect you even from my own biological relatives." I'm hit with a sudden realization. "Hey, you don't mean one of them—"

Before Warren can confirm, he lets out a loud gasp.

"Oh." The wakwak's black-and-purple lips form a perfectly round O shape. He looks down at his chest, where an arrowhead is poking through. "Lulu! Don't trust your—"

Warren suddenly glows blue, then dissolves into mist, taking with him my hopes of finding the Maligno to save Mom. The arrow falls to the ground with a loud clang.

I drop to my knees. "Noooooo!"

CHAPTER TWENTY-ONE

The Nosy, Starry-Eyed Lady of the Sky

GREAT. WE'RE BACK AT SQUARE ONE. NO LEADS. NO WITNESSES. NOTHING. After all that trouble, our best chance of finding Mom is now on his way to the Underworld.

Haribon, Papa, and the Maharlikan soldiers had arrived in time to apprehend the shooter. But he turned out to be just some criminal who had a score to settle with the wakwak. Or so he said.

"Do you think he was telling the truth?" I ask Haribon, leaning on the balcony railing outside our room. "It seems too convenient that he shot Warren just before we could find out who the Maligno is possessing."

Thanks to the duck, Kitty, Bart, and I got to hang out

in my room as soon as we returned to the Balay Dayao compound. Yep, even Bart. My biological family wasn't pleased about me having boys in my room. But Haribon argued that Bart and I wouldn't be alone, and my friend wasn't sleeping over anyway, so they finally agreed.

"Perhaps. But it is suspicious," says the duck, looking up at the night sky. "I'll have to look into the wakwak's background to be able to say for certain."

Hay. More work for us to do. But it's hard to hate Warren the wakwak. There's no denying that he kidnapped Mom, but he had no choice. I wouldn't hesitate to do the same thing if my loved ones were threatened.

"Ate, do you remember the last thing he said?" Kitty chews on her fingernails. "About your biological family—"

"Yeah. I know." I sigh. There's no point delaying a conversation that's bound to happen soon anyway. "Unless there are cousins or other relatives I haven't met yet, or Warren is lying to us . . . the Maligno host is either Kuya Yani, Tita Ligaya, or Papa."

"How do you feel about that?"

I avoid looking at my sister. "Sad."

Kitty reaches for my hand. I take it without hesitation, holding on as if she'll disappear too. Not to be melodramatic, but with the way things are going, she might be the only family I'll have left.

"You know, Lulu, I've been living in Maharlika City for a very long time," says Haribon. He sits beside me, so close that I feel his feathers on my skin. "I've seen every member of your family grow up from baby to adult. They're good people. Even though the Maligno has a hold on one of them, I am certain your relative's soul is fighting with all their might to break free."

"What do you mean?"

"Don't give up on them," says the duck, tilting his head to stare at me with his beady eye. "They're still there. They're not lost to you yet."

"We'll get them back, Ate," Kitty promises. "We'll kick out the Maligno from your relative's body so you can have them back." She gives my hand a squeeze and bites her lower lip. "I just hope that when all this is over . . . um . . . you'll still want to live with me and Mom. We don't have a palace like this, and you'll have to share a room with me—"

"Duh! Of course I'll still want to live with you and Mom." I pull my sister in for a side hug. "We'll go home to Inarawan once we're done here."

Kitty smiles. She looks so much like Mom when she does. It makes me miss Mom even more.

"Dinner's here!" Bart calls from inside the room. I tell the others to go ahead, since I'm not hungry yet. But the truth is, I've lost my appetite.

From my balcony, I can see most of the island. It reminds me of Metro Manila at night, like that time when Ate Mariel treated me, Kitty, and Bart to a fancy dinner at a cliffside restaurant in Antipolo City. Except here, the lights are blue instead of yellow, and the heavens have way more stars than any sky I've ever seen.

It's humbling to think that this island city is just a small speck in the universe . . . the universe I'm supposed to protect and save.

"Penny for your thoughts," Haribon says as he waddles up beside me. "The food is getting cold. If you're worried about your mother and what the wakwak said—"

"Do you think I can do all these things?" I blurt, the words I've been wanting to say finally rushing out. "I want to promise Kitty that everything's going to be all right, but I can't. We still haven't found Mom. And now I have to rescue one of my family members from the Maligno's hold. I can't even save my family, so how am I supposed to save the universe when that time comes?" I continue, running a hand through my hair. "Wars, famine, disease, chaos in the Underworld, gods losing powers . . . How am I supposed to fix all that? I'm only eleven, Haribon! I'm not cut out for this. Maybe the Anito made a mistake picking me."

There's an odd kind of relief to finally being able to say these things out loud.

Ever since Tita Cecile told me I'm a Salamangkero, I just kind of accepted it. How could I not? It gave me superstrength and an ability to wield magic, stuff I figured would be useful in our search for Mom. It *was* pretty handy and kept us alive on our way to this island, and it even got us close to finding Mom.

But it never really occurred to me that I might actually have to do a whole lot more than that. Like, there really is a possibility that the Maligno can bring chaos to the Realms, and I'll have to be the one to fix it.

Haribon jumps up and flaps his wings, landing gracefully on the railing. He looks me straight in the eye. "Lulu, I understand it is not easy for you to have faith in others. But you should at least trust yourself. Do you?"

"I don't know, Haribon. I really don't know."

"Well, you'll have to." The duck tilts his head to the side. "You really won't be able to do anything unless you do."

Before I can think of an answer, a shooting star appears in the sky.

"It's a bulalakaw!" I exclaim, pointing at the streak of light. "Maybe if I wish for guidance, I'll know what to do."

"A bulalakaw doesn't grant wishes— Ay!" Haribon shakes his head. "Never mind. If it's going to make you feel better, go ahead and make a wish."

"Little shooting star," I pray, bringing my clasped hands up to my forehead. "Please help me with this Salamangkero thing. I have no idea what I'm doing, and I just really want to know why the Anito seem to think it should be me."

The balcony glows with bright yellow light. The light

gathers behind me. I turn to look, and I see it forming into a figure. Then the light solidifies into a pretty girl who looks about the same age as I am. She has dark skin and a flat nose like me, but her black hair is superlong—it reaches her ankles. And her eyes . . . looking into her eyes is like gazing at the Milky Way. Bright, twinkling, and captivating.

I gasp as I recognize her. "You're the girl in the posters at the karaoke place!"

"Yes, Lulu, that's me. The owner is a fan of mine," she says, laughing. The stars twinkle behind her, kind of like those fairy lights programmed to blink in time with the Christmas song playing in the background. She turns to the duck. "Hello, Haribon. Your new body seems . . . less fierce."

Haribon jumps off the railing and lands on the balcony floor. He gives the girl a respectful bow and steps back. "Lady Tala."

The girl is Tala, the goddess of stars.

"Ate, what's going on?" Kitty and Bart join us on the balcony. By the way Bart's bowing, I guess he already knows the girl is a goddess. I introduce him and Kitty, nonetheless.

"I never thought you'd be a great babysitter, Haribon," the goddess remarks with an amused expression. She pats me on the shoulder. "Don't take it personally. The Omen-Bringer usually joins a Salamangkero when they're already grown-up. You just happened to be the first kid Salamangkero he's ever accompanied."

Haribon lowers his head. "The Maligno escaped sooner than expected, my lady."

"Yeah, I know. I've been watching these three since forever!" Tala disappears, then suddenly pops up behind us, as fast as the twinkle of a star. She puts an arm around my shoulders and Kitty's. "Your relationship is, like, goals for me. And your friendship with Bart . . . also goals! Maybe one day I'll have friends like you three."

"You said you have fans." I raise an eyebrow. "Can't they be your friends?"

"Well . . . not really." Tala stares at her bare feet. "It's hard to know if they really want to be friends with me or if they just like me because they're a fan and I'm a goddess."

"You can be our friend," Kitty says, smiling at Tala.

The star goddess's lips quiver. "Really?"

"Yeah!" Kitty and Bart nod. Even Haribon bobs his head.

"No," I say.

Everyone turns to look at me.

"No, I mean, we don't have to ask her to be our friend," I explain hurriedly. As nice as this girl is, she's still a goddess who can turn everyone on the balcony into ashes if her temper goes supernova. "It's just that I feel Tala is already our friend. I'm pretty sure she's the one who saved us at Mount Banahaw. That light from the star. It was you, wasn't it?"

"Yes, it was me!" Tala hugs me and Kitty tight, then releases us just as fast. She does a quick dance on the balcony. "Hooray! I have friends!"

Kitty, Bart, and I exchange a grin. Carmen the bully seems like a distant memory now. Because in this world, there are beings who actually want to be friends with us.

When Tala is done dancing, she makes herself comfortable on the balcony railing, perching on it like Haribon. "Anyway, since we're friends now, I'm going to grant Lulu's wish."

Haribon lets out a raspy quack. If I didn't know better, that's the duck equivalent of a laugh.

"I wished on a shooting star," I mumble, avoiding Bart's and Kitty's curious stares. "Haribon said it isn't real."

Bart snorts. "You wished on a bulalakaw?"

"Why? What's wrong with wishing on a shooting star?" Kitty asks.

"Wishing on a shooting star is a Western concept, my friends," Tala explains kindly. "Your ancestors feared bulalakaws. They believed them to be firebirds bringing pestilence to the land. Anyway, it doesn't matter. We're friends, so I'm going to help you any way I can."

"Are they really diseased firebirds?"

But Tala doesn't hear my question, because she's already busy summoning the stars.

"Wow!" Kitty gasps. "It's like a meteor shower!"

"A meteor— Wait, don't do that!" I say. I don't want to

be the cause of the next great extinction just because a goddess wants to help me.

"It's not a meteor shower," Bart says, his jaw dropping in awe. "Those aren't asteroids. They're—"

"Santelmos!" Kitty claps excitedly. I don't bother asking how she knows. I'm sure it's something she learned in school, which I should probably know too but simply forgot or slept through. Thankfully, Tala spares me from Kitty's you-should-pay-attention-in-class-next-time lecture and explains what they are.

"That's right!" Tala beams. The goddess of the stars really is pretty. But she's not my type. For some weird reason, my gaze falls on Bart. The little orbs of light make him appear . . . um, well . . . cuter. "Santelmos are usually just spirits of the dead bound to the place where they died. My santelmos used to be humans in the Middleworld who dedicated their lives to studying or worshipping my stars and have chosen to serve me in their afterlives. They will help you understand."

Tala waves her hand, and the santelmos begin to grow brighter and brighter. The goddess claps and the santelmos explode into tiny specks of light, settling on the balcony floor.

"I may be alone in the sky, but I have watched the Realms for many, many years," Tala says, taking a handful of the light confetti. "My stars hold my memories of the past. Watch carefully, my friends."

Especially you, Lulu, says Tala's voice in my head. *My star memories will show you the answer to your question.*

The santelmo confetti on the floor begins to form three-dimensional drawings of a precolonial battle between two tribes—one human, one giant. It's like watching a diorama coming to life.

The human tribe is led by a woman on horseback, her sword glowing bright blue. A falcon flies behind her, putting out the eyes of her enemies with its talons and sharp beak. The humans win the battle, and they cheer on their warrior princess as the last of the giants is sent to the Underworld. "Urduja! Urduja! Urduja!" They chant the woman's name.

The figures disintegrate. This time, the confetti shows a familiar scene—a man trapped between two boulders as large and tall as a ten-story building. It's Bernardo Carpio.

"Kuya Bernardo!" says a man who appears before the trapped hero. "The plan. Do not forget the plan."

"It is not going to work!" Bernardo's voice is low and drips with self-confidence.

A Philippine eagle appears in the sky, saying, "Your Highness, let go and jump up. I will catch you!"

"I can do this, Haribon!"

Haribon?!

"Let go or you'll die, Kuya," the other man begs. "Please!"

"Nooooooo!!!"

The giant boulders crush Bernardo. Thankfully, we don't see the painful last moment, but we do hear the other man's and the talking eagle's anguished cries.

The light diorama changes to a beach scene, featuring a different man this time. It must be during the Spanish colonial period, as the rolled-up breeches and shirt he is wearing were popular with common Tagalogs during that time. The man is sleeping on a hammock tied between two coconut trees while a rooster frantically tries to wake him up. But the man stirs only when a lady in a baro't saya upends his duyan and he falls to the ground.

"Juan, my brother was waiting for you this morning!" She tells him he can't be lazy if he wants to be the Salamangkero: "Di ka puwedeng tatamad-tamad kung gusto mong maging Salamangkero."

"You call me lazy, and yet you expect so much of me," the man named Juan says. "Can I not be the Salamangkero?"

"Yes, of course, but—"

"Wonderful! Best of luck finding a new one. It has been a pleasure knowing you, Dian Masalanta." Juan gives the woman a bow and returns to his hammock.

The scene changes once again. This time it shows Manong Sol and a man in bloodied clothes with a parrot sitting on his shoulder—Andrés Bonifacio. "You have been wronged, brave warrior," says the sun god. "But we brought you back to life. Your descendants shall become as great and as brave as you, and they shall protect the Realms when the slumbering evil awakes."

"Yes, Lord Apolaki. It shall be done."

The scene disintegrates. But it's not over yet. The santelmos form another scene. This time, it's shown through a window. A boy, about six or seven years old maybe, looks over the crib of a baby girl as he holds an ice pack to his black eye.

"You can keep kicking and punching me, but I'll never, ever leave your side," he says. "I'll always be your kuya, your big brother. I love you, bunso."

The scene changes to a gathering under a balete tree. The same baby is now in the arms of someone very familiar—Tita Cecile.

"What's done is done," says the goddess. "Tatay and I made a mistake."

"I'm the only one who was tricked by that evil spirit, daughter," Sitan says, appearing in my line of sight. "Not you. It is not your fault that the baby has been separated from her family. Do not worry. Once we catch the Maligno, he will suffer the worst punishment Kasanaan can offer—"

"Still. It's both our responsibility, Tatay." She touches her nose to the baby's. "I will protect her with my life until she is old enough to come back to the City on her own."

Manong Sol comes into view. "She might need to heed the calling sooner. The Realms—"

"I don't care. I have a bond with her now. You can ask your sister if you doubt it." Tita Cecile holds the baby tight. "I'll protect her as long as I can."

"You're the goddess of broken homes. You *can't* be a mother."

"Then I'll find someone who can be her mother while I keep her safe."

"I will do my best to hide her memories of magic," says another familiar voice. It's Anagolay. "But Apolaki, anak," she says to Manang Sol, "you need to help the child. She must be ready when the time comes."

"Yes, Mother. I will make sure she grows up to be the great warrior we need. She will be the greatest of all Salamangkeros."

"It is settled, then," says the booming voice of an unfamiliar man. The diorama doesn't show him, though. "Apolaki, send a message to Mapulon to move his dambana near you. You two will need all the help you can get."

The baby starts to cry.

"Shh . . . it's okay, little Lulu. I've got you, kiddo. Shh . . ."

The baby is me?

Diorama baby Lulu spins until the scene changes again. This time, five-year-old diorama Lulu is being taught Sikaran by Manong Sol at his home in Sagitna Island. The sparring ring is surrounded by glowing Salamangka, like a boundary.

"Kick the target without taking the banana plant off its roots, Luningning," says the sun god. "You need to be precise with your strength. Concentrate!"

Diorama Lulu does a spinning back kick, and the scene changes. My diorama version is now seven years old, and she's on the roof deck of our apartment building with Mom, Kitty, and Bart.

"It's one of your songs, Lu," says Bart, cranking up the volume on his phone. "BTS!"

"Ooh! I like that one too. Louder, please. It's 'Danger,'" Kitty says, pulling diorama me and Mom to the more spacious, uncovered area of the roof deck. "You're going to love this!"

Mom pulls diorama Kitty and Lulu to her in the middle of dancing, squeezing them tight. "I love you both so much!"

"Mom! We can't breathe."

I wish I didn't let go of Mom. I'd do anything to get another hug from her right now.

The santelmos show us more recent memories. Battling the wakwak. Surviving Mount Banahaw. Holding our boat together as the sea god tries to break it apart.

Then the figures disintegrate, and the light show is over. The santelmos return to their orblike shape.

"You were raised and loved by gods, magical creatures,

and humans, Lulu," Tala says between heavy breaths. "Unlike your predecessors, you've learned to love all beings in the universe—in the Upperworld, the Middle-world, the Underworld, and the In-Between. You can bring them all together. We don't want it to be you. But the fact that we feel this way makes it even clearer that it *should* be you. I— Oh."

Tala holds on to the balcony railing. I grab her hand so she doesn't fall over.

"Are you all right, my lady?" Haribon asks as he and Kitty look on, concerned.

Bart isn't saying anything. I follow his gaze and see he's looking at my hand that's holding Tala. I yank my hand back.

"I think I need to rest." Tala touches her chest. She takes a deep breath, exhaling slowly. "I must leave you now, my friend. I have shown you what I can. But remember, even though it should be you, the choice of accepting or letting go of the Anito's gift remains in your hands. It's still up to you. Just don't forget who you are, no matter what path you take."

I nod. It's not an easy decision, but I know it's going to be the right one.

"Thank you so much!" Kitty exclaims. She pats the goddess on the shoulder. "You really don't look well. Are you sure you're okay?"

Tala looks like she's going to burst into tears any minute now. "We're really, truly friends?"

"Of course," says my sister.

"Yes." Bart and Haribon bow in response.

"Wonderful!" Tala smiles as brightly as her twinkling stars. "Call on me anytime! Just . . . not in the morning. At least for now. It takes a lot for me to stay awake in the morning, and it's even harder now with my powers being so wonky. Take care, my friends!"

Then, in a flash of bright light, Tala and her santelmos are gone.

CHAPTER TWENTY-TWO

Don't Leave Grumpy Cats Behind

I'M NOT GOING TO LIE. THE SANTELMO LIGHT SHOW IS A LOT TO PROCESS. But like I said, I know what I have to do.

I feel the Salamangka surge through me as I open my right hand. The blue light forms a small flame floating above my palm.

I choose to keep this power. To protect my loved ones—humans, creatures, and gods. To stop the Maligno from destroying the Realms. To keep the peace in the universe.

I know what I have to do, but telling my sister I want to do it is a totally different story.

"Let's go inside," Kitty says. She doesn't wait for a reply

and walks right in. Haribon, Bart, and I join her at the coffee table, where our barely eaten dinner sits cold.

Bart is the first to break the silence. "Haribon really is a haring ibon. A bird king. So cool."

Haribon puffs up his chest. I guess that's the duck version of flexing muscles. Cute.

"Right?" I say, grinning. "And Bernardo Carpio! Can you believe it? He was a Salamangkero. Just like me!"

"No. You don't have to be the Salamangkero, Ate."

All of us turn to look at Kitty.

My pulse quickens. Here we go. I *knew* she wouldn't like my choice.

"Tala said so herself: you can choose not to." Kitty purses her lips. She reminds me of my math teacher whenever I forget to submit an assignment. "You saw the scenes," she says. "There's a guy who turned it down—"

"Yes, someone did. *Juan Tamad.*" I narrow my eyes. Bart puts a hand on my shoulder, but I shrug it off. "Don't tell me you didn't get the connection. Every cautionary tale about laziness that we studied in school features this guy. You know, like that one where he's mistakenly buried alive by monkeys because he did nothing but sleep all day? You want me to be like that?"

"Don't mock me. You know that's not what I meant." Kitty's eyes narrow and her nostrils flare—a bad combination. "Why can't we just find Mom and go?"

"And then what?" I ball my fists, and they glow blue.

“Just let the Maligno keep using my relative as a bodysuit? Keep causing chaos?”

Haribon steps between us and spreads his wings wide. “That is enough. Let us all just go to bed and discuss this tomorrow with cooler heads.”

“No.” Kitty crosses her arms over her chest. “I will not sleep until I talk some sense into my sister.”

“Sense? You’re the one being unreasonable! Didn’t you pay attention to Tala and her light show?” I fling my glowing fist, accidentally releasing the Salamangka at a flower vase. The rose petals burst into flames. Oops. “I’m not going to give this back. I’m going to be the Salamangkero.”

Kitty stands up to help Haribon and Bart put out the fire. “Now look what you’ve done. Your carelessness is really going to get us killed.”

Okay. I am a bit worried that I did something that could have set our room on fire. But I’m too angry. Thankfully, though, Haribon and Bart extinguish the flames before Kitty can assist them.

“You’re making me super angry!” I say. “It’ll be all your fault if we end up dying in a fire.”

“My fault?” Kitty says. “How can this be *my* fault? ARGH!” She pulls at her hair in frustration. It’s not fair. If I do that, I’ll pull off every strand on my head. She has it so easy, and she has absolutely no idea. “*You* were the one who chose to make this hard on both of us. You could have just given that power back, but *no-ooo*. You had to pick the path where you can show off and be the hero."

Oh.

I see. So this is what all this drama is about.

"You know as well as I do that that's not the case." I stare Kitty straight in the eye. "You're jealous."

Kitty's lower lip trembles. She opens her mouth to speak but changes her mind. Without a word, she grabs her bag from the bedside table and heads for the door.

"Where do you think you're going?" This is really getting out of hand. Kitty is making a huge deal out of something so simple. "We're not done yet."

"We are. We are so done talking. It's pointless arguing with someone as self-centered as you." Kitty swings the door open. "I'm bunking with Paloma and Gamila. Or wherever. As long as it's not here!"

"Fine!" I say hotly. If she thinks I'm stopping her, I'm not.

"Fine!" Kitty looks over her shoulder to glare at me. "Take your medicine!"

"I already did." Actually, I haven't yet, but I don't want to admit that I need her to remind me. "And I'm your ate! You should—"

BANG! Kitty slams the door.

"She's so disrespectful! I'm going to make her—" I feel a tug on my shorts. I look down and see the duck pulling on the hem. "What are you doing?"

Haribon releases my shorts. "Just let her go. You're both too upset right now."

"She's just so frustrating!"

"He's right, Lu," Bart says in a quiet voice. "Let Kitty go."

I glare at him. "What? Are you going to tell me to give back my powers too?"

"No, I won't tell you what to do. But I'm not going to lie and say I'm happy it's you."

"Why? You don't think I can handle it?" I hope he doesn't say I can't because it will hurt, but I *need* to hear him say it anyway. Kitty, who's been a supportive sister since forever until now, doesn't seem to think I can. If Bart doesn't believe in me either, I'd like to know now that I'll be handling this Salamangkero thing all by myself.

"Of course not." Bart's jaw clenches. "I'm certain you can handle anything. But I'm your best friend, Lu. I'll always be worried about you and, at the same time, support whatever you decide."

"Thanks." I breathe a sigh of relief. I'm so glad he thinks that way.

"Anyway, I'd better head out and catch your sister," he says. "She doesn't know where Paloma's and Gamila's rooms are. The barracks is quite big; she'll surely get lost." He says good night to Haribon and heads for the door. "See you tomorrow, Lu."

It's a great feeling when you know you have friends you can depend on.

"I'm guessing you're not sleepy yet." Haribon tilts his head. "Go get your belt bag."

"Why?" I ask the duck as I take an anti-epilepsy tablet

from the pillbox in my belt bag and down it with a glass of water. Thankfully, Bart and Haribon didn't use up the entire pitcher of water when they put out the flames from the flowers I burned with Salamangka.

Haribon shakes his feathers. "We're going for a walk."

I've gotten so used to talking to Haribon that there are times I forget he's a duck. This is not one of those times.

When he said we were going for a walk, I expected a stroll around the courtyard. Or, at most, around the whole Balay Dayao compound. But no. The duck's idea of a walkathon is to make me jog nonstop from the main house all the way to Bonifacio Park and around the Sacred Lake while he flies by my side.

"Can we stop for a bit?" I gasp, holding on to the railing around the lake for dear life. "Are you trying to kill me?"

"No. Just tire you out," the duck says, looking at me with his beady stare. "Are you still angry?"

"I'm sweaty, exhausted, and possibly dying of thirst." I turn to my right. "Meow, can I have water—oh."

"She's not here." The duck flies up three feet and lands on the other side of the railing. "Climb over the fence. The water in the lake is clean."

"Is this legal?" I ask, but I follow the duck anyway. "If I get in trouble for this, you're bailing me out."

The duck flaps his wings. "I'm the Omen-Bringer. This is official Order of Apolaki business."

"You're making that up." I drink a handful of cool lake water. It's refreshing and sweet and has an aftertaste I've never had when drinking water. If I tried this in any of Metro Manila's rivers, I'd probably sprout an extra arm or grow scales or something. That's assuming I survived the severe pooping. "This is good. So refreshing!"

"Told you." Haribon dunks his entire head into the water. I can see it's taking every bit of his self-control not to dive right in. "I'm not making up the Order of Apolaki," he says. "Paloma and Gamila are part of it. Bart's grandfather is one of its generals. Your brother is one of its officers and your father is the leader. We answer directly to Lord Apolaki. Since you're the Salamangkero, you're automatically part of it."

I smirk. "What are you, then? The mascot?"

"No. I already told you." The duck shakes his feathers. "I'm the Omen-Bringer!"

Haribon settles on the shore of the lake. He's close enough that the water touches his feathery chest every now and then, but far enough to keep relatively dry. I sit beside him, following his gaze to the giant tree on the islet in the middle of the lake, Bathala's Tree.

"Before I became the Omen-Bringer, I used to live with my own kind. We're tigmamanukan. Omen creatures. Batala, our land—"

"Bathala?"

"Batala, as in, *bah-tah-lah*," the duck says slowly. "Batala is a place—not the Supreme God. The Almighty Bathala's name has an *h* in it like *bat-hah-lah*."

"Got it. Okay, so why aren't you in Batala, then? Did you get locked out or something?"

"Batala is similar to Maharlika City in the sense that it's a land in the In-Between, protected by magic. But omen creatures like myself can go back there anytime." The duck pauses. "I chose not to return just yet."

"Why?"

"Because of you," Haribon says without hesitation.

"Hey, I didn't ask you to—"

"You didn't, I just chose to. Even creatures are given free will; it isn't solely a human concept." The duck narrows his eyes. "Urduja, Bernardo, Juan, Andrés, and now you. I chose to be by every Salamangkero's side from beginning to end. But you need to remember that this isn't your burden alone. You have me. You have allies. You have friends. And most especially, you have your sister."

I look at Bathala's Tree to avoid Haribon's gaze. Patches of glowing blue light momentarily appear between the balete's oversized vines. Back in Caloocan, that would have alarmed a lot of people. But here in Maharlika City, where there's an abundance of Salamangka, it's perfectly normal.

"Do you know the hardest thing about being immortal? It's outliving everyone you care about." Haribon moves to sit closer to me, so close that the feathers of his right wing touch my skin. "My body withers and dies; their bodies wither and die. Still, I choose to be reborn so I can be with the next Salamangkero. Even though I know I'll be broken when they leave me, the friendship and the good times we'll have are very much worth the heartache."

"I'm sorry."

"Don't be. It's a known fact that being left behind hurts a lot." Haribon looks up to meet my gaze. "Can't you see how Kitty feels, Lulu? Like Bart, she will support whatever you decide. But she's afraid to lose you to this new life you'll have as a Salamangkero."

That's ridiculous. "I want her to be a part of it. I won't leave her behind!"

The duck tilts his head in my direction. "Then tell her that. Talking about it will go a long way."

"You're right." I've been so focused on how I feel that I didn't notice I've been neglecting my sister. She needs to know that I can't do this without her. "Let's go, Hari—"

BANG! There's a loud explosion behind Bathala's Tree.

Haribon and I drop to the ground. The duck covers my head with his wings. "Stay down."

From the ground, we see a flurry of soldiers running in the direction of the compound.

Oh no. Kitty and Bart!

I get to my feet and hold out my arm. Haribon flies up to it, climbing onto my shoulder. He's got great balance for a duck. Which isn't surprising, after all, because he once was a brave Philippine eagle who fought with Bernardo Carpio in battle. "Hold tight, Bird King."

We hurry back to the main house as fast as we can.

CHAPTER TWENTY-THREE

Battle-Ready, Bulletproof Duck Scout

THE MAIN HOUSE IS IN CHAOS.

The soldiers are boarding up the windows while the household staff are packing all the family heirlooms and valuables they can save. The living room has been turned into a makeshift armory, arrows and swords strewn all over the sofa and coffee table. Gamila is manning the evacuation, shouting orders at her walkie-talkie. In the dining room, Paloma and Tita Ligaya have a glowing three-dimensional map (kind of like Tala's light show) spread out on the table while they discuss strategy.

Two men—the two men who are supposed to be the leaders of this warrior clan—are visibly missing.

"Where are Papa and Kuya Yani?" I ask.

There's a buzzing sound as Tita Ligaya wheels over to meet me and Haribon.

"Wow, Tita," I say. "That wheelchair is awesome!" It's made of gold and pearl and hovers a foot above the ground as it glows with Salamangka. Attached to the armrests are two huge cannons and a bunch of buttons that probably hide even more awesome weapons.

"Thank you, anak." The lakambini's lips form a grim line. "I believe your brother has been looking for your father."

Haribon shakes his feathers in irritation. "The Supremo is missing?"

"Don't judge him too harshly. It is not cowardice that made him leave, but the need to protect his children," says Tita Ligaya. "Gamila will tell you what happened."

The lakambini bows to Haribon and me before returning to the dining table map.

What in the Realms was that? I thought she was cool.

I don't know about Tita Ligaya, but leaving right in the middle of an attack on your city—your home—sounds very much like cowardice to me. Manong Sol would have chased me to the ends of the Realms if I did something like that.

A familiar whiff of sea salt and caramel reaches my nose. I turn and find Paloma standing in front of me. Behind her, as usual, is Gamila.

"Omen-Bringer, you need to evacuate with Gamila and the trainees," Paloma says. "It's not safe for you here."

"I can manage." The duck huffs, obviously offended. "I've been in more battles than your ages put together, young lady."

Paloma simply shrugs, her gorgeous black hair bouncing on her shoulders. It's like watching a shampoo commercial in the middle of a . . . well . . . terrorist attack.

"Where's my sister?" I ask. "She said she'd be bunking with you."

"She was. She's safe, don't worry." Paloma nods.

I breathe a huge sigh of relief. Thank the gods!

Paloma's walkie-talkie beeps. "Excuse me."

"Bart evacuated with her as soon as we heard the explosion," Gamila recounts in her usual reassuring tone. She's wearing a hijab of an unusual material—rubbery, with a pearl-like sheen. "Your aswang friend seems pretty nifty with the spear. So we were assured your sister is in good hands."

Trust no one but your sister and your friends. That's what Amanikable said. Bart definitely has my trust. He's back to being one of my Peanut People again, and I'll give him a hug when I see him.

A *friend* hug, of course.

"He's the only one we could trust to protect your sister," Paloma says, lowering her voice. She looks warily around her. "It's hard to know who's with us. The evil spirts are great at hiding. A group of possessed soldiers planted a bomb at the compound's south gate. The explosion took down an entire wall."

"But the gods aren't in the best shape," Gamila says, pursing her lips. "It's like what happened in the Underworld. Explosion. Attack. Escape."

Haribon and I exchange glances. Chaos. The Maligno is seeding chaos.

"There's one thing I don't understand. . . ." I furrow my brows in concentration. Something's still missing. I need to figure this out. "Why force entry into a compound that's practically a fortress?"

"Komandante Yani believes they might be after a relic in the vault," Gamila answers. "We have soldiers guarding it now. But the lakambini believes otherwise, so we're also sending out troops all over the City and asking reserves to protect their homes."

"You should call on your retired soldiers."

"We have."

"Okay, then." I square my shoulders. "How can we help?"

"Battle gear crash course first." Gamila points at my shirt. "There's a button on the left hem of your shirt. Press it."

I do as Gamila says. Sure enough, pearly white sleeves appear on my arms. They're very lightweight, but tough like oyster shells. "Cool!"

Paloma nods at Haribon. "You need to protect the Omen-Bringer," she says to me.

"Hoy!" The duck wiggles his cute, fluffy butt in irritation. "I said—"

"Yes, yes. You've seen many battles." Paloma waves his complaints away. "But now you're in the body of a duck, and you're going to need extra protection."

I tug at my shirt. Maharlikan crafters are great at making battle-ready clothes. "Didn't you make him a bulletproof duck vest or something?"

"He has one, but he's too embarrassed to wear it." Gamila tosses me a vest. It's like a dog's vest but made with the same rubbery, pearl-like material as Gamila's hijab.

"I am the Bird King; I do not wear ridiculous human outfits!" Haribon flaps his wings, as if his bird king–ness isn't clear enough.

"Hay naku, suotin mo na lang kasi." I tell him to just wear it already. Before he can protest, I grab him from behind, holding him down as Gamila puts the vest on him. He tries to struggle, but of course he's no match for the magical strength of the Salamangkero.

Gamila beams at Haribon. "Now you look battle ready!"

A small smile touches Paloma's lips. She really is pretty when she smiles. But looking at the dressed-up Haribon, I can't help but remember Bart in Tannie mode. An image of the black puppy in seasonal dog clothes makes me smile.

I guess this is what happens when you're close to death. You reminisce about the people you love, the ones you'll leave once you move on to the Underworld.

"Kagawad Paloma, we need help with the windows!" a soldier calls from the other side of the room.

"We got this," I assure her. Paloma gives me a grateful nod as I take one of the wooden boards. It doesn't weigh a thing, but I've seen that three soldiers are required to lift it, so it must be heavy. I bring the board across the room, the duck waddling behind me. "Did you know that while BTS is the English acronym for Beyond the Scene, the band still uses their original Korean moniker, Bangtan Sonyeondan?"

"This compound is about to burn to the ground," Haribon hisses. "You expect me to listen to random facts about your favorite band *right now*?"

"Bangtan Sonyeondan roughly translates to 'Bulletproof Boy Scouts.'" I set the board down and clap dust off my hands.

"And I need to know this because . . ."

"You're a BDS." I burst out laughing. "Bulletproof *Duck* Scout!"

"That's not even funny. Just board up that window and let's go. I'd rather watch you in battle than listen to your pathetic jokes." Haribon's head feathers fluff up in irritation, making me laugh even harder. He starts pecking at his vest, but he can't remove it. Like I said, the Maharlikans really know how to design battle gear.

As I lift the board into place, I notice movement in the garden between the main house and the trainees' mess hall.

"This is demeaning, embarrassing—"

"Shh! Haribon, come up here."

Without hesitation, Haribon flies up to my shoulder. "Is that the Supremo?"

"I don't know."

At the far end of the compound, a man is pushing his way through a wall of bamboo grass. He's trying to get into the space between the tree trunks.

"It's too dark," I complain, squinting. "I can't see—"

Right on cue, the stars in the sky twinkle at the same time. The light they radiate illuminates the man's face.

I stifle a gasp. Haribon's right. It *is* Papa.

"Thanks, Tala," I murmur. Having a friend in such high places really does have its perks. Anyway— "What is he doing? Where's he going?"

"AH-TEH!"

My heart sinks at the sound of a familiar voice.

Kitty runs past the dining room and into the living room, where Haribon and I are. The duck has barely gotten off my shoulder when Kitty throws her arms around me. Behind her is Bart.

No, no, no! She shouldn't be here.

"Hoy! Bakit andito pa rin kayo?" I demand to know why they're still here. "You should evacuate!"

Bart wipes sweat off his forehead. "I'm sorry, Lu. But he has her."

"I don't . . ." I gulp. I hope he doesn't mean what I think he means. "What do you mean?"

Kitty takes a step back to meet my gaze. "Ate, the Supremo took Mom."

No way. "How can you be so sure?"

Bart shows me a piece of paper. "He dropped this on his way out to the garden."

With shaking fingers, I read the note. The note that's obviously, 100 percent meant for me. My heart sinks lower than the lowest level of the Underworld. It says:

Meet me at the foot of Bathala's Tree when fire burns in the sky.

I have your mother.

CHAPTER TWENTY-FOUR

A Mother for the Sword

I WANT TO THROW UP.

I can't believe it. My biological father, the Supremo, is the Maligno's host—he's the one who kidnapped Mom. It sounds like the plot of a TV family drama, but it's actually happening in my life. To *my* family.

There's a tug on the hem of my shorts.

"Focus, Lulu," says Haribon, his beak full of cloth. "Don't let your emotions overwhelm you. We need to save your mother."

Haribon's right.

I need to study the facts. I take a deep breath. "Okay. Papa dropped the note, but that doesn't mean he's the one who wrote it. He could have found it and gone to find out whoever it is himself."

"He left once Komandante Yani told him that the possessed had broken through the gates," Bart says in a quiet voice. "Komandante Yani followed him."

"They were gone longer than they should have been," Kitty says, "but Gamila wanted us to evacuate, so we went with the trainees." Her voice sounds hoarse. She brings out her water tumbler and takes a drink. "We were somewhere in the barracks when we heard a soldier say that your brother was injured."

"Papa wouldn't hurt Kuya Yani—"

"Komandante Yani ordered his men to find your father and arrest him," Bart mumbles. "We couldn't believe it either, so we broke away from the group to look for the Supremo ourselves."

"We saw your father on the west side of the compound, and he dropped the note along the way." Kitty bites her lower lip. "Your father looked like he was in a really bad fight, Ate."

"I've known your father since the day he was born, Lulu," Haribon says. "He would never abandon his troops during an attack. Unless—"

"—he's been possessed," I finish for him. I lean on the windowsill before my knees buckle. It's hard to deny it, especially when there are witnesses. Even I saw him skulking about. The evidence is clear—Papa took Mom and hurt Kuya Yani.

Haribon climbs back up onto my shoulder and gives it a reassuring squeeze. "We'll bring him to the lakambini and she'll get the Maligno out. A katalonan like her can do that."

"No. *I'll* find a way." I glance in my aunt's direction, remembering how just moments ago, she insisted her brother wasn't a coward. I grab Bart's arm. "Dude, can you bring Kitty— Meow, what do you think you're doing?"

"I'm going to fight with you."

"No."

"Yes." Kitty brings out her bow and takes an arrow from her Pringles container. She sets the arrow to stun mode. "I'll spot you from behind. And I've always had the better aim between the two of us."

As hard as it is for me to admit, Kitty has a point. Still— "You might get hurt."

"So could you." Kitty continues to fill her canister with stun arrows. "You're just superstrong, Ate. But you're not invincible."

I rub my temples. Kitty really is testing me. "We don't have time for this. Bart, can you just drag her to safety or something?"

To my surprise, Bart doesn't say anything. He simply tests out the tip of his sibat, waving the spear aloft.

"Bart!" I say in a louder voice.

"I heard you." But Bart still doesn't look up.

"My sister—"

"No, Lu," says Bart, his voice firm as he finally meets

my gaze. His irises turn red. I'm once again reminded how dangerous an aswang he can be. And . . . well . . . kind of cute. "Let your sister fight."

"Fine. Let's just all die together."

If Kitty is scared of getting hurt, she doesn't show it. To her credit, she's really trying her best to put on a brave face.

Kitty, Bart, Haribon, and I follow my father's path through the wall of bamboo. Beyond it, there's a hidden door that leads to an underground tunnel. It's hard to see, but the glowing balls of Salamangka every few feet light the way.

The walls of the brick labyrinth are damp with water leaking from the ceiling. I'm guessing we're walking beneath the compound moat, but I don't ask Haribon to confirm. I worry that the sound of my voice will carry through the tunnel, and my father will know we're onto him.

I don't know how long this tunnel is, but we've been walking for at least twenty minutes now. We're all sweaty and thirsty by the time we finally see the end—where we see my father entering a door.

I gesture for us to slow down. Bart and I get our weapons ready as Haribon nudges the door open with his beak.

To our surprise, the door reveals a moss-covered stairwell leading up to a forest area.

"Bathala's Tree," Haribon murmurs. "We're on the islet of Bathala's Tree."

Sure enough, we see the giant tree towering over all others in the middle of this tiny piece of land. Even from ten feet away, the balete's oldest vines are as wide as a refrigerator. The spaces they create are big enough for a man to crawl into, to hide . . .

"Please help me!" someone cries.

. . . Or to keep someone prisoner.

Papa runs to a cage made of small intertwined vines. He tries to pull them apart, but the vines don't budge. He takes a step back, revealing the prisoner.

"MOM!"

Bart and Haribon try to stop me and my sister, but we shrug them off. I run to my father and disarm him, letting Bart bind his wrists and ankles. Surprisingly, he doesn't struggle or try to fight back.

"Mom!" Kitty sobs. "You're alive."

"My sweet buko pies," Mom says in a voice that sounds like her throat is dry because she hasn't been getting enough water. Her eyes are bloodshot, and she has cuts and bruises on her arms. Seeing them makes me angry.

"GET OUT OF MY FATHER, MALIGNO!" I shout, feeling the Salamangka surge through my body. My balled fists glow with blue light.

"What do you mean, anak?" Papa stares at my glowing hands warily.

"It's not him, buko pie," my mother croaks. "He didn't hurt me."

Kitty reaches through the intertwined vines to take our mother's hand. "It's okay, Mom. Ate and Haribon will find a way to get you out of there and free the Supremo of the Maligno."

"No, really. It's not him!" she says.

I gently pull my sister from the cage. "Mom, stay in the corner. I'm going to try to lift . . . this . . . vine . . . AHH!"

I lift the vine, and some blue light comes out, but the vine snaps back down again.

"Oh, bunso. You must preserve your strength and stop wasting it on that futile attempt." It's Kuya Yani speaking. He comes out from behind the tree and climbs over the large vines, landing in front of us. He smooths down his shirt and fixes the knapsack hoisted on his shoulder.

One by one, his soldiers come out of the shadows. Archers. Infantry. Kuya Yani's loyal regiment, minus Paloma and Gamila.

I slowly make my way back to Kitty, Bart, and Haribon. The hairs at the back of my neck stand up. My "Lulu-Tingle" is ringing alarm bells. Something doesn't feel right.

Mom lets out an audible gasp. "Girls, leave now! It's him!"

Kuya Yani's troops point their arrows and swords at our group.

What in the Realms is going on?

"No way." I shake my head. Kuya Yani can't be the one possessed by the Maligno. "It can't be you!"

"Well, it is me. Mind you, it hasn't been easy." The Maligno rolls his head. When he looks at me again, his brown irises have turned red, and his face is contorted with a grotesque smile. "The City is well-protected, and I needed someone from the Bonifacio family who knew where you were hidden in the Middleworld. But none of them wanted to risk your safety, so I had to plant visions in Yani's mind that he must check on you. His loyalty and his need to protect you almost cost me my plan. My prison in the Underworld dampened my powers so it took some time to push him, but he broke eventually. He secretly left the City to check on you, unknowingly leading me to where you were and allowing me to take over his body once I broke free."

"Hay. Sabi na nga ba." The Supremo heaves a long, sad sigh. He looks defeated. "I knew it."

"Papa?" I turn to face him. "What do you mean?"

"Bravo, bravo!" The Maligno claps his hands. "Since when did you know?" he asks the Supremo.

"I've suspected since you insisted that Lulu open the vault." The Supremo hangs his head. "I never considered the possibility of my own son being possessed until you mentioned that. My Yani would have recognized his own sister, the same way Ligaya and I knew it was her."

"You truly deserve the Supremo title, Papa." The Maligno lifts the agimat out of his shirt and waves it at me. "Thanks, by the way, baby sis. I wouldn't have gotten this back without your help."

Papa gasps. "But I went back in to check on the agimat! It was still there!"

"A great craftsman believes in my cause," the Maligno says, "and he created a perfect duplicate of the stone for me." The Maligno in my brother's body smirks. "You would never have known the difference."

"You used me," I say through gritted teeth. I can't believe I fell for it so easily and didn't even suspect a thing. He insisted on testing me with the opening of the vault. But all along, he was the one who was carrying the despicable evil spirit. Had he tried to open the vault himself, he'd have been found out. He needed me to open it for him.

The Maligno needed me so he could take his agimat.

"Leave my son's body, Maligno!" Papa shouts as I break his bonds.

"You're an evil, evil man," I say to the Maligno. I grasp the hilt of my buntot pagi in my pocket with one hand and the folded balisong with the other. He'll pay for this. "Is that why you took my mom? To make me get that disgusting thing for you?"

"That, and one other thing. We'll discuss that in a bit. Let me introduce myself first." The Maligno bows theatrically. My brother's body emits black smoke, black smoke that momentarily gathers to form the silhouette of a man.

"Hello, Salamangkero," says the smoke. "It is I, Restituto, the great sorcerer who brought Bernardo Carpio to his knees and sent him to the Underworld. It is also I who has weakened the gods. They are so eager to keep mankind in the dark, they used up their magic to deceive the humans. And now look at them. They are nothing but useless, drained little gods!"

Restituto goes back to Kuya Yani's body, making his eyes glow red again. "You shall now do something for me, Lulu Sinagtala."

"You serious?" I snort. The Maligno hasn't spied on me well enough. If he had, he'd have known he'd never be able to make me do anything for him. "Why would I do that?"

"Because you want your mother back." Restituto touches his agimat, and blue light comes out of it. It circles the tree, then drops to the roots. The Salamangka lights up a section of the vines, which reveal a trapped saber—a sword once used by the Spanish colonizers of the Philippines. "Free my sword, and I shall let your mother go."

I take a step back. My mother for a sword. He just wants his sword, and I get my mother back.

"Lulu, it's a trick. Don't do it!" Haribon hops onto my

shoulder. He pecks at my hair and flaps his wings in agitation. "Trying to remove it could kill you. And that is the same weapon he used to channel the magic that trapped Bernardo Carpio!"

"It's true." The Maligno shrugs. "But I'm also the only one who can get your mother out of that cage."

Now I can fully understand why Warren the wakwak agreed to kidnap my mother. The Maligno gave him no other choice. His mother or mine. Obviously, he'd pick his mom. And I'll do the same.

"I'll do it. I'll get the sword."

Haribon sighs, defeated. He flies off my shoulder and lands in front of me.

"Lulu, no! Don't!" Mom sobs. She turns to the Supremo. "Stop her, don't let her do this. She's your daughter! This tree . . . it's too powerful. The effort could kill her."

At my side, Kitty is sobbing. Bart's face is streaked with tears.

Will the worlds end once I give the Maligno back his sword? Probably not.

It will be difficult to stop him from wreaking havoc, though. And I might actually die trying to fix things.

But this is Mom we're talking about. I promised my sister we'd get her back, and I have no intention of breaking that vow.

I hold the vines clutching the sword and pull them apart with all my soul and being.

My muscles scream in agony, but I hold on.

"AHH!" With one hard yank, the vines finally come loose.

Restituto reaches from behind me and pulls the sword out. "Thank you!"

My knees give way. But Kitty, Bart, and Papa catch me from behind. Haribon gently pecks at my cheek.

"You promised," I manage to croak. "You said you'd let Mom go."

"Yes, I did." Restituto brandishes his sword and points at Mom's cage. "A promise is a promise. Unlike the gods, I keep my promises."

The intertwined vines that form the bars ebb away.

"MOM!"

Kitty and I run to our mother. We sob as we hug her tight.

"My girls," she cries. "My sweet buko pies."

"Touching, touching," Restituto says. "How very touching."

Kitty, Bart, Haribon, Papa, and I form a protective circle around Mom. He will not lay a hand on her ever again.

"Relax. I just want to talk." Restituto raises his hands in mock surrender.

"Fine. Talk." I'll let him talk, all right. I'll let him talk long enough that I can gather enough strength to rip that disgusting maligno out of my brother's body.

"I was betrayed by my people. Then betrayed by my

Spanish allies. Humans know nothing but betrayal—just like their gods." Restituto spits on the ground. "The gods have done nothing but sit on their thrones in their dambanas, expecting fealty while giving nothing back. They torture our brethren, claiming to be experts on what is wrong and what is right. I say enough of that!"

There are grumbles and angry shouts from his troops. "Enough! Enough! Enough!"

"The Realms belong to people and creatures. We will put the gods where they belong. In nothingness and in death!"

"Death! Death! Death!"

These men, these supposedly possessed men, rally behind Restituto like mindless drones and overzealous members of a disturbing and very messed-up fandom. A fandom willing to kill. A fandom of corrupt souls determined to rule the Realms. It's the worst fandom of its kind.

"Join us, Lulu Sinagtala. Join us and be free from constant servitude to the gods." Restituto offers me his hand. "With your powers and mine together, we can easily dispose of the gods. We will rule the Realms together and create a new universe."

"Join us! Join us! Join us!"

What Restituto just said reminds me of something I've heard before. *He shall rise to power once again. And the worlds are ours.*

It was never about freedom. It was all about power.

"The Anito has already given me this," I say with a smirk, waving my Salamangka'd fist at him. "So, no thanks."

"You will die, then." Restituto scowls. He nods at his men. "Kill them, except for the child. Maim her enough that I can finish her off myself and use her soul's Salamangka to open this portal."

Kitty, Bart, and Papa hold their weapons aloft. They activate their handheld shields, which glow with Salamangka.

I ready my balisong and buntot pagi. "Get behind us, Mom."

I spin the stingray tail just like Tita Cecile taught me. This time, I spin even faster. Faster and faster until the buntot pagi forms a shield of glowing blue light.

Restituto's archers pull on their bowstrings.

"Would appreciate some godly help here," I say, looking up at the stars. "Tala! I would like to live a little longer, please."

The stars twinkle bright in response. *Close your eyes, my friends. In three . . . two . . .*

A great ball of light explodes at the foot of Bathala's Tree—a blinding light, like a star going supernova.

CHAPTER TWENTY-FIVE

Enemies Then, Enemies Now

TALA'S BLAST NOT ONLY STOPS RESTITUTO'S MEN FROM SHOOTING AT us, it also disarms them as the starlight melts their weapons.

The light from the exploding ball gathers to form the silhouette of a young girl: Tala.

The goddess of stars gasps, staggering backward.

Luckily, Kitty catches her. "Tala!"

Restituto really thought his plan through. It's evil, but genius. He made sure to incapacitate the gods so he could do whatever he wanted.

I glance in his direction. He's managed to deflect Tala's starlight, but I'm pleased to see him scrambling to get his troops back in order. Tala gave us time; we have to make good use of it.

Papa steps in front of me and bows. "Let us know your orders, Salamangkero."

"Papa—"

"You are the Salamangkero." He squeezes my shoulders. "You were trained by Lord Apolaki himself, the god of warriors. No one is better to lead us than you."

I nod. I'm going to get us through all this. "Tala, you need to rest. Stay with Mom. Haribon, can you make sure Mom and Tala—"

Haribon bows. "I will protect them with my life. Come with me!"

"Be careful, my sweets," Mom says, putting Tala's arm around her shoulders and lifting the goddess before following the duck.

As Haribon ushers Mom and Tala to safety, he pecks at something on his chest. Two tiny mechanical arms burst out from the sides of his vest, zapping Salamangka at anyone who tries to stop them. The duck's enemies get stunned and fall to the ground.

Haribon quacks as he waves the mechanical arms in glee. "This is quite impressive. I think I will have shoes made."

A vision of Haribon in a duck vest while wearing duck shoes pops into my head. I push the distracting (and hilarious) thought away to address my remaining companions.

"Papa, Bart, take the left side. Kitty and I will take the other." I ball my right hand into a fist and make it glow with Salamangka. "Be careful. We got this! Now move close to me. I'll scatter our enemies a bit."

I drop to a knee and punch the ground with my glowing fist. Remembering my training with Manong Sol, I focus energy into my punch. It creates a wave on the ground like Restituto's tremor. But instead of causing a Realms-wide catastrophe, my focused wave only upends our enemies. "Gosh, I'm so awesome."

Bart snorts. His expression then softens. I know it's not a good time, but he's really cute with his eyes so intense like that. "Good luck, Lu."

"You too." I crack my whip at an attacking soldier, and he falls. I turn and hit another one with the hilt of my bal-isong. Slowly but surely, we inch toward Restituto, who's barking orders from his vine shelter like the bossy cow-ard that he is.

Papa reaches him first, with Bart close behind.

"Ha! It's far from over, little girl!" Restituto says, slash-ing at Papa, who narrowly avoids getting hit. Restituto lunges at Bart, who instantly transforms into a dog and doesn't get stabbed.

"You're going to pay for that," I growl. My maligno-possessed brother lunges for me again, but this time I'm ready. I spin and kick the sword out of his hand.

"Ahhhhh!" Kuya Yani, the real Kuya Yani, screams in

agony. Then, just as suddenly as he started, he stops and laughs hysterically, Restituto in control of his body once again. "Your life would have been different if Sitan hadn't listened to my whispers that your birth meant his doom. He wouldn't have ordered his daughter to take you from your family."

I pause. "His daughter?"

"Yes. Mansisilat is the one who removed you from the City." The Maligno laughs again, angering me even more. "Your beloved tita Cecile."

"Don't listen to him!" I hear Haribon shout from behind a tree.

I ball my fists, and they glow with Salamangka.

"Anak, calm down," Papa says.

"He's messing with you, Lu!" Bart calls to me. "Block him out."

"Ate, please . . ." Kitty cries.

"It was you who ruined my family!" I scream at the evil spirit. I'm breathing heavily. The Salamangka on my fists glows even brighter. "It was because of you my entire life was full of secrets and lies!"

Before I can make a move, however, Papa jumps between us. "Luningning, don't!"

My brother, Kuya Yani, his strength amplified by the Maligno's hatred-fueled power, kicks Papa into a balete vine. There's a loud, crunching sound as his bones break on impact.

CHAPTER TWENTY-SIX

My Family versus the Universe

"PAPA!" KITTY AND I RUSH TO PAPA'S SIDE WHILE BART ENGAGES THE Maligno. He brings out his sibat and deactivates its blade, turning it into a staff.

"I will be fine. Do not worry about me," my father says, wincing in pain. "Help me up, please."

Kitty supports his back, helping him sit.

"Stay here," I tell him. "Haribon is on his way."

"No. I have a plan," Papa says. His face crumples in pain, but he forces himself to straighten up. "HOY MALIGNO! Leave that boy alone and listen to me!"

Restituto, using my brother's body, punches Bart, who lands a few yards away. My heart drops, but thankfully Bart stands up and reclaims his staff.

"Bart, stop," Papa orders. My friend does what he's told, but the evil spirit doesn't heed the call for a cease-fire and grabs Bart by the collar. "Let him go, Maligno! I will make a deal with you that you cannot refuse."

That catches Restituto's attention. He lets go of Bart's shirt and puts him down on the ground.

"Take my body. Bayani is only eighteen—he is young. If you possess me, you will also have the advantage of my experience."

"Papa, what are you doing?" I ask.

He's trying to save your brother, Lulu, says Tala's voice in my head.

"Be quiet. This is between him and me," Restituto says, studying my father. "Your body is broken, but once I take over, it won't be an issue. Possessing you will give me access to your knowledge. All your knowledge. Even your secrets."

Papa seems to hesitate a bit. But he squares his shoulders and says, "Yes. You will know everything."

"Don't," I say. If Papa goes through with this, he'll give the Maligno a huge strategic advantage. He'll have Papa's knowledge of Maharlika as its Supremo at his disposal. It'll be much harder for us to stop him. And I might lose him. "That's a terrible, terrible idea."

"Can I at least say my goodbyes?" Papa asks the Maligno. "It might be a while before I have control over my body again."

The evil spirit snorts, waving his permission. "That's for certain. You will die my servant, Bonifacio spawn."

Papa holds me by the shoulders and pulls me close.

"Listen to me, Luningning. Lulu. Anak . . . you and Yani are both my children. I made a promise to your mother that I would protect you both with my dying breath—and I intend to keep it. Please, do as I say," he says. Then, lowering his voice, he adds, "Once he's in my body, kill me before he fully settles. He will be weak during the transition, and my spirit will drag him all the way to the Underworld."

Did I hear him right? Did he just ask me to *kill* him?

"Use your balisong. I love you, anak. I wish we had more time together," Papa says, squeezing me tight. Then he lets go. "I'm ready. Take me, Restituto."

I hold on to my father, but it's no use. The process has started.

The Maligno leaves my brother's body, which instantly drops to the ground, snaking its way to Papa.

As the black smoke gets absorbed by my father's body, he takes my hand one last time.

"Do it now, anak. Kill me now!"

You're not a killer, my friend, Tala's voice whispers in my head. *That is not you. Remember who you are.*

I meet my father's gaze as I bring out my balisong and flip it open. Mom always said that the eyes are the windows to one's soul—and I can see Papa inside, very clearly. He's in there. My family. My father.

It's okay. We'll defeat the Maligno some other way.

I believe Tala.

"Papa," I say, my voice breaking. "I'm sorry."

I plunge the knife into the ground, falling to my knees.

I can't do it. I just can't abandon him. I'll never, *ever* abandon family.

Even if it means chaos in the Realms.

There has to be another way.

Papa stands up, dusting his pants, injuries forgotten. The Maligno has taken full control. He takes his agimat from my brother's slumbering body along with his knapsack, flinging it over his shoulder.

"Ah. This man has so many secrets," he says, cracking his neck. He picks up my balisong, studying it. "Government secrets. War strategies. Family secrets. And my favorite of all—Lulu secrets. Oh, not just Lulu secrets. Lulu and Tagalog gods kind of secrets. The things I now know are going to make your head spin, Salamangkero."

"Get your filthy soul out of him!" I scream as tears run down my cheeks. "Give him back!"

"ATE, WATCH OUT!"

Too late.

Everything happens like a slow-motion sequence in a movie. I see the blade of the knife I was supposed to stab Papa with flying straight at my chest.

The Maligno not only inherited all the secrets of Maharlika, but Papa's knife-throwing skills as well.

Resigned to my fate, I close my eyes and brace myself for the pain.

I hope it won't hurt for too long. Make it a quick death, please.

No, friend. I got you.

I open my eyes to find a ball of light in front of me. It solidifies into the form of a young girl. A young girl with a dagger in her chest. "Hi."

Tala.

"This is even better," Restituto says, smiling an evil smile using my father's face. He stabs Tala again, this time in the back, with his saber. He turns his blade and pulls it right out.

The goddess gasps and falls to the ground.

"NO!"

Restituto lifts the sword, which is covered with glowing blood the color of pearls. He twirls the saber, and its tip siphons Tala's Salamangka. I try to hold on to the light, to no avail. The blade glows blue as it absorbs the magic.

"I had a blast, but I have to go," the Maligno says, pointing his saber at the balete vines, encasing them with Tala's Salamangka. The giant tree glows blue, and a doorway forms within the vines. "Rest in peace, Tala. Goodbye, everyone!"

"STOP RIGHT THERE!"

Tita Ligaya, Paloma, and Gamila have arrived with the

Maharlikan elite squad. Blue light encases Tita Ligaya and her wheelchair. But before the lakambini can attack, it's already too late.

The Maligno steps inside the portal, and the vines close behind him. Restituto is gone.

CHAPTER TWENTY-SEVEN

Ashes to Ashes, Dust to Stardust

Even before we officially met, Tala has been my light in the dark. All my life, I've never walked outside without the stars shining bright. They lit my path when the streetlights were out, they let me and Kitty play even at night.

Tala has always been with me, watching and twinkling. Shining as bright as her stars.

But now, as she lies in my arms, her light has dimmed. Her usually glowing gown is dull and covered with pearly-white blood. Her sparkling eyes have lost their shine.

The goddess of stars is dying.

"I'm so sorry, Tala." I pull her closer. "I should have listened to Papa. I should have stabbed him like he said I should. I'm so sorry."

"No, no, no. Don't think that. It was the right thing to do. You're a good person, Lulu, my friend." Tala gasps for air. "This was my choice."

"I'm so sorry."

"Don't be." Tala touches my face with trembling fingers. "Don't cry. This isn't the end of our friendship. I promise I'll see you again. I'll be in a different form, and I may not be the same Tala you know, but I'll remember you. I'll never forget that you were a friend to me."

To please her, I will myself not to cry, but it's hard. Her last wish, and I can't even grant it.

"Shh." The goddess wipes away my tears. "Don't carry the worlds on your shoulders alone, Lulu. Not everything is on you. Not everything is your fault."

Tala coughs. "Stay with me, my friends. Please stay with me to the end."

"We're here, Tala," Kitty says, stroking the goddess's hair. "We're all here for you."

"If you're feeling lost, look up to the heavens. My stars will guide your way. My friends. My dear, sweet friends . . ." Tala flickers, then she breathes her last. The stars in the night sky wail, their cries of grief heard not by our ears but by our souls and hearts.

Tala's body floats into the air. It glows with bright light one last time before finally dissolving into stardust.

The goddess of stars is no more.

CHAPTER TWENTY-EIGHT

It's All about Technicalities

For Tala's send-off, all of Maharlika gathers around in Bonifacio Park as Tita Ligaya and her katalonans light a pyre at the foot of Bathala's Tree. Members of Tala's fan club, the Starlights, sing a song for the goddess as they hold on to each other. We light candles and hold them up to the sky.

As the pyre and candles burn, little specs of light rain down from the night sky. It's as if the stars are crying for the loss of their queen.

The Maharlika elders create a flag in honor of Tala. It's adorned with a five-point star and words in Baybayin, the Tagalog script: "Tala, Ilaw ng Maharlika." Tala, the Light of Maharlika. They hang the flag beside the City's flag, the one with Manong Sol's symbol. It's the greatest honor they can give to the goddess of stars.

The mood in the compound is just as somber. Everyone, from the household staff to the military to the ordinary people, feels the loss of their Supremo.

But he's not gone. Papa's soul didn't leave his body. And I'm sure he's fighting the Maligno for control with all his might.

When I chose not to follow his instructions to end his life, I made a promise that I would get Papa back. And that's a promise I don't intend to break.

"Thank you for taking care of my children," Mom says to Tita Ligaya. Tita Ligaya and Kuya Yani take turns shaking Mom's hand as they finally "officially" greet each other. If only Tita Cecile and Papa were here, it would be the perfect family reunion. But this will do, for now.

Mom, Kitty, Bart, and I stay in Maharlika City until Christmas Eve. The Maharlikans generally don't celebrate Christmas. This holiday was brought to the Philippines by Spain, and the scars of Catholic abuse in the Spanish colonial period are still very fresh in the minds of the people in this city. But the Balay Dayao household celebrates it anyway, just for me.

I keep wondering whether all Restituto's supporters are really possessed. Or are some of them acting on their own accord? I bet I wasn't the first one he ever asked to join him.

Before the malignos became evil spirits in the Underworld, they were people. People with corrupt souls. Beings who just really wanted a part of Restituto's power.

Maharlika. Noble warrior. This is a city of noble warriors—supposedly. Can they still call themselves noble after what has been and is yet to be revealed?

Do they still deserve to be called noble warriors?

Kuya Yani has taken every opportunity to apologize to my mother. But you know Mom. "There's nothing to forgive," she says. "I know it wasn't you. It was Restituto."

It's actually harder for me. I spent time with that bad Yani, and I've seen what he did under Restituto's control. I'll need some time to get over that, so I avoid him as much as I can.

I'm going down the steps of the main house to meet Kitty, Bart, and Haribon for inihaw when I run into my brother. "Hey."

"Hey."

"So, um, I'm heading out," I say, looking away from him so he'll take the hint that I'm not in the mood to talk.

"Wait. Don't go yet."

I stop and turn to face my brother. I really don't know what to say to him. I mean, the last time we were together was when I was still a baby (a baby who apparently gave him black eyes). But studying him now, I can see that he's very different from the Maligno. He doesn't have that air of cunning about him. He's more like Papa, who had the leader vibe and was serious but approachable and kind.

"I know what you're thinking," Kuya Yani says, biting his lower lip. "I should have fought the evil spirit out of me."

"You couldn't have."

"I should have tried harder." My brother shakes his head. "I could see everything he was doing, but I felt powerless to stop him."

"Restituto has been stewing in his anger since the time of Bernardo Carpio, Kuya. That's like, even further in the past than the Philippine Revolution. His anger would have made him far stronger than the usual sorcerer."

Kuya Yani nods. A smile touches his lips. "You've grown up into a smart girl. You used to scream a lot when you were a baby, and I couldn't understand why your little tantrums gave me several black eyes."

I grin. I've seen that memory. "We have a lot of catching up to do, Kuya."

"We definitely do." Kuya Yani brings out something small and paper-like from his pocket. "I couldn't buy you a Christmas present in time with all the things Tita Ligaya and I have had to take care of because of what happened recently. So I thought you might want to have this."

It's an old photograph of our family. My mother is seated on the throne while holding newly born me in her arms. Haribon is by her feet, standing proud. I suppose this is before Tita Ligaya's spinal injury because in this photo, she's standing behind my mother with Kuya Yani and Papa.

“Don’t worry, it’s real,” Kuya Yani assures me. He puts a hand on my shoulder. “I’ll instruct housekeeping to get rid of all the fake things in your room, so you don’t have to see them when you visit. From now on, we’ll make real memories. We’ve lost so many years together because of Restituto. We can’t let him take any more from us. If you’re okay with that, of course.”

“I’d like that.” Then, before I change my mind, I throw my arms around him. I feel him stiffen, so I wait for him to let go. But he doesn’t.

Instead, Kuya Yani holds me tighter, tucking my head under his chin. His voice cracks as he speaks. “I’m so glad, bunso. I’m so glad.”

Do you know that feeling when you’re in a boring class, and thirty minutes seem to go by really, really slow? But those same thirty minutes seem like such a short time when you’re watching a cool movie. My time in Maharlika City is like the second one. Just when we’re starting to have fun, it’s time to go.

After saying our goodbyes to Tita Ligaya and Kuya Yani, we gather our belongings (and our Christmas presents) and leave. Paloma is driving our boat while Gamila follows behind on this amazing underwater and surface jet ski. We come across mer-people who greet us along the way, and Gamila almost runs into a bunch of glowing squid and giant jellyfish.

"I fixed your phone," Bart says, handing it over to me. "I was able to save all the songs in your music app. Just wait to play them until we get to the port island."

"Why not play a song now?" The god of the sea appears on Bart's side of the boat, along with his giant sea horses. My friend looks like he's about to pee—or has peed—his pants.

"I thought you hated my music," I say wryly. "Last time I played BTS, you nearly killed us."

Mom gasps audibly. "What?"

"Oh, hello. You must be the girls' mother. I'm Amanikable, the god of the sea." Amanikable reaches across Bart to shake Mom's hand. Bart looks like he's about to faint. "Play your music," the deity says to me. "I would love to listen. I was just in a bad mood that day."

Bad mood? It was more like temper tantrum of the tempest.

Still, I play "Euphoria" on my phone. Amanikable closes his eyes and rides the waves beside us, humming as Jungkook beautifully belts out the song's English and Korean lyrics.

We reach Sagitna Island before "Euphoria" ends, all thanks to Amanikable.

I shake my finger at the sea god. "Can you not dump seawater on us like last time?"

Amanikable gives Mom a sheepish look. "I was just teasing them. It was only a tiny splash of water."

We pat the giant sea horses and bid Amanikable goodbye, watching them as they dive back into the sea and disappear.

"Ooh! What did you trade to get on the sea god's good side? I was so sure he'd drown you!" a familiar squeaky voice says as we alight from the boat. "Hello again, Lulu Sinagtala and friends."

"Gavino." I sigh. "Not everything in the Realms can be bought, you know."

"Not in my world." The duwende shakes his head. "I believe you owe me a boat."

Everyone, except for Mom and Haribon but including Kitty, brings out and points their weapons at the duwende and his kapre goons. If the duck had been wearing his battle vest, he would have activated its mechanical arms and used them as Salamangka zappers.

"No, no. I got this," I say, gesturing at my friends to lower their weapons. They do so reluctantly. I step up to the dwarf.

"Our contract is pretty clear, kid," Gavino says with glee. "You didn't bring back my boat in one piece, so I get to keep all your magic."

"The one piece, Lu," Bart whispers in my ear. His breath smells like lemon drops. "Don't forget the one piece."

"Oh yeah!" It's as if a bulb has lit up in my head. I rummage through my pockets and find that one little piece of wood I got from Gavino's dead boat. "Here's your one piece."

"What's this?"

As soon as the sliver of wood makes contact with the duwende's hand, all the magic from Anagolay that he took from me swiftly returns to my agimat.

"That's not fair!" he says.

"Like you said," I say, smirking, "it was *in the contract.*"

"You will pay for this, you little brat," Gavino snaps. He turns to his goons. "Kill every one of them and toss their bodies into her new friend the sea god's domain. Spare them no mercy."

We all bring out our weapons. Even Haribon is leaning forward in attack mode, ready to fight.

But before anyone can make a move, a bright ball of light explodes between our group and Gavino's. "ENOUGH!"

The light fades, solidifying in the form of Manong Sol. He looks really scary, with all these little flames dancing on his skin and his eyes glowing like fiery coals. He's still old, yes, but outright terrifying. No wonder a lot of magical beings fear him.

Gavino and his crew are no exception. They hold up their hands in surrender, with the duwende stepping forward, his head bowed.

"Lord Apolaki, Your Greatness," he says, bowing way too theatrically to be sincere. "This girl and I have a contract. She cheated me! She stills owes me a boat—"

"And you shall have it." Manong Sol snaps his fingers. "The boat is already in your warehouse, where you shall now return."

"But, Your Greatness—"

Manong Sol gives him a smoldering stare. Like, literally smoldering. With fire and all.

Gavino does the smart thing and walks away with his goons. He grumbles something about the boat disappearing when the sun falls. But the kapres cover his mouth and carry him away.

"You're welcome!" Manong Sol's flames disappear. He's back to normal, non-smoldering Manong Sol now. We bow to him respectfully.

"You did well, Luningning," Manong Sol says, a hint of a smile on his wrinkly lips. "All of you did. I'm very proud of you."

Paloma and Gamila look like they're going to start flailing like fangirls. Geez.

"I believe everyone deserves a reward."

"We don't need a reward, my lord," Paloma says, bowing again. "Serving you is our honor."

"No, no," I say, pushing Paloma aside. "We want the reward!"

"Of course you do." Manong Sol rolls his eyes. "An all-you-can-eat seafood buffet. How about we take a break from saving cities and have lunch?"

Steamed crabs, grilled oysters, clam pasta, baked mussels with cheese and garlic, fried calamari, salmon sashimi? Now, *that* is a mission from the god of warriors that I'm more than willing to fulfill.

"You're on! Lead the way, Manong Sol."

CHAPTER TWENTY-NINE

Merry Christmas from Our Family to Yours

MANONG SOL AND BART WENT BACK TO INARAWAN STREET AHEAD of Mom, Kitty, Haribon, and me. The four of us stayed at the sun god's house in the In-Between to rest a bit before heading home. I would have preferred to visit Boracay Island instead, but Manong Sol said our mission's not done yet, so it's just the Sagitna Island beach for now.

We only stayed there for a couple of hours, though. Mom is eager to go home. I guess Kitty and I are too, and Haribon is excited to explore the "new Middleworld." The last time he was in our world was during the time of Andrés Bonifacio, which is, like, more than a hundred years ago. Thankfully, Maharlika City adapts technology from our world, so the duck won't be too culture shocked.

But the moment we step out of the portal in the Sangang-Daan Tree, it's not Haribon who is surprised. For the first time ever, Mom, Kitty, and I see Inarawan Street without the Balabal.

We walk up the sloped road and see our neighbors for what they really are—aswangs, tiyanaks, manananggals, wakwaks, tikbalangs, duwendes, kapres, engkantadas . . . not even one of them is human. And that's totally fine—no, not fine. It's great! I'm so happy I can see everyone's true selves and they don't have to hide from us anymore.

Everyone says hello and Merry Christmas as we walk by. It's still very much Inarawan Street, but just a bit different and a whole lot more magical.

"Come on, my family," Mom chirps. "Let's go home!"

I let Mom, Haribon, and Kitty walk ahead to our apartment building. Manong Sol is sitting crisscross applesauce on a bench outside Bads Bunny with Bart. A thread of Christmas lights falls from the store sign and startles my best friend, who suddenly transforms into Tannie the shih tzu. Ate Mariel leaves the cash register with only her torso and batlike wings. She flies up to the Bads Bunny sign and fixes the lights.

Yep. We're home, all right. This is home. *Our home.*

I jog to catch up with my family. "Mom! Meow! Haribon! Wait for me."

Mom puts a huge pet carrier for Haribon to use as a duck house into my shared room with Kitty. The duck is ecstatic, because this means he is now officially a Sinagtala.

But there are still things left unsaid between Kitty and me.

It's the night before Christmas, and Kitty is busying herself by working on our school project that's not due until after the New Year. Haribon gives me a look and leaves the room.

It's now or never.

I clear my throat.

"Yes?" she asks.

"Do you want me to take down some of my posters?" I blurt out. Ugh. I'm really terrible at this. "If you'd let me keep one each of Jungkook, Rosé, BTS, and Blackpink—"

"No, no. It's fine. Our room wouldn't be our room without them." Kitty puts down the glue. I take it as a sign and sit beside her. "I was really hurt that you would think jealousy is the only reason I don't like it when you do dangerous things," she says.

"I'm sorry," I say, staring at my fingers. "I didn't mean it. I know you're just worried about me."

"That's not the only thing." Kitty fiddles with a marker. "I feel like you don't need me anymore. You have your powers, your magical friends . . . all I can ever do for you now is remind you to take your meds on time. Like that's any help in protecting the Realms."

"Are you kidding? My meds are important!" I take her hand in mine. "Seriously, Meow. You know I tend to forget my meds when I'm distracted. Can you imagine me battling the Maligno and I suddenly get a seizure? And also, Bart and I need an archer to cover our backs!"

"Well, if you put it that way . . ."

"Best of all . . ." I squeeze Kitty's hand. "You keep me grounded. You're my constant reminder of why I'm doing this."

"Oh, Ate!" Kitty throws her arms around me. "I'll never stop worrying about you. That's what sisters do; we worry about each other. But I realize now that being sisters also means supporting each other. I can't say I'll ever be okay with your decision to be the Salamangkero, but it was your choice to make, not mine. I'll stay by your side if you want me to."

"Of course. You've always been with me, Meow. I . . . I don't know what I'll do if you aren't." I bite my lower lip. "We may not be sisters by blood, but we're more than that—we're soul siblings."

"Yes. Soul siblings. I love that." Kitty gives me the biggest of smiles. "I love *you*, Ate. We're in this together. I will never, never, ever leave your side."

⋆ ⋆ ⋆

"Merry Christmas!" Kitty's face is the first thing I see when I wake up the next morning. She hands me a glass of water and my epilepsy tablet.

It's like any other Christmas morning, until—

Quack!

Haribon's feathery head pops up from the foot of the bed. "Merry Christmas!" he says. "Hurry up, Lulu, there are so many gifts waiting for you."

That's enough for me to hurry downstairs. Well, after brushing my teeth, of course.

"Merry Christmas! Slow down, girls," says Mom, grinning. "The doorbell's been ringing all morning with all these deliveries. Anagolay sent us a huge box of bibingka, sapin-sapin, and other delicacies. I'll prepare us a plate to try them all. Go on. You can start with the unwrapping."

"And hot chocolate?" I ask. Christmas morning isn't Christmas morning without a mug of piping hot tsokolate eh.

"And hot chocolate." Mom winks.

"Hooray!" Kitty and I cheer.

Mom's right. The space under the Christmas tree is definitely more packed this year. We find presents from the usual neighbors, but also odd, random gifts from deities and magical creatures.

Tita Marites and Tito Tolits sent us gift cards for haircuts and mani-pedis at their salon. Amanikable sent me a piece of live coral inside a Salamangka snow globe, with a note that reads "To the Salamangkero, her sister, and the dog. Always remember to bring BTS music if you want to cross my seas alive. PS: Jungkook is the best!" Well, good to know he won't try to drown me again. *And* I've managed to convert him to becoming a BTS fan too!

Sitan didn't send me anything, but he gave Kitty original K-drama merchandise. Which is fine. I don't care.

If Tala were around, she would have sent me something. But then again, having been friends with the star goddess is more than enough of a gift already. And I miss her very, very much.

Then there's Tita Cecile's gift. Having her with us again would have been a better present, but her recorded message will do for now. My heart aches at the sight of her familiar face materializing on the surface of the water.

"Merry Christmas! Thank Bathala you're all okay. Sis, I'm so sorry I couldn't take care of the kids as I should have. Kitty and Lulu . . . I hope one day you'll forgive me for everything I've done." Projection Tita Cecile hangs her head. "I'll make it up to you when I get back. Unfortunately, I must stay here in the Underworld for a bit longer. Tatay is heartbroken that all three of my siblings are rebelling against him, and we're still working overtime to repair the breach the evil spirit created during the prison break and the destruction of the Hill of Despair. But I promise—no, I swear to you as a goddess making an oath with a human—we'll be together again. I sent you some goodies to tide you over until I get back, and they should arrive right about now. . . ."

Ding-dong! Ding-dong!

Mom opens the door to reveal a duwende pushing a giant balikbayan box.

"ULS delivery!" says the dwarf. "Underworld Logistics and Shipping is dead set on serving you. Please sign here."

Mom affixes her signature to the duwende's tablet.

"Thank you." He hands my mother a flyer. "This contains our service rates. We deliver anywhere in the Realms, even in the In-Between. With corresponding fees, of course. Kindly note that delivery to Kasanaan has additional hazard fees, and please be reminded that we are not allowed to deliver to corrupt souls in the process of completing their sentences. We hope to be of service to you again soon. Enjoy your parcel, and Merry Christmas!"

"Sorry you had to listen to the delivery guy's long spiel," Tita Cecile apologizes from the projection. "There aren't many delivery options from where I am in the Underworld. Anyway, inside the box, you'll see a special mobile phone I asked Aman Sinaya to create for us. Feel free to use that to video call me anytime. It's much faster than sending these marble message things.

"I hope you like the stuff I sent. Kiddos, Silverio told me about what you did. I'm so proud of you. We'll have a proper celebration when I get back." Tita Cecile dabs the tears from her eyes. “Don’t let the duck poop all over the house, okay? I love you, sis. I love you, kiddos. Merry Christmas!”

Tita Cecile’s image disappears. Kitty and I dive right into the balikbayan box.

A balikbayan box is a huge cardboard box full of goodies. Overseas Filipino workers typically use them to send stuff to their families back in the Philippines. The box is usually oversized like this to accommodate shipping everything in one go.

Tita Cecile’s balikbayan box from the Underworld is full of snacks, candies, chocolates, clothes, and toys. And of course, the special mobile phone she mentioned. She even included a nice duck bed for Haribon to use.

In the afternoon, Manong Sol arrives with Bart and Ate Mariel. They bring food and more gifts.

“Suit up, Luningning. Come to the gym with me for one round,” the sun god says right after we open our presents. “With the Maligno on the loose, you can’t slack off.”

He doesn’t have to tell me twice. I put on a pair of my favorite gym shorts, sneakers, and Ate Mariel’s Christmas gift—a customized T-shirt with a combined print of Jungkook and Rosé, the two most gorgeous beings in the whole wide Middleworld. I leave the Jungkook pillow Bart got me for Christmas on my bed, but Kitty and I are wearing the matching gold bangles he also gave us. A Salamangka shield materializes from the bracelet when you tap it, kind of like the energy shields the Wakandans use during battle in *Black Panther* and *Avengers: Infinity War.* It's perfect for training!

For the first time ever, Manong Sol lets Kitty and Bart train with us. Kitty practices shooting arrows while Bart and I spar.

"I have taught you combat, and I am glad you're good at it," Manong Sol says. "It's time for you to learn more about the power you hold. Your Salamangkero abilities go beyond superstrength, Luningning. But today, we shall hone your battle skills further. We must be prepared when we meet Restituto again."

I hold my balisong and buntot pagi aloft between Kitty and Bart as images of red-eyed warriors appear around us. One by one, the projections solidify into dangerous foes. "You two ready?"

Bart and Kitty answer at the same time. "Ready!"

We might be kids, but we're strong. We're going to practice and practice until we're so good, the Maligno will regret he ever met us. He will return my father to me whether he likes it or not.

I twirl the butterfly knife around my thumb as I square my shoulders. I'm Lulu Sinagtala, and I'm the Salamangkero. I have the strength of Bernardo Carpio and the magic of the Anito. I'm coming for that Maligno, even if it's the last thing I do. "Let's do this!"

GLOSSARY

The Philippines is a melting pot of diverse regional cultures, each with its own colorful history and tales of magic and legendary heroes. Tagalog mythology is just a fraction of the greater Philippine pantheon. There are so many more stories from different regions to read about and pass on.

Mind you, I'm not an expert in Tagalog mythology. The descriptions and pronunciations here are based on what I know—from stories I've been told by my elders and people I've met in my travels, anecdotes I learned when I was in school, and tales I've read during my research. I hope that at the end of reading this glossary, you'll find yourself exploring the subject more on your own.

DEITIES

Amanikable *(Ah-MAH-nee-CAB-leh)*

The god of the sea. In some stories, Amanikable is known as the patron of hunters. It is said that a beautiful mortal woman named Maganda, whom he loved, rejected him. Because of this, Amanikable seeks revenge on all mortals, wrecking boats and drowning people every now and then.

Aman Sinaya *(Ah-MAHN-see-NAH-yah)*

In the *Lulu Sinagtala* world, Aman Sinaya is a brilliant inventor and a nonbinary deity of crafts. But in the myths, Aman Sinaya was the god of fishermen for the early Tagalogs. They prayed to him when they cast their nets, nets that were said to have been invented by Aman Sinaya himself. This story of him being the craftsman of such a vital tool in the livelihood of early Tagalogs inspired me to depict Aman Sinaya as a deity who creates amazing stuff.

The deity's gender varies in the stories too. Some believe Aman Sinaya is a goddess, born from the soul of a maiden who drowned and became a water deity. There are others who contend that the deity's name actually implies they are male. Aman Sinaya comes from "Ama ni Sinaya," which means "Father of Sinaya."

Anagolay *(Ah-nah-GOH-lai)*

The goddess of lost things. She is the mother of Apolaki and the daughter of Mapulon. Early Tagalogs prayed to her whenever they needed help finding something they'd lost.

Apolaki *(Ah-poh-lah-KEE)*

The god of the sun and patron of warriors. He is Anagolay's son. In some sources, though, he is the son of Bathala.

Bathala *(Baht-HAH-lah)*

The god of gods. He is the supreme god and the creator of the worlds.

Mansisilat *(MAHN-see-see-laht)*

The goddess of broken homes and one of the four agents of Sitan. It's said that seeing a happy family puts the goddess in a very bad mood. She enters a home disguised as a healer or a beggar, then pits family members against each other until one of them leaves.

Mapulon *(Mah-POOH-lohn)*

The god of seasons and health. It's important to note that the early Tagalogs relied on the predictability of the seasons for a good harvest—a good harvest meant people would be healthy and full. So that makes Mapulon vital to the people's survival. He is also known as the kindest deity.

Sitan *(See-TAHN)*

The god of the Underworld. He oversees the souls in that realm and is in charge of rewarding or punishing them. Interestingly, some say it is possible that Sitan isn't a god but a collective of demons, or forces of hell who torment sinners.

Tala *(TAH-lah)*

The goddess of stars. She is said to be one of the daughters of Bathala and a mortal woman.

MAGICAL CREATURES

aswang *(ahs-WANG)*

A shape-shifting creature that usually falls under one or more of these five categories: vampires, viscera suckers, were-dogs, evil witches, and ghouls.

duwende *(doo-WEHN-deh)*

A creature similar to goblins, elves, or dwarfs. They're known to use their magical abilities maliciously if you offend them, but they may bring presents if they like you or if you become their friend. So if you ever encounter a duwende, be sure to be respectful and nice. Who knows? Maybe they'll give you an enchanted gift the next time you meet!

engkantada *(EHNG-can-TAH-dah)*

A dryad who guards natural habitats like mountains, forests, or seas. They are fairylike and usually have light complexions and may have blond hair. People tend to be wary of them, as they resent humans who trespass on their realms.

kapre *(KAH-preh)*

A tree giant. They're hairy, dark, and muscular creatures with strong body odor who like to sit on branches of huge trees to smoke. They're not evil, but if you cut down the tree they consider their home, you can bet they will seek revenge.

maligno *(mah-LEEHG-noh)*

An evil spirit. They tend to focus on a particular person they want to harm. In some places in the Philippines, people attribute sudden illness or death to the evildoing of a maligno.

manananggal *(mah-nah-nahng-GALL)*

A vampiric creature with batlike wings that can separate its body at the waist. They're most vulnerable when their body is separated. Sprinkling salt or crushed garlic on the segmented lower body will prevent the manananggal from rejoining their two halves. And if they don't become whole again before sunrise, they will perish.

santelmo *(sahn-TEHL-moh)*

A ball of fire believed to be the spirits of the dead. It is said that if you see a santelmo in the forest, you should resist the temptation to follow it. Because if you don't, you'll surely get lost, and the only way to escape is to have another person help you. The best thing to do is to simply light a candle in the place where you found the creature. That way, their spirit will find peace and finally move on.

tigmamanukan *(teehg-mah-mah-NOOH-kahn)*

An augural bird. Ancient Tagalogs believed this creature was sent by Bathala himself to give a good or bad omen to one's upcoming journey. If the tigmamanukan flies right, your journey will be a success. If it flies left, you'll never return. See? This is why everyone (especially Lulu) should listen to Haribon—the Omen-Bringer knows best!

tikbalang *(tick-BAH-lahng)*

A creature with the head and hooves of a horse and the body of a man with oddly long limbs. They are usually benevolent beings who sometimes play tricks on travelers passing under their home tree without saying "excuse me," leading the unsuspecting people astray and making them go around an endless circular path. It's said that the only way to break a tikbalang's spell is to wear your shirt inside out to confuse the creature.

tiyanak *(tee-YAH-nahk)*

A bloodthirsty creature that takes on the form of a toddler. It lures its victim into the forest by crying like a baby. When the victim picks it up out of concern, the tiyanak reverts to its true form and attacks.

wakwak *(WACK-wack)*

A birdlike vampiric creature. Unlike the manananggal, it can't separate its torso from its lower body. It has sharp talons and wings similar to a bat's. If you hear the flapping of a wakwak's wings and it's loud, it means the creature is far away. The fainter the sound, the nearer the wakwak is to you, so watch out!

ACKNOWLEDGMENTS

I've always felt that we Filipinos frequently got relegated to being the sidekick or the vague-brown-character-in-the-background in international spaces—we were rarely the heroes. Me writing and publishing a book for kids featuring a superpowered, dark-brown, and epileptic Filipino girl who encounters magical beings from Tagalog mythology in Metro Manila was a near-impossible dream. For years, I kept putting off working on this story for fear of getting told that the world didn't want it, and that it should be tucked away in a drawer, never to see the light of day. But with the encouragement of people who believed in me more than I did myself, *Lulu Sinagtala and the City of Noble Warriors* became a reality.

Truly, I have a lot to be grateful for. So let me start the thank-you parade by expressing my utmost gratitude to you, dear reader, for continuing to support my work. Because of you, I get to keep writing about dark-brown and flat-nosed Filipino girls like me. Thank you, thank you!

It's also humbling to find out that many great people are involved in publishing this book, and even more so knowing about the hard work they put into it.

I'm utterly grateful for Megan Ilnitzki, editor extraordinaire! I'll be honest and say that at first, I felt scared writing in a new genre and doubted myself. But I realized I didn't have anything to worry about, because Lulu and I were in wonderful hands with you, Megan. Thank you also to Jenny Ly. You two should be called the Patron Deities of Authors with Ugly Drafts, because without your magical touch, my manuscript wouldn't be the book that it is today. I became a much better writer working with you both.

My amazing Harper team—especially Sabrina Abballe, Patty Rosati, Mimi Rankin, Samantha Brown, Genessee Floressantos, Shannon McCain, Lia Ding, and Lauren Evans—thank you for bringing *Lulu Sinagtala* to kids everywhere. To Caitlin Lonning and Alexandra Rakaczki, you have my deepest gratitude for taking good care of my words. To Joel Tippie, many thanks for the fantabulous book design! And of course, to Marianne Palita—thank you so much for bringing Lulu, Kitty, and Bart to life with your amazing cover art.

I'm also super lucky to be represented by rock-star agents. To Claire Roberts of Claire Roberts Global Literary Management, thank you for giving Lulu's story a chance to be read all over the world. To Alyssa Eisner Henkin of Birch Path Literary . . . I hope you never get tired of hearing me say "thank you, Alyssa, you're the best!" Because you *are* the best, and I will always be grateful to have you by my side, supporting me and championing my work every step of the way.

Writing isn't easy, but it helps to have friends I can fangirl with when the stress of deadlines gets too rough. To Nina, Khursten, Cla, and Anj . . . thank you, ladies—not only for the Bangtan hangs and parties, but also for introducing me to the online communities of Borahae From Manila and Titas of BTS. I've loved BTS for years but only within the confines of our home. I'm so glad I finally found other safe places where I can scream about how awesome BTS is and fangirl as much as I want without fear of being judged. Thank you, fellow ARMYs. Apobangpo!

To Rae and Isabelle: thank you, besties! No matter how busy we all are with our lives and careers, I'm so glad we always have each other.

Many thanks to my parents, who have appointed themselves my unofficial social media post–sharers and online cheerleaders. To my younger sister, Joyce, thank you for taking care of my needy pets whenever I'm on a deadline, and for being my first—and hopefully not my only—loyal fan. I'm very lucky to have such a supportive family.

Last but not least, thank you to my husband, Marc, who never reads any of my books but will tell everyone in all three Realms that I'm such an awesome writer. I had the courage to chase my dreams because of you. None of this would have been possible without your love and support. I love you, forever and always.